CHANGED

A DEMON HUNTER ROMANCE #3

CARRIE THORNE

Published by Thorny Books

Carrie Thorne

https://carriethorne.com/

Standalones

The Christmas Bet: A Double Feature Christmas Standalone.

Enjoy free books, first looks,

review team access,

and occasional hellos from Carrie?

Let's do this: carriethorne.com/newsletter

For my littlest niece. Fearless and unstoppable.

Prologue

Belltown, Seattle, Fifteen Years Ago.

One more taste before sunrise. Drunk on the bliss of the night, on that heartrending instant when you knew nothing would ever be the same—and not just because the sex had been life-altering—Bennett rose to kiss her again. The tip of her fang grazed across his lips as she taunted him. Adair smiled and trailed her fingertips over his jaw before giving in to the kiss. Warm and tangy, their breath entwined.

In stark contrast to the quiet of the stolen moment, the piercing shrill of sirens rattled the air around them. The crisp breeze over the rooftop served as a reminder that winter was heavy in the air. Beneath him, the sandpapery roof scraped against the skin of his back. Adair slid off and readjusted, then snuggled atop him, resting her head on his shoulder.

His voice filled with gravel, and coated with satisfaction, he said, "I knew training on the roof was risky, but the rocks digging into my ass have officially sealed it for me. I'm getting a bigger place. Something with room to train, add a gym, library, design my own living quarters. Maybe some outdoor furniture for more comfortable rooftop sex."

"Or we could try a bed next time. You know, like normal people?" He felt her wicked grin against him as her fingertips trailed along the ridges of his abdomen.

"Normal? I can't say I am familiar with the concept."

"I am well practiced at normal. What better way to blend in?"

"Fair point." He grinned, tracing the contours of her arm.

Melted into him, she tormented him with her touch–and not just because he wanted to go again, well, he did, but if she had a clue what she did to him, the corny thoughts in his head, she'd run far and fast. She sighed. "I suppose demon hunters don't have time for normal."

"I had the choice to live a human life, but it wasn't for me."

She shifted up to her elbows and grinned at him. "It suits you. Slayer of monsters by night, and debater of the nuances of ancient languages in the lecture hall by day."

"I should have picked something more interesting, but it is useful." He tipped his head up and pressed his lips to hers before lying back down again, hoping she couldn't feel the flutter in his chest at the simple affection. "What about you? You have an eternity to do whatever you'd like."

"I enjoy experimenting with normal, but there are only so many careers that don't involve daylight. Perhaps I'll try my hand at graphic design." She settled her head back on his shoulder and wrapped her arm around his waist.

"You kicked ass the other night when we ran into those werewolves. If you wanted, you could try out life as a demon hunter for a century or two. Quinn and Lana are open minded and would be on board with you joining our team. My parents would flip if they found out about us in any form, but they'd come around."

"Bennett. It's more than that. I don't give a damn what your parents think, nor your friends. They're hunters; they won't ever see past what I am, anyway. And sure, I can fight. Even vampires don't last as long as I have without survival skills. But you were raised for this. You make a choice to dedicate your life to protecting the fricking world. I wasn't. I didn't."

On his eighteenth birthday, Bennett had accepted his heritage, suffering the inelegant ceremony in which his parents, grandparents, and a few other demon hunting families gathered and watched him writhe around on the ground as his ancestor's demon blood activated within him. While the others chatted and congratulated each other on his success, he lost his lunch. His skin prickled, sweat drenched his skin, and he fought the embarrassing tears of fear and pain as he transformed. It was like going through puberty all over again, multiplied by infinity, but within the course of an hour. Okay, so his mom and the other hunters in the room had tried to soothe the ache, acutely remembering the misery of the change. Especially the moment you believed you wouldn't survive it. Because not everyone did.

When it cleared, they'd left him to recover blessedly alone while they shared cake and champagne. Breath coming easier, mind clearer than ever, he'd sat on the cool concrete of his parents' patio. Cold was no longer painful, but simply a nagging reminder that he ought to move inside, eventually. Having prepared for the life of a demon hunter since infancy, Bennett was well trained in combat, but the strength running through his veins was intoxicating.

He'd wandered the first few years, traveling the world, learning the ropes as he tested his limits. But he'd missed home. So, four weeks and two days ago, he'd rented a simple apartment in Seattle. The place was exactly where he needed to be. The nightlife was vivid, the parties wild... and he knew vampires walked among them.

Demon hunters didn't have keen smell or sight like vampires, certainly better than humans, but nothing one would call extrasensory. He simply knew.

And he'd been so right. Three weeks ago, he'd met her.

Trained well, he suspected the club was full of bloodsuckers. Bennett had been compelled to scope it out. Innocent in appearance, graceful in her movements, yet swift and assured, he'd known what she was. With the satin dress that clung to her body like sinful second skin, her sun-kissed hair, the dappling of freckles across her cheeks, and pink lips that formed a natural pout, she'd been a walking vision of all his fantasies come true. No doubt about it, she was absolutely a vampire; her allure seemed designed to tempt him.

Falling right into her trap–willingly and intentionally–he'd followed her to the dance floor and splayed his palm possessively over her abdomen as she leaned into him, their hips swaying together in a fluid, erotic rhythm.

But she hadn't been at all what he was expecting. Instead of deigning to sink her teeth into him, she didn't make the move. Not to say she didn't make some moves. He had regretted that his first solo vampire slay was going to be such self-torture. But he'd been trained well. Vampires would do whatever it took to lure in their prey. And he wasn't about to blow it by falling for her charms.

She didn't struggle when he held the knife to her throat, but asserted her vegetarian status, her innocent blue eyes swimming with honesty. Vampires had survival instincts stronger than any other as the only immortal breed outside the demon realm. So naturally, he hadn't believed her at first.

When the dust settled from their battle of wits, he'd learned they had the same goal. Well, similar. She wanted to maintain her safety in this corner of the world and was seeking to clear the area of bloodsuckers. He wanted them annihilated.

"Bennett?" Adair murmured, her porcelain skin warm against his. Yet her voice was colder than the sleet that teased in the air.

"Yeah?" Fuck. He knew that tone. Well, not from experience, but he'd known it was inevitable. She'd made it clear he was little more than a dalliance. As she'd put it, minutes before thrusting her tongue down his throat that first time, their ages, and lifestyles were insurmountable barriers.

He'd scoffed. Sure, she was five centuries older. What guy wasn't younger? Yes, he was a few months shy of twenty-one, and she was his first, but he knew what he was getting into. Adair looked no older than her early twenties, and would for the rest of eternity. As a demon hunter, he'd age a few more years, then hold steady for at least two or three hundred years. At least they'd look the same age for a few hundred years.

Interrupting him from his memories, waking him as he'd been falling asleep, Adair finally murmured her question, "You know this can't happen again, right?" Her sunny brown hair tickled his skin as she sat up.

"Why not?"

"*Why not?* Come on." She gestured to herself in general, but his eyes drew right to her breasts, spectacularly perky... he grinned with pure postcoital, no-longer-a-virgin euphoria. Gliding the tip of her tongue over one of her razor-sharp canines, she bit down until a drop of blood clung to her tooth before she licked it away.

He sat up and embedded his hand in her beachy waves, cradling the back of her neck, and pressed his lips to hers. Without force, without plea. The blazing hot fire the simple connection stirred was off the charts. Didn't matter that he had nothing for comparison, human or not. He knew. They shared something extraordinary.

"Bennett, you're a sweet guy, but..." she trailed off, looking at the glow of sunrise threatening in the distant sky.

Thumb tracing his hand along the curve of her jaw, he shook his head. "I am a sweet guy. And I'm not an idiot. I'm not expecting white picket fences." An ache in his chest, his breath grew heavy as he accepted the inevitable.

"This was a mistake. I'm sorry."

The last trace of hope exhaling from his empty lungs, he shook his head. "It wasn't, but I know where you stand." Regrettably.

She slipped her feet into her panties. "Please say you won't go after them alone. Call in your mother's team or something."

Teeth gritted tight, he grabbed his jeans and shoved his feet into the pant legs, lying back on the rough surface of the roof to pull them over his hips, the sharp pebbles digging into his skin. He kept his hand over the goods and tugged up the zipper, not giving a fuck where his underwear had gone. "Hell no. First, demon hunters don't join forces with any hunter outside their own team once their parent has trained them and deemed them ready. Second, they won't understand that you're not like other vampires and will go after you too."

"You don't have a team. Come on, you told me yourself, Quinn hasn't accepted the demon blood yet, and Lana is away at college."

"I'm not calling for my mommy and running from the first decent fight of my life."

"There are too many of them."

"Fight with me. I know you've got the skills."

"We won't survive it."

"What about your brother, isn't he getting back into town soon? Quinn will accept the gift when she turns eighteen in a few days, and

Lana can be here at a moment's notice. We've been training together since we were in diapers, and I know they'll be game to dive right in. With your brother too, we can take them." He was floored that her brother, her actual biological brother, was part of her life. Bennett didn't even have a sibling, but his parents were in their reproductive prime, so maybe someday. But it was different now that he was old enough to have his own.

His jaw dropped, and whatever she'd been saying melted right out of his ears. She pulled her top over her head, closing her eyes and running her fingers through her hair. Before tonight, she had gifted him with a few third-base make-outs, but something about tonight had been special. Maybe she'd agree to a few years of more nights like this–

"Bennett?" She raised an eyebrow and cleared her throat when he didn't look away.

"Huh? Sorry," he muttered, sporting a sheepish grin as he raised his gaze to meet hers.

Adair wasn't merely alluring because of her natural predator appeal. Something in her azure eyes and freckled cheeks gave her an air of naivete, but her wicked grin and sinful body promised so much more. And, well, damn, he knew that was absolutely true thanks to tonight. "He's up in the highlands, and there's no service at the castle, but he promised he'd be back by the twentieth."

"Where you were born?"

"I wish. Our home crumbled long ago. This one was much more solidly built by the descendants of our cousins. We invested a lot to restore and modernize it." She held her breath. He knew there was more to it, but she shook her head. "I can't let three young demon hunters get killed by some old friends of mine."

"Old friends?"

"Very old. They're experienced, they're smart, and they're vicious. Even with three, you don't stand a chance. So Logan and I will lend a hand–"

"Great. You and me, your brother, Quinn, and Lana. We've got this."

She glanced to the sky and clenched her jaw before letting out a controlled exhale. "We finish this, then I'm out."

"You have better things to do with your eternity?"

A wicked shine flashed in her gaze. "Deflowering a newbie demon hunter is one thing." She rose to her feet and extended her hand. "But keeping him on the hook? Not my style."

As he met her grip, the shock of the connection sent heat radiating up his arm, surging through the rest of him. She'd surely had plenty of lovers, didn't she realize this sort of thing wasn't your run-of-the-mill affair?

Maybe she did. As he stood, she took a long, heavy breath, her eyes drifting over his shoulders, trailing down his abdomen where her tongue had been an hour ago.

"Adair?" he teased, biting his tongue as he watched her blush. So vampires could blush. Good to know.

She cleared her throat and looked up at him. "Sorry, I, uh, I think I'm hungry. Sun's coming up soon anyway, and I'm not looking to get a tan today."

"Sunset again? My place?" he asked. Not that it would be her place, as she wouldn't even let him know where she lived.

She nodded, backing away. Reaching down, he snatched his shirt from the ground and watched her strut away.

IT DIDN'T TAKE LONG. Having never been foolish enough to observe demon hunters at work before tonight, Adair could say with certainty that their reputations were well earned. An inexperienced team, one of which was only days out of the change, yet the three hunters sliced through the lair.

Extracting her knife from the chest of a fallen vampire, Adair checked the room for the next threat. But the remaining bloodsuckers weren't going to last much longer.

Fast as lightning, a vampire sprinted across the room and leaped on Bennett's back.

Bennett snapped his head back and crunched its nose. With a howl, it dropped to the ground.

Shield bashing into the vampire in front of him, he spun and lowered to his knees, his sword gutting the first, then drove back into the neck of the second.

Quinn swung her great sword and a vampire head hit the ground and rolled under the tablecloth.

Axe striking into the chest of another, Lana slammed it to the ground and finished it.

And Logan. Ever the warrior, stealthier than in his clunky days as the Scottish raider, Adair's brother snapped a neck and cleared the far corner.

Adair inhaled deeply and caught a familiar scent. She gritted her teeth and crossed the bloody backroom of the club.

Bennett finished off his prey and ran to catch up. He nodded to the door, silently asking what had caught her attention.

She moved to unlock the office door, withdrawing a pin from her hair.

Before she got the chance, Bennett nodded to the door. "May I?"

With a shrug and a curious nod of her head, Adair stepped back.

He kicked the door, and the hinges snapped on impact. The door crashed into the room with a deafening clatter.

A bullet whizzed toward them, aimed straight for Bennett's forehead.

Adair gripped his shirt and tugged him out of the line of fire.

Not fast enough.

The bullet struck his shoulder. Bennett recoiled and growled, glaring down at the blood trailing from his wound.

Simpering with a sardonic smile, Sonra whimpered, "Adair. It has been too long."

Bennett stopped in front of Sonra and glanced back, waiting for Adair's okay, despite the blood oozing from his shoulder. It had to hurt, even with his abilities, but he didn't let on that he was even fazed by it. Too sweet for his own good.

She shook her head, drawling over her name in return with a mockingly sympathetic cadence. "Sonra. It hasn't been nearly long enough. Foolish as ever. I would have thought someone would have silenced you for your recklessness by now."

Sonra panted with excitement. "It doesn't matter anymore. We will rule this world." She smirked knowingly and looked to Bennett. "All thanks to you."

Adair ached, watching the woman she once considered a dear friend, now so caught up in the evil that the demon side of her craved. "It doesn't have to be that way. Finding our place doesn't have to be so complicated; the world isn't what it used to be."

Sonra pulled back her lips. "No, but it could be so much better." Snarling, she raised the gun and pointed it straight between Adair's eyes, smug and not having a clue what was coming.

Slamming his shield into Sonra unceremoniously, Bennett knocked her flat and finished her off with a fluid sweep of his sword.

The others came sauntering in, their clothes stained with blood, thrill and relief mirrored in their expressions. Logan nodded to Adair. "Let's go. Calloway will come when he finds out it was you."

"Good." She nodded, holding her breath as she looked over the bloody scene. Her stomach rolled, imagining how she'd once reveled in being on the other side.

Lana called in the local coroner's team to take care of the bodies and coordinate clean-up as they sped away from the scene. Sunrise threatened on the horizon, the gray glow of morning teasing at the corners of the sky.

Bennett's hands glided smoothly over the wheel, taking every turn with a confident leisure as he drove them back to his apartment. He reached across and rested his hand on her thigh, a smug grin as he rode on cloud nine, pleased with the success of his first big mission. Adair shook her head and grinned, utterly and completely charmed.

Quinn, Lana, and Logan crashed in sleeping bags on the apartment floor, wiped out from the long night.

Adair tugged Bennett by the belt and shut the bedroom door behind them and had him undressed before they reached the bed. The adrenaline from the night pumped through her, the urgent need for him thundering in her veins.

Fingertips trailing along the angle of her jaw, Bennett slowed them down. With a savoring leisure, his pace, his attention to detail was intoxicating. Patient, attentive, he made love with her all day... like they had all the time in the world.

She did.

He didn't.

As the last scrap of daylight faded around the edge of his window blinds, she laid her head on his shoulder. A fat tear beaded at the corner of her eye. She eased up and took one last look.

The front door slammed open and shattered her silent escape. A furious roar shook the walls. Thundering closer, the demon threw open the bedroom door, and the growl threatened the structural integrity of the building.

1

Breath fast and unsteady, Bennett jerked up and scanned the room. Safe. Home. Alone. He flicked off the smooth white sheet and buried his face in his hands, rubbing his eyes until the dream faded.

Damn, when had his beard gotten so ragged? Since Typha and his disembowelment, he hadn't bothered with niceties like haircuts. Quinn had always cut it for him. And asking her now? No fucking way. Beyond her normal snarky, she'd gone from months of cranky pregnant woman to sleep-deprived new mom.

Not his problem anymore.

As he rose to his feet, he guarded the nagging pull in his abdomen. Although physically healed months ago, the blistering sensation of his gut healing itself from the inside out had yet to fade. Rapid healing was great, as the injury should have taken his life, but the close call still haunted him. That was the life of a demon hunter. Potentially centuries long, but it could be ended damn fast in combat.

Each strike of his bare feet over the cool concrete ricocheted off the high ceilings of the empty building. He'd considered renovating the rest of the warehouse. He could make a killing, cashing out on the trend of urban lofts in the area, but he preferred the privacy and anonymity of the discrete structure. The ground floor had evolved into an elaborate training room for the team, so the investment had at least paid off in that respect.

Through the floor-to-ceiling windows, the gray of the Seattle sun wasn't telling if it was sunrise or sunset. Not that it made a difference normally, but today... today he had to travel.

He clicked the coffee pot to brew on his way past the kitchen and lumbered into the bathroom. The slope of the brick tile floor declined as he crossed into the walk-in shower and flipped the knob to steaming. Palms pressed flat against the wall, he bent forward and let the heat pool above his broad shoulders before washing away the useless memories that were nearly fifteen years expired. Those pouty lips still haunted him.

After a brilliantly long shower, almost enough to make him feel as half-human as he was, Bennett snagged a towel from the heated rack. Sparing half a glance at the mess he'd become, he shook his head and stalked out. Over these last few months he hadn't been idle, despite minimal demon inactivity and the team hunkering down for some well-deserved quiet.

Any given day, and he could take a few vampires without a fuss. But with the gift of enhanced strength and endurance from his demon-mother ancestor last year, he could sit on his ass for a month straight, then walk out and knock a werewolf on its ass without breaking a sweat. Still, not his style. He'd always been the first one to hit the training room floor. But after last year? When he wasn't hitting the streets, he was in his gym from sunrise to sunrise to ensure no demon would bring him so close to the brink again.

Not bothering with a towel or bathrobe, he trudged into the kitchen. His phone blinked with an alarming blue light to let him know he had a message. Not that he needed to check it to know exactly what it said.

He poured a cup of black coffee and took a long, mind-melting pull. Without a second glance at his phone on the counter, Bennett strolled across the open floor plan to his dresser and tossed on a pair of distressed jeans and a black t-shirt that clung to his tight abs, then added tan leather chukkas and a matching belt. When he could stall no longer, he skimmed the barrage of messages and sent a quick thumbs-up to the group and let them know he'd be there in ten.

Not bothering with the little-used freight elevator, he steadied his coffee and dashed down the steel staircase to the main floor. He dropped into his McLaren, the cargo bay door rising as he fired up the engine. He turned onto 4th, crossed the wide spread of railroad tracks, and slid in front of an exhaust-puffing semi onto Marginal Way. A few safety checkpoints at the airfield, and he slipped into his hangar.

Lana was waiting for him, eyes rolling and hands on her hips. Dark hair flipped to the side, miniskirt and spike-heeled boots not giving the slightest nod to the brisk morning, she shook her head with an ornery smirk. "Sleep in a bit this morning?"

"Sorry," he muttered, continuing his clipped pace toward the private jet.

Arms folded over his chest, Vann's expression remained stern. "Ready?"

Bennett nodded. "Let's go."

Astrid was already in the cockpit, poring through her latest training manual with her typical intensity. Blond hair smoothed out of her face, she offered him a brilliant smile. "Hey." She nodded, then back to her book. "Thought you were at your place in BC?"

Shit. He'd been a total ass and dodged a dinner hangout a few nights back, claiming he would be off the grid for a few days. Usually when things got tough, or even blissfully quiet, he retreated to his parents' home north of Victoria. Well, his home now. They'd built the sea-side structure shortly after he was born, and after thirty-five years, they decided the home they had built to raise him in was truly his, and they were ready to turn over a new leaf. "I was going to, but, I didn't go."

"Oh." She pursed her lips tight, worry drawing her eyebrows together.

"I'm fine."

"I know," she said with a soft smile. "When you're not, don't hide, okay?"

He nodded, then turned back into the cabin. Exploring the ins and outs of the jet with vibrant curiosity, Bodie grinned. "Is the landing strip at the ranch big enough for this?"

Bennett leaned against the wall and folded his arms over his chest. "An experienced pilot in a pinch could land there, but you wouldn't need something this big. I got this to fly the whole team, plus all our gear, anywhere in the world. If you invest in a sturdy prop plane that can handle your Montana winters, you won't need much."

"Fair point. Probably not as fast, though." Bodie bit his lower lip and grinned like the first time he'd driven Bennett's McLaren.

Unlike Vann and Quinn, who had ragged on him for the lack of subtlety in his toys, like the jet and the car, Bodie had gotten a kick out of all of it. Raised in isolation on his pack's Montana ranch, Bodie had only recently discovered the joys of fast toys. No wonder he'd taken right to it; as the wolf, Bodie was fearless. The corner of his mouth quirking up, Bennett let the lightness of the moment and Bodie's easy manner tame his mood. "True."

On the flight to Eureka, his friends joked and hung out, taking the edge off his angst. Astrid was the eternally attentive student and handled most of the flight herself, sporting an eager grin the entire time. Hell, she didn't even need him in the cockpit.

The drive to Quinn and Ryan's home was gorgeous in the chill wind. The isolated structure stood proudly on the hillside, dreamily looking over the Pacific. A year ago, if anyone had told him his girlfriend would dump his ass, declare their relationship as boring, then days later fall for the son of the king of the demon realm and bear his child–after telling Bennett she wasn't ready for marriage or children? Oh, and let's not forget his guts getting sliced out of him when he'd convinced the team a little recon wouldn't hurt, her crying over his dying body before she was blasted across the fricking arctic and into the arms of her soulmate...

He rubbed his hands over his face and shook away the redundant self-torture. He'd known Quinn was right about them. Friends-to-lovers wasn't always a true love story. Besides, destiny had played a strong hand in bringing it all to pass.

Fate was a bitch like that.

As they parked the SUV, Ryan met them on the front step. Barefooted, dressed in an old white t-shirt and faded jeans, with the bleary eyes of a new dad, Ryan managed a sleepy grin. "Hey guys. Quinn's been going nuts waiting for you. Of course, she and Skye are passed out now."

Lana bounced up the steps and spun Ryan for a giddy hug, whether he was ready or not. The rest filtered in a bit more sedately. With high ceilings, massive windows, wood beam ceilings, and plank floors, warmed by plush area rugs and overstuffed furniture and a fire roaring in the hearth, the home was exactly what Quinn had always wanted. The rest of the team had already seen the place, helping with the big move a month or two back, but Bennett had been on a solo recon to investigate a possible leviathan that turned out to be as ridiculous of a rumor as it sounded.

"Fiona and Quentin left this morning?" he asked Ryan.

Nodding as they walked in together, Ryan said, "It's been a whirlwind, both our moms here for the birth, happy as anything I've ever seen, then Quentin flew back from his latest mission last weekend and they stayed until today, then Fiona and my mom will take turns coming to help when I go back out to sea."

"Bet you guys need some time to yourselves. I think Lana's planning to move in, but I'll drag her out with the rest of the team when we leave."

"As much as Quinn loves the company, yes, please, I'm looking forward to a few days alone with my family before I ship out."

"Go catch a nap while you can."

The others were already heading down to the basement, which apparently was filled with bedrooms and a gym dedicated to training. Quinn had wanted a comfortable place for the team to crash anytime and for however long they needed.

Ryan hesitated, his eyes black as midnight, and the circles under were equally dark.

"Go. You're dead on your feet."

"I've fought monsters for days on end, but up rocking and pacing and changing diapers? Way more exhausting." Ryan ran a hand over his stubbled beard before turning and heading to the bedroom. "You guys can make yourselves at home, fix whatever you want for lunch."

Bennett chuckled under his breath. Strolling to the windows, he looked out over the endless ocean, at the fog blurring the horizon and spreading onto the expansive field of yellow grass and wind-sculpted trees. Some might see it as desolate, but it was remarkably soothing. Sunshine, Ryan's mother, had made an impact, dotting the patio with brightly colored noninvasive plants to bring life to the patio. The others laughed and chatted downstairs, already at home.

Running a hand over his face, Bennett couldn't decide if he wanted to sit or stand... or run screaming. He wanted to hate Ryan for stealing the life he'd envisioned for himself. But, turns out, Ryan was a tough guy to hate. And loved Quinn in a way that Bennett never could.

With his mother and her father on the same demon hunting team, they'd been best friends since infancy. And they wanted the best for each other, even though that wasn't together. They'd really only dated two years, so they'd been friends for far longer than they'd been lovers. Still, the downshift was never as easy as the move forward.

Soft steps padded out of the nursery, the sweet whimpers of a newborn and her mother's soothing coos erasing the anxiety that had clawed at him all morning.

Turning, he caught sight of his ex. "Hey," he said with a smile.

"Hey." She grinned back, her sleepy smile about knocking him flat with hundreds of memories of when she'd looked at him like that.

"I made your husband snag a nap. Guy's a wreck."

"How'd you get him to take a break? I've been trying for days. I honestly don't think he's slept in the two weeks since she was born." Rubbing a sleepy face against her mother's chest, Skye wound up with a pitiful cry.

"As he was about to fall asleep on his feet, I think he was done arguing." Bennett slid off his leather jacket and tossed it onto the entry hook. Holding out his arms, he reached for the precious package that crashed her cranky head into her mother's sternum.

Quinn smiled and passed her to him. Cradling her close, he held her like a little football and rocked her in his arms. Sweetest little thing he'd ever seen. Dark, onyx eyes like her father, burgundy fuzz atop her head and bow-shaped lips already hinting at a wicked sense of humor like her mother. She was everything Quinn deserved. Amazing and sweet and fricking adorable. Lowering to the corner cushion of the couch, Quinn pulled her legs under and melted in.

"You did good." Bennett tapped his fingertip on the little one's nose.

Reading him as easily as she always had, Quinn's smile was affected by the lines across her brow.

He bit his lip and shook his head before she could say it. "No. Let's not go there. You were right all along. I was set on the perfect life and thought that was you and me. This..." he glanced around the house, toward the main bedroom where Ryan had escaped, and down at the infant in his arms, he shook his head. "this is incredible. We would never have had it quite like this."

Tiny black irises with silvery-blue flecks swam with sleepiness in his arms. Stroking a finger over her little nose a few times, adding a soft *shh*, she fell asleep in his arms. Propping her up against his broad shoulder, Bennett moved to the recliner and savored the genuine innocence that couldn't be beat.

"You're a natural."

"She's a good baby."

Wrapping a throw blanket over her legs, Quinn sighed. "I know nobody else is even close to ready, but I wish she was going to have a little friend. Like we always had each other."

"We were lucky. While our parents planned the next skirmish or toasted together at the holidays, you and I were the only kids."

"And eventually I was egging you on until you cussed and spit and Lizzy and Jonathan were horrified."

He laughed, careful not to wake Skye. "My parents were so pissed when we figured out how to get those swords down."

"Even worse, the weekend after I turned eighteen? You were, what, twenty? Lana was nineteen. Our first big mission together, and we marched straight into the lair a few blocks down from your old apartment? Fighting alongside two vampires?"

"Your dad was livid. When Quentin found you and Lana in sleeping bags on my living room floor, a naked vampire in bed with me, and her brother in the kitchen sipping his evening coffee with blood for creamer?"

Laughing to the point of snorting, Quinn threw her head back and took a few minutes to calm down enough to respond. "I don't think I've ever been as afraid of a demon as I was of my dad when he found us that way." She pushed her lava-red hair out of her face and added, "You never said how Lizzy reacted when he told her. She had to have been pissed."

Gnawing in his chest, he flashed back to last night's dream. His subconscious felt the need to torture him regularly, near nightly the last few months. "Yeah, you could say that. Mom was full of warnings, mostly about how deceitful vampires can be, and Dad gave me the man-to-man lecture about not letting my dick do the thinking. I didn't speak to them for weeks, convinced they were too narrow-minded to see that true love knew no borders."

A scowl stirred Quinn's midnight blue eyes.

He shook his head, taking a long sniff of the sweet baby smell of Skye's fuzzy head.

"I know it sounds crazy, but why don't you look her up? I know you–"

"She made her feelings quite clear," he whispered, careful not to disturb the snuggly package that nuzzled into him. "You know me. I thought she was my fricking soulmate, but I was an inexperienced fool. Then I thought you were the love of my life, but I was wrong again. Oh-for-two."

"Seriously. You and I have been best buds for forever. It was only natural to see if there was more. We were wrong, but it was a worthwhile experiment. You were different back then. With her."

"I grew up."

Swinging her hips as she strolled up the stairs, Lana grinned and aimed straight for him. "So sneaky up here, stealing all the baby time for yourself."

Bennett forced a smile and rose to his feet, passing off the sleeping bundle, only a little smug when she pouted at the loss and Lana had to sing her calm. He stalked into the kitchen to pour a scotch big enough to knock him on his ass and into dreamless sleep tonight, wishing his demon hunter blood would let him get drunk, just once.

2

Pioneer Square, Seattle

Sun-kissed chestnut hair tickling her shoulder blades, electric blue dress hugging her hips and clinging to her torso, Adair clicked past the bouncers as they opened the velvet gate for her. In full swing, the Seattle club was hopping. A bass-heavy techno rhythm vibrated the floor beneath the carefree dancers that were grinding in the dim light.

Pink and blue spotlights glowed over the common areas, diffuse against the matte black floor. A cluster of hot-young-things fell silent until she passed. Whispers. A dark-haired one jogged to catch her. "Hey, if you're not here with anyone and, you know, want some company, come on and join us for a drink? Or a dance?"

Adair trailed her hand across his shoulder. "Not tonight." Leaning to whisper in his ear, she closed her eyes and scented his tangy pulse under his skin. "Go. This isn't the club for you and your friends." Open only a few days, the club already reeked of her bloodsucking brethren.

Withdrawing, she continued her path until she reached the corded-off stairs. To the guard, she smiled, flicking her tongue over a sharp canine. With a subtly fang-bearing smile in return, he opened the gate, greedily sweeping his gaze down the length of her. Jackass.

Overlooking the club, the private lair was dark, with only low hanging pendant lights that neither she, nor the VIPs, needed to find their way. From an overstuffed black leather couch, arms, and legs sprawled wide, either in a blatant offer of tasteless sex, or declaring that this was his territory, the boss spoke, "To what do I owe the pleasure?"

Adair masked her disgust, drawing her lips tight. How had she once thought him irresistible? As striking as the day she'd met him, timeless in his immortal body, he was still long and lean, but more toned now, and he sported a ponytail and freshly shaven face. She didn't want to imagine what he'd been up to while he'd been off the map, but judging by his smug smirk, it wasn't anything good. "I had to see for myself if the rumors were true. The great Calloway, returning from the darkest corners of the earth to bring blood to my territory."

"I missed you." He grinned wide, his teeth gleaming whiter than his pasty skin. A foursome of half-dressed vampires with flushed cheeks emerged from behind the curtain, the scent of their shared meal ripe on their skin. One woman draped herself over Calloway, the others making themselves at home in the cozy sitting area.

"Missed me?" Adair snorted, holding her ground. "Oh, I'm sorry. Last time we saw each other I had a knife embedded in your jugular. Was that what you were lamenting? I'll be happy to do it again."

Those pale eyes glimmered with what might actually be tears. "I never got over you, but at least I had Sonra."

Adair's gut wrenched, her poker face threatened failure.

"Yeah, you know what I'm talking about."

"I had little choice, with all the noise she was making around here. Really, I couldn't let her go on and risk our secrecy."

Running a hand over his powdery brow, Calloway forced an exhale. "You're not wrong. She was... foolish. But she was mine, and it is my duty to punish those that ended her without my consent."

"So you rose from whatever ashes you were hiding under for vengeance? Beneath you."

"Ah. I believe you and I are not on the same page. It has been too long since we caught up. I'm so glad you came."

"I know you've been off the grid for a while, but there's this fancy device called a cell phone. You could have called, texted, emailed, posted." She gritted her teeth, resisting the fist-clench that throbbed in her knuckles.

He laughed as if she were the greatest comedian, his winning smile turning her stomach. "Would you have responded? Would you have come if you knew it was me? This is so much more fun in person." Abruptly, his lips turned into a full sneer. "Sonra was a fool. But she was on to something. And I'm not just talking about this prime location. I mean, look at this place? Rare sun, damp streets, and I've always wanted to live on a boat."

"Get to the point." Adair began to regret coming, as her presence seemed to be more of an ego-stroke for him than the threat she'd intended.

"You've been naughty. Really, grinding with a demon hunter? I figured at least you wouldn't be so foolish as to trust one."

"This may be news to you, but the universe does not revolve around you. I don't give a damn where you've been, burrowed in a hole in Antarctica or baking in the Saharan sun. I live my life how I want, regardless of your location on this planet." Smug son-of-a-bitch.

"I don't think you quite realize the implications of your little affair."

"So I got to deflower a demon hunter while kicking your cronies out of my territory. Fun times. But I can't imagine how that's relevant now." She risked snapping the heel of her stiletto if she couldn't calm down. Forcing her pulse to slow, she teased her fingers in her hair and pasted on a blasé expression. "I didn't come to chat. Sonra was a lovely, but stupid woman. I can make one quick call, and you'll have a serious demon hunter problem. Or, you and your little followers can flutter away and leave my territory."

"You still don't get it, do you? I'm not here to infringe on your territory. Sonra was passionate. She was adventurous in a way you never will be."

"And now she's dead. And I'm not."

"As the light faded from her eyes, she used the last of her strength to send me one final message. That my life's work was coming to fruition."

She folded her arms over her chest and bit her cheek.

"I'm here because this is where fate has determined the story will begin. I have spent the last two centuries reading and learning, planning a better future for all of us. A life where we won't have to hide in the shadows."

Fuck. He relished in a good plan. She'd been part of his plan once. It hadn't turned out well for either, but she'd known he wasn't finished. "Always restless. That's the trouble with such a long life, you need to appreciate the little things." She shrugged.

"Oh, I do. Seemingly such a little thing, you swapping sweat with the sweet little demon hunter–"

The half-asleep woman at his side shifted against him, sliding her bare leg along his, her mouth turning into a wicked grin and pale eyes sparking with life. "Sweet? Little? Oh honey, he's a vicious warrior. Yum. I'd be willing to give up humans for a ride on that one."

Adair swallowed the nausea *that* image invoked. Initially, she'd watched Bennett from afar, telling herself she was ensuring that he was safe. But after he'd taken up an active dating life, she hadn't been able to handle the details and didn't even know if he still lived around here, if he'd changed his number, or if he'd started a little demon hunting brood of his own by now.

Calloway shifted his position and slid his hand up the slut's thigh possessively. "Milan, please. The hunter may act fierce, but he is still young and foolish."

The slut tipped her head back and laughed. "Fresh and brave and full of naughty ideas. If those shoulders are any hint at the rest of him, I would love a taste of his–"

Clearing her throat before she had to endure the end of the sentence, Adair interrupted. "Okay. Lovely chat. I'd like to get home before sunrise. You've been warned."

Calloway shifted the curvy leg off his lap and leaned forward. "I wish you had come sooner, so you could watch firsthand. I wonder, who will hunt the hunter?"

Bile rose in her throat as she imagined the multitude of reasons he might be suddenly targeting Bennett. And here she thought she was done with Calloway fucking with her life. She held her expression bland but knew Calloway could feel her pulse pounding under her skin.

Like a fascinated student becoming the teacher, he expounded, "I'd never heard of a demon hunter being changed, and I'm sure, like me, you've heard any attempt would be unsuccessful. And if the attack fails? None of us wants to be the target of hunters, so few have ever tried."

"And here I'd heard you took out an entire team a few centuries back."

"I don't like to brag–" *liar*, "–but that rumor is true. Took dozens of us, the best of the best, but I survived." *I*, not we.

Regret darkened her vision as she imagined how many he'd let die, vampires or not, in pursuit of his plan. Although she had no wish to return to that life, she'd had friends she'd abandoned when Logan had found her and offered a freer, peaceful eternity.

Calloway leaned back into the couch and snickered, tracing his tongue over his teeth. Still smirking wide, his pale eyes locked onto Adair. "But that's not what I'm talking about. I stumbled upon a prophecy. You know how those demon hunters love recording the predictions from crazy old seers."

"Oh boy. Please tell me you're not falling for one of their attempts to bait you into something?" She folded her arms over her chest, cocking her hip out to the side. One clue. Come on. Did he have Bennett already? Where?

"I can tell the difference. This was genuine, from the library of a fool that thought he could take me alone." He sighed, satisfied as he relived the memory. "*There will be a hunter changed. Fated to crave as the vampires do.*"

A frigid chill stiffened her spine. Steadying her voice, she shook her head as if he were daft. "Demon hunters can't be changed. And even if this 'prophecy' comes to pass, that passage says nothing about the hunter's fate once turned. I crave human blood, but that doesn't mean I drink the stuff. And I sure as hell wouldn't join your dimwitted minions."

"Changing a demon hunter alone is a worthwhile experiment, but I have much bigger plans for him. Whatever his preferred drink may be."

Closing her eyes, she took a long inhale, refusing to suppress the memories that still ate away at her, of the bizarre thrill inherent to

vampires that had led her to destroy so many lives. Successfully resisting human blood had taken years of practice, of accepting what she
was, what she had been, and not acting on those cravings. "You intend
to change a demon hunter, hoping they will succumb to your thrall
like a typical progeny? And not just any demon hunter, but one that
is stronger than average, even more than when we took out a handful
of your friends in one night? You're going to get your ass kicked."

His pale eyes danced with merriment. "Oh, your lover hasn't only
grown stronger since you took him last. I've been watching. He's
developed a bit of a temper. But, although he could be a hell of a killer,
I don't give a fuck what he eats, who he answers to, or who all he kills...
or doesn't."

"Is avenging Sonra really worth the risk?"

He nipped his lower lip, licking off the drop of blood and closed
his eyes and smirked. "Sonra brought on her end, you're not wrong.
I would have ended her myself for her lack of subtlety. But as her
death was in the name of my goal, she deserves vengeance. Lucky
me, the prophecy pointed to your little playmate. See? Fate. I've been
dreaming of the day I get to rip out your heart like you ripped out
mine."

Her pulse accelerated, her heart about to beat out of her chest as
adrenaline screamed at her to take him out now, before he could do
any damage. Frozen in place, she calculated her odds of getting out
of there alive if she tried. The bodyguards, the vampires that listened
keenly on their conversation... Today was not the day.

Sitting up, he leaned forward and rested his elbows on his knees,
unblinking. Knowing her well, he saw right through her. "You're too
late. It's already done."

Arresting in her chest, her heart refused to beat. "Where is he?" she
seethed through gritted teeth.

He wasn't saying more. And she was out of time. She turned on her pinpoint heel and stalked toward the exit.

"Adair?"

She held her position but didn't turn back.

"If at any point you think you might get a happily ever after? Know that I will be right there, ready to take it from you."

She took off, heels not even touching the ground, needing to find Bennett before he hurt someone.

3

INDUSTRIAL DISTRICT, SEATTLE, THREE DAYS AGO.

DOWNSHIFTING AS HE NEARED home, the garage door opened, and he pulled into his warehouse. Glancing around the vast, hollow space, he crossed toward his living quarters, his footsteps echoing off the steel walls. Dim lights swung overhead as a gust of wind rushed through in one last furious blow before the room sealed shut.

At the foot of the stairs, he halted and turned, opening the door to his training room rather than turning in for the night. No padded flooring for demon hunters, the concrete was roughened by years of training, mostly by him, but the team joined him often enough to make a few respectable dents. Bypassing the wall of weights and machines, most of which he'd broken and had yet to replace, he crossed the abraded floor. He pressed his thumb to the lock and shoved open the garage-style door, unveiling a wall of weaponry, mostly filled with those passed down through his family for generations. Plus a few sharp objects he'd picked up along the way.

They'd landed as the sun was setting, the clouds lowering to coat the city in freezing mist. Lana had crossed to the next hangar over, hopping into her plane to fly home to Sitka. Astrid and Bodie planned to spend a few more nights in their Elliott Bay home before returning to Montana to catch up with Bodie's werewolf pack. And Vann had driven home to San Francisco.

When they'd left Quinn, Ryan and little Skye, they'd stood waving goodbye from the front porch, an adorable family unit. Skye had been cradled in Quinn's arms, nuzzled against her neck. Protective despite his heavy lids, Ryan had wrapped his arm around them, a kiss for each.

Too restless to settle in for the night, Bennett snatched his favorite sword and shield, tempered and re-tempered dozens of times since his great-grandfather had aided his team to victory in the vampire uprising of 1483. Perfectly balanced, the sword was like an extension of his arm. It was always risky, bearing the unsubtle weapon in public, but few were foolish enough to walk in this neighborhood at night, unless they were looking for trouble of their own.

Stalking out of the warehouse, he took a long inhale of the cool air. He ventured into the fog that grew thicker as darkness encompassed the city. He kept the area clear of demons, but maybe he'd get lucky.

Crossing the tracks, he passed homeless encampments, factories that had been shut down with the latest downturn of the economy, and bypassed what looked to be an impressive drug deal. He fired off a tip to a detective he knew; he had bigger fights to find.

Shattering the relative calm of the night, a scream of terror that only inhumanity could incite, unwittingly beckoned him. Taking off at a sprint, arms pumping at his sides, thighs burning at the intensity of his pace, he ran deeper into the frozen mist.

Past the old transfer station along the waterfront, an abandoned warehouse hummed with demon activity. Halting at the nearest bay door, he listened. Laughter, shuffling. A handful of vampires.

Nagging in his chest, his instincts urged him to call for backup.

Another cry of terror. Shit, how many humans did they have in there? No time.

Astrid and Bodie could be here within fifteen minutes. These people didn't have fifteen seconds.

Letting the adrenaline heat his veins, fuel his rage, he gripped the hilt of his sword. Closing his eyes, his mouth turned up in a satisfied smile.

Sliding the door open, he saw the crowd. No more than eight vampires. Nothing he couldn't handle.

He stalked inside, letting his footsteps echo through the hollow cavern and off the high ceilings, alerting his quarry.

Eight wide-eyed, blood-dripping sets of teeth turned toward him, while six victims lie whimpering on the table.

"You guys must be new in town." Nodding to the humans on the table, he softened his voice. "Go. There's a cop two blocks north." Scrambling, those that were still conscious helped the others, holding pressure over their bites as they limped away. He added as they passed, "Not a word about what happened tonight. My anonymity protects me so I can hunt them."

A few wary nods as they shuffled past.

The vampires stalked closer. He tightened his grip on his shield. "Well? Let's get started. I mean, I've got all night, but you don't." Fuck, he needed a good fight. Too long without, and he'd grown twitchy.

Snarling, three ran for him. Easily slicing through the throats of the first two, he bashed the next across the room and readied for the next. The others sprinted toward him with inhuman speed, surrounding him.

He rolled his shoulders and stood waiting in the center of their circle.

A livid screech from the fiercest of them threatened to shatter the windows above. The vampire rushed toward him, believing its speed would deliver the advantage.

Rotating, he nailed it in the face with a roundhouse kick.

He ducked to dodge the blow from the next, driving his sword into its gut.

Arcing in a fluid motion, he disabled another.

Each bash of his shield, each swing of his sword, and every closed-fist punch at close range as he gripped the hilt... all tempered the fire that had been brewing in his gut this past year.

After crunching the nose of one that popped up to its feet, he turned for the next.

Too fucking late. It lashed at him with its fists, baring its sharp teeth in a blatant threat. He juked, but the swift hit hammered his ribs and knocked him back.

Fuck these guys were fast. Holding his ground, Bennett winked at the last of his prey.

Rapidly cooling as it trickled down his skin, his own blood pooled at his lip from a blow he hadn't been fast enough to dodge. Licking it off, he tasted the coppery drip, shaking his head and rolling his eyes. "Mmm, tasty. Sorry, but I'm not sharing."

Unfazed, the remaining vampire grinned, the room eerily silent like the calm before the storm.

Thundering from above, from behind, hooting and chirping with a revelers' glee, they came.

Without pause, he sprinted for the door. Yeah, he'd needed a good fight, but he didn't care to die tonight.

Seven vampires, twice the size of those he'd ended, pounded through the bay door.

Eight more.

His heart surged into his chest; his adrenaline boiled as the hunter became prey. Another six strolled in the side door.

Loose gravel slipped under his feet as he changed direction. Pumping his arms faster, he scanned the room. Aiming for the stairs, he spun in place.

Ten more from who the hell knew where. These weren't foolish newbies. As a unit, combat ready, unusually patient, they surrounded him.

Fucking trap.

He stilled, his breath coming fast. His shirt clung to his sweat-soaked skin, chest rising and falling. Bracing his legs, he tightened his shield and rolled his shoulders.

Blocks away from home, his team scattered, his temper peaked... the trap was very, very deliberate. Calculated and designed for him alone.

They closed in.

Diving, he skidded on his hip and out of the bullseye center of the bloodsuckers.

The first lashed out. He slipped under, blocking him and driving his sword into the next.

He flipped over his shoulder and leapt to his feet. One by one, they dove at him. A shrug, a bash with his sword, he knocked them back.

Between blows, he searched for an out that didn't exist.

Foolishly naïve, the largest of them popped back to his feet and roared toward Bennett. Crunching under the impact of his elbow like a walnut shell, he shattered his nose, then spun and slammed his shield into the next that thought herself clever enough to catch him off-guard.

As one, another cluster of vampires lunged to take his legs out from under him. As he struggled to stay on his feet, he slammed his shield back. In a calculated move, three of them wrenched his sword from his hand. Red-hot sparks blasted from his shoulder. His eyes burned with a furious pain.

Ignoring the searing sensation of his shoulder hanging loosely out of its socket, he swung his shield around and flattened any in his reach. The move bought half a second to snap the loose joint back into place. The ripping grit of it spliced black stars across his vision. Blinking, he shook his head to bring the fight back into focus.

Another mass of them closed in. Bennett dove for a slide tackle out of the fray and took off across the warehouse.

Fast as fuck, a cluster caught up to him, latching on to his neck, his waist, another dangling from his foot. Kicking, he smashed its face under his boot.

His sword unreachable, he fisted one in the throat, shoving another by the chin while he pummeled a pair with his shield. Rolling out of reach, he snapped back to his feet.

He knocked the next that came for him with the full force of his shield, the flailing body flying at a concrete pillar. Cracks sprouted through the support on impact, rattling the steel roof.

The metallic taste of blood coated his tongue, his vision blurred as his face swelled from a few fractures. Almost halfway done, only fifteen more to go. Blinking, he tried to clear his head until he could see halfway straight.

He wasn't making it out in one piece.

A big guy with dark hair and a neck thicker than his own thigh sprinted after him, arrogance flashing in his pale eyes.

Wiping the corner of his mouth, Bennett grinned. Jagging at the last second, he spun and grabbed the asshole's arm and heaved him into the post. At the force of the massive vampire's body blasting into it, the pillar shattered. Above, the roof creaked and bowed.

As they surrounded him, closing in to finish him off now that he was well and truly trapped and broken, one muttered something about this not being as easy as they'd been led to believe.

Bennett took off for the next pillar, the crowd following as he'd hoped. Never stopping, movements erratic as he was no match for their speed, he kept them guessing. Skidding to a halt, he waited.

Cracking his shield against the skull of the next, he sent it flying against the pillar that crumbled on impact. The roof tumbled further. A flutter of hope rattled in his chest as he sighted the next two pillars. Might take him out with them, but he'd survived worse than a building falling on top of him.

Gaze scanning with desperate calculation, he lined up the vampires in his path. Two pillars. And still another seven vampires blocked the exit.

Before he could make it to the next pillar, laughter obliterated his last flicker of hope. He knew before he saw.

A dozen more strutted in.

The rest was a fucking blur, and not just because he couldn't see a damn thing through his swollen eyelids. Too many, too fucking fast.

Lights out, darkness closing in.

Couldn't run on his shattered ankle.

Couldn't think through the excruciating throb of concussion.

Arms and legs of a dozen-and-a-half vampires pinned him down. Bent rebar and concrete shards from the shattered pillar dug into his back. Gasping against the pressure, he fought to take in a full breath. Filled with lead, he couldn't lift his hand to at least rip out the throat of the mouth-breather hovering over his head.

Dozens of razor-sharp teeth sunk into his neck, his arms, his legs, burning as they tore into his flesh. Ripped from his lifeless arm, his shield crashed into the rubble as it was tossed aside.

Hoarse, he slurred, "Why?"

"The prophecy." As his life drained into the mouths of the greedy monsters, the same rumbling voice chuckled, "Now open wide."

His body numb, unmoving, his mind in and out of consciousness, he felt the unmistakable viscous, warm fluid wash over his lips. A thumb pulled down his chin, and the coppery taste of blood poured down his throat. Heavy on his arms, his legs, his head, the surviving vampires pinned him in place.

Coughing reflexively, he gagged and spit, but it was too much.

Not another fucking prophecy.

4

Now.

FURY SCORCHED THE BACK of his throat. Forcing his eyes open, Bennett pulled air in and out of his lungs, the sensation so exquisite, it felt as if the cool night wind imprinted into every cell. He flexed his fists. No ache, no splintering zaps. His fractures healed, his wounds gone. As if nothing had happened. But everything had.

How long had he been out? Big fucking blur. Flashes of pain and blood and... Hunger. Desperation.

That unquenchable thirst.

At the thought of another taste, he craved like nothing else. His skull thundered, a heaviness choking him that would only be relieved by the heady nectar.

Across the room, a cluster of vampires bitched and griped. Crystal clear, like a violin solo in an empty opera house, he could hear the whiny one shifting her feet in place over the gravelly floor while the other exhaled a heavy sigh. "He should have completed the change already. If you fucked this up... Your instructions were clear."

The other grumbled, "Calloway's a fool if he thinks this is going to work. No demon hunter has ever been changed and this must be why. He's fed off two dozen of us, fourteen already dead, and the rest of us need to feed if we're to keep up with him." A long pause. "Look at me. I'm pale. I'm hungry. The bastard broke most of my ribs, trying to drain me before the others knocked him out again so I could get away. He's getting stronger and we won't be able to subdue him much longer. Where are my reinforcements?"

"Fuck. I've never seen a human require more than a few pints to complete the change. I've got another ten vampires coming to help. Go feed, there's a college party a few blocks down with some decent targets. I'll tide him over until the others get here."

The whiny one's voice lightened at the mention of a hearty meal. Bennett could still taste the buttery warmth of her blood on his tongue. "I... have you ever seen anything like this? I mean, what happens if his body rejects the change?"

"We'll find out."

He closed his eyes as the others rose to take a lunch break. Nine exhausted vampires struggled to stand.

"Be careful," she said.

"I can handle it." She man's voice hummed with amusement.

A smile teased at the corners of his mouth; Bennett was looking forward to taking out the vampire with an ego bigger than his own.

The sleepy voice hissed with a derisive sarcasm. "Of course, the inexorable Blayk can change anybody." Pausing, the vampire seemed to remember her place on the food chain. "Seriously, be careful. Go feed him before he wakes up all the way, or he'll be too strong. I know you changed most of us, you know the risks, but he's... don't let him get his hands on you."

Now.

Bennett rose from the rubble and cleared his throat. "Thanks for the lovely time, but I have better places to be."

Nine half-speed, groggy vampires turned from their path and trudged toward him.

Wait for it.

Grinning, Bennett took off, like running on a cloud, his feet skimmed over the ground as he noiselessly closed the distance in half a heartbeat.

With a few easy neck-snaps, he cleaned up the room. Might not be fully changed, but the power coursing through him? The speed, the pure sensation of even the air on his skin... invigorating.

When the last of them hit the floor, Blayk stood with his hands on his hips, waiting.

Bennett rolled his shoulders and sauntered toward him. "So sweet of you, offering me a little drink to tuck me in for another nap."

The corners of Blayk's lips drew up. "Looky you. Not a trace of thrall for your sires, huh? He'll be so disappointed. Hate to spoil your plans, but you're not going to last long without another infusion."

Hands on his hips, Bennett snorted, "Infusion? Is that what you call it? I've survived worse than vampire blood shoved down my throat. Nasty business." While his words decried the revolt he should be feeling, his throat lurched with a yearning. Exhilaration rushed through him as he felt the vampire's pulse pounding, the need for the relief nothing else would provide.

"Sure. Try going without. Let me know how you feel in a few hours." Blayk shrugged. "I mean, you're pretty tough, but I can feel it. It's too late. Ignore it now, and you'll be dead within hours. Although maybe a day or two, for you. Let me finish it, and I can show you how powerful you can be."

Instinct pounded in Bennett's brain, that sharp vampire survivalism battling with the bullheaded demon hunter. "When it's done, do you really think I'll let you live?"

"You will if you want to know whose idea this was and why. He seems to think there's some grand prophecy you'll fulfill for him." Blayk pulled down the neck of his shirt, revealing his pulse bounding under his skin. "Some people don't know how to appreciate what they have."

Furious, desperate, knowing the choice was already taken from him, he moved in. Jerking Blayk's head back, he sunk his razor-sharp canines into his jugular.

Warm and tangy, like an ancient wine, the blood filled his mouth, his veins, clearing his mind. Rushing through him, a desperation to complete the change, he squeezed, sucking what wouldn't come fast enough.

Laughing, his voice hoarse as Bennett drained him, Blayk whispered in his ear, "Company's coming." A pair of heavy-duty engines revved as they neared.

Eyes heavy, the intoxicating vampire blood too much to handle, Bennett dropped Blayk and fought the impending sleep that had held him comatose for days. Stumbling backward, he blinked and shook his head. Fuck; no wonder vampires didn't feed off each other.

Ears still ringing from the ironic gratification, Bennett took off. Legs pumping at full speed as he battled the sandbags filling his limbs, he sprinted into the night. Blayk's laughter transitioned to a pissed-off trail of expletives, his footsteps fading in the distance as he realized he was too slow, too late, and too drained to catch Bennett.

As headlights rounded the corner, drawing closer, Bennett ducked into the alley. As if lead weights filled his eyelids, his eyes fluttered shut, and he shook away the drugging effects of the vampire blood as he struggled to stay awake.

A few more blocks and he'd be home.

He wasn't going to make it that far.

Limbs growing heavier by the second, Bennett turned into Tent City. Passing through, he stole an unattended blanket and crossed into the next alley. Legs about to collapse beneath him, he dove behind a dumpster. Pulling the blanket over his body, he succumbed to the exhaustion.

THE SUN THREATENED ON the horizon. She knew she was too late to save him. But there might still be time to stop him.

Bennett as a vampire? He was already stronger and more stubborn than most. Add vampire speed and senses? He'd be unstoppable.

She pulled out her phone and crossed her fingers that he might answer this time. Nope. Straight to voicemail. Her stomach sunk in her abdomen like deadweight. Dammit. If he'd changed his number, some poor soul had a dozen messages to call her back immediately. With other fun tips, like *don't eat anyone*, and *lock yourself up and I'll find you*.

She dove into her Porsche and fired up the engine. Windows tinted, including the windshield. A doctor's note in the glove box claimed the skin allergy she often used to fit in amongst humans. Came in handy.

Pinstriped roads warned the temperature was well below freezing, and the de-icers had been at work all night. After uselessly sweeping the area around the club, she drove to Bennett's old apartment in Belltown. A long shot, but it was a starting point.

She skipped the elevator and tore up the stairs. Outside his door, or what used to be his door anyway, she tried to catch his scent, but demon hunters were impossible to smell. Handy for them, but damned inconvenient for her.

Nothing, but she caught scent of a woman that wore too much perfume.

Ignoring the annoying ache in her chest that Bennett might be dating some annoying perfumy bitch, she knocked. As the door opened, the sun glared into the hall. Adair stepped back and sported her chipperest smile. "Hi, is, uh, is Bennett around?"

The tall brunette's face scrunched. "I think you have the wrong apartment."

"An old friend of mine used to live here. You wouldn't happen to remember a prior tenant by that name?"

The woman shook her head. "No, but I've only lived here a few months." She glanced up and down the hall to the other units. "I think Mrs. Sanderson in 702 has been here the longest."

"Thanks. Have a good day." Adair gave her sweetest smile and hurried to 702.

Doubting she'd get lucky, Adair knocked. A wrinkly faced woman with a gray bun swung open the door. "DoorDash?"

She shook her head. "Um, no."

Mrs. Sanderson moved to slam the door in her face.

"Wait. Mrs. Sanderson? Do you recall a man named Bennett that lived in 712, about fifteen years ago?"

"What's it to you?"

"Long story."

"Well in that case." The woman gestured with melodramatic sarcasm, then waved her hand in front of her face like she was brushing away a fly from her face. "Actually, I wouldn't be much help anyway. Bennett moved away probably ten years ago, but I remember him like it was yesterday. Handsome one, always a smile for me, used to help me cart my groceries up the stairs when the elevator would break. Strong as an ox, that one."

"That's him."

"Aren't you a little young to be tracking down some guy? He'd be quite a bit older than you."

Adair smiled softly. While she may be stuck in the body of the foolish twenty-three-year-old she had been, she felt every one of her five and a half centuries. And Bennett wouldn't have aged more than two or three years since he'd lived here, and wouldn't age much more than that over the next two or three centuries. "You really don't know where I could find him?"

"Used to be a girl in 708 that was a police officer. Real pretty thing. They dated for a short while around the time he moved out. I recall she said he'd been looking at places in the Industrial District."

"Okay, bye." Adair didn't bother with final farewells, silently cheering at her good fortune.

She flew down the stairs and hopped back into her car and took off. *Okay, think.* Bennett wouldn't be easy to take down. And it would take a lot of vampires. Someplace in the Industrial District would be an ideal place for a large-scale paranormal ambush.

Turning, she left Belltown. Up and down the streets, she checked every alley, every face. Her stomach growled as she realized she hadn't eaten all day, and her stomach had been too testy to eat before confirming what she had suspected: Calloway was in town, he was pissed, and he had a plan.

What if Bennett was burnt to a crisp somewhere, or surrounded by bodies he'd drained? And when he realized what he'd done? He'd never forgive himself.

If his humanity was too buried and the vampire side took over? Fighting the demon inside had seemed impossible, until she'd seen how her brother had mastered it. She'd never be able to take him alone.

After crossing back and forth over the broad tracks, passing homeless encampments, in and out of vacant parking lots, she clenched the steering wheel, vibrating with frustration. As the sun set behind her, she found a warehouse with a buckled roof and its bay door teetering off the track.

No one had taped it off; something was up.

As the sun had yet to make its final descent, she drove straight inside and slammed on the brakes. Blown away by the state of the building, she struggled to take in the widespread destruction. Inhaling deeply, she caught the scent of dozens of vampires. All dead.

No. More subtle, but fresher, alive... Blayk.

Fuck. Clenching her jaw, she took sharp breaths as she realized the extent of things. Sonra. Calloway. Blayk. The old gang was back together again... and they'd brought her back into the fold.

No sign of him now. No bodies. The ground was wet with icy patches that had frozen in the shadows of the unseasonably cold night.

Crumbled concrete and steel rebar littered the ground. She glanced up and saw the gray glow of daylight teasing through the cracks in the roof where two of the support pillars had collapsed.

A glint of steel under a pile of rubble caught her eye. Stalking closer, her heels clicking with each step, she reached and grasped her hand around the hilt of Bennett's sword.

Whatever had happened to him, he still smelled like nothing. Enough demon hunter remained to leave him undetectable. But judging by the destruction... he wasn't the same.

Shit. Back to square one.

She jumped in the car and took off.

5

BENNETT EASED THE FOUL-SMELLING blanket from over his head. Although darkness penetrated the alley, dawn threatened on the horizon. Not a soul in sight.

He rubbed his hands over his face and took a long inhale. Rising to his feet, he searched for signs of Blayk or any of the others. Not a trace of vampire on the air.

Clear as day, seeing each pebble and each footprint in the frost, the grime coating the street sign at the end of the alley, his eyes assessed his surroundings at rapid speed. Stalking toward the street, he felt his steps lighter, his movements fluid, precise.

And he thirsted. Feverish, furious, his thoughts focused on one goal. No longer a hunter, he was pure predator.

Tilting his head up, he sniffed the air. The corners of his mouth turned up as the scent shot a thrill prickling over his skin. Passing a few jackasses that were high as kites on something revolting, he kept moving.

There. The scent grew stronger as he neared a distribution plant. A foolish young security guard strolled along the parking lot on the other side of a chain-link fence, whistling a chipper tune as he walked his beat.

Footsteps silent on the icy path, Bennett stalked closer, the craving growing blinding, his focus on nothing but his prey. Scaling the fence, he leapt over, landing silent as a cat on the pavement.

Sticking to the shadows, Bennett closed in on his quarry. The enticing scent beckoned him nearer, faster, relief already surfacing as the craving that clawed through him was about to be satisfied.

No clue as to his fate, the man didn't have time to react until it was too late. Taking the guard by the neck, Bennett jerked him close.

Struggling, punching, flailing, the guard panicked. Undeterred, Bennett tuned in to the pulsing under his skin, then sunk his sharp teeth into flesh. Warm, savory nectar flowed as he drank deeply, the burning in his throat easing, relief flooding his veins.

The guard stopped fighting as he grew pale. Bennett's thirst was nearly quenched.

"Please," the guard whispered with what little energy he had left.

At the guard's voice, something seemed to stab into Bennett's temple like a knife to the conscience. Clenching his eyes shut, he tried to ignore it. *Fuck, he was still so thirsty, only a little more...*

The body he held grew weaker, heavier in his hold as he lost the strength to stand.

Bennett opened his eyes, assessing the blood red marks on the pale neck. His eyes welled with a clouded rage, his own panic clenching in his chest, flashing him back to the sensation of being crushed under the weight of the vampires as they drained him. Loosening his grip, he lowered the guy to the ground.

A gruff edge to his voice, he murmured, "Go home. Tell anyone what happened, and I'll track you down and take the rest."

The guard sat with eyes wide, a hint of color returning to his cheeks.

Taking off at a sprint, Bennett scaled the fence and landed on the concrete sidewalk. Feet never stopping, he took off toward home.

Cresting over I-5, the rising sun teased its arrival. As he crossed the final block, he scanned the parked cars for tinted windshields or darkened SUVs. Clear. But those fuckheads wouldn't be far. What were they waiting for? Or had he taken out enough of them, that they were forced to regroup?

He rested his thumb on the lock and the moment the latch clicked open, he ducked into his warehouse. Pounding up the stairs, he swung open the door to the loft. His phone sat on the kitchen counter, the light flashing with a new message.

Fuck no. He stripped off his bloody clothes and stuffed them in the fireplace, lighting the kindling and watching until the tainted fabric blazed.

Running his hands over his face, he froze as blood smeared across his palm. His, the vampires', his victim's, all blended together and caked into his beard. Stomach roiling at the revolting absurdity, he wanted to vomit but knew it would only make things worse; the hunger would return that much sooner.

Stalking into the bathroom, he flipped the shower nozzle to blazing hot and scrubbed until his skin was agonizingly raw. He grabbed scissors from the drawer and cut away at his beard before shaving his face clean. He tugged his overgrown hair back.

As the mirror defogged after the hot shower, his face came into view. He'd expected to see the pasty complexion of a vampire, but found his skin unchanged. His eyes were a few shades paler than his normal espresso, and his pupils were more alert.

Peeling back his lips, he felt the snarl rumble in his throat. Longer, sharper, his canines were pure beast, designed to feed. Backing away, he looked to the massive wall of windows to see the morning sun casting a glow around the edges of the curtains.

He threw on some fresh jeans and a t-shirt, tossing a sweatshirt on his bed as he tugged on his boots. He needed to get a move on, but where would he go? His place in BC? Hell no, his parents might still be there. How about calling in the team? *Hey, guys, I was a fucking idiot and walked into a trap, and, well, now I'm a monster.* No thanks. That conversation could wait.

And what fucking prophecy?

He lumbered up the spiral staircase to the loft's loft, as Lana had titled it, into the library that Astrid had spent weeks helping him to plan and fill years ago. His stomach churned as he considered how to break the news.

For him, for them... not right now.

Staring blankly at the wall of books, he rubbed his hands over his face. Freezing, he glanced down at his palms, letting out a sigh of relief that they were clean. *Out, out damn spot.* Fuck. Days ago, he was drowning in self-pity. Now he was drowning in self-beratement. Couldn't catch a damn break.

And when the craving struck again? He needed to find blood. Fast.

Burning in the back of his throat at the very thought of it, he imagined a little more human blood. No one would know. It's not like he was going to kill anyone...

He absolutely would. A few more seconds, if that rip-roaring headache hadn't rattled his progress, he would have drained that security guard. Delivery service would be fantastic, but to request a pint of blood?... Groaning as he envisioned the possibilities, of ordering some breakfast... starting with the delivery driver...

Shaking his head, thinking of *anything else*, trying to block the thought from his mind, Bennett turned on the loft's single pot brewer and sipped a cup of black coffee while he stuffed a stack of texts that *might* be helpful into a box. Adair had only needed blood every few days; he'd make some calls and pick up something from a butcher on his way out of town. Hell, he'd lick a raw steak if he had to.

What was Blayk saying about another infusion? Fucking shit, that taste had been different from the guard. Like literal lifeblood, where the guard had been closer to mana or ambrosia or something irresistible, the vampire blood had been critical.

Dammit, stop thinking about it. His throat burned, his mouth watered at the thought of another taste. Vampire, human, cow… any of the above would ease the hunger that was growing stronger by the second.

Reaching to the next shelf up, he grabbed a few more books on vampires, but he doubted anything in here told of the change. Slice a belly, shatter a neck, then call in the coroner to cremate. Demon hunters didn't exactly care how the vampires spawned each other, instead focusing their efforts on eliminating them.

He needed help. Dashing down the stairs, he lifted his phone from the kitchen island and glared. Cringing, his stomach wrenching in rebellion, his throat burned as the craving knocked him on his ass. Breaking out in a cold sweat, he collapsed to his knees.

ADAIR SCANNED THE AREA, looking for… anything. Something. A glimmer of hope that he was alive and not ravaging the local population in a frenzied killing spree. Expanding her circle, passing dozens of not-its, she finally found what she was looking for. At the edge of the industrial district, a few restaurants and converted lofts dotted the row, civilization increasing with each block closer to downtown.

About damn time. An old warehouse looked decrepit at first glance, but she could see where the structure had been subtly updated. Hopping out of the car, she stuck to the shadows, the overcast sky toasty as a tropical island, but tolerable for now. At the garage door, she searched for a lock she could pick, a window she could bust open... anything.

Flipping a rusted-over panel, she found a sleek electronic doorbell. Pulling in a lungful of oxygen, she pressed the green button to request entry. Watching the camera, she silently pleaded for him to be here, safe and peaceable inside.

He didn't answer, but within a few seconds, the garage door smoothly retracted, revealing a cavernous bay. He was here. Her heart tripped in her chest, and a heavy moisture pooled behind her eyes. Parking in the middle of a cluster of flashy cars, she turned and saw the garage door closing behind her.

Targets, dummies and a whole lot of open space. Clearly a well-used training area. To the left, she saw the finished areas. A gym, well equipped with weights and mirrors for serious training. And a metal staircase next to a freight elevator. Climbing the stairs, she kept her treads silent. Easing the door open, she sniffed for signs of anyone but Bennett, and was relieved to find nothing more than a fire in the hearth and coffee in the brewer.

The left wall was dominated by floor-to-ceiling windows that overlooked the city. Along the adjacent wall, an impressive fireplace was the focus of a trio of couches that surrounded a wide ottoman atop a plush white rug. An identical rug anchored the open bedroom on the opposite wall, the bed neatly made with white sheets and a fluffy comforter with a wintry impressionist painting over the bed, a wooden double-wide walnut dresser to the side. To the right, a long dining room with seating for six bordered a granite, brick and stainless-steel dream kitchen. Further along, a door to what looked to be the bathroom, and to the right, a triple-sized walk-in closet or something.

Her gaze landed on a spiral staircase that led to a loft above. Dashing to the top of the stairs, she found a cozy library overlooking the rest of the living space and a box of books tipped over on the floor, but he wasn't there either. Where was he?

A low, whimpering growl rumbled from the closet beneath her. Tearing down the staircase, she threw open the closet door. Locked in heavy iron chains and hooked to a steel support beam, Bennett sat on his knees, tugging, yanking at his bindings, his wrists raw and bloody. Tears streamed down his face.

She inched toward him, swallowing the burning pit of resentment for the creeps that would snuff out such a steadfast light.

His eyes were bloodshot, their natural, vibrant brown now a dull dirt and as lifeless as his ashen complexion. He shook his head as he growled, "Don't."

Lowering to her knees in front of him, she stayed out of biting distance. "I know you're hungry," she crooned. Hair wild, shirt ripped over a torso that had seriously bulked up since she seen him last, his body tensed with restrained rage.

He bared his teeth and let out a fierce rumble. Those canines confirmed it all.

Jerking against his bindings, the veins of his arm bulged as he strained to break free. One bolt had already snapped off the wall, but he'd been smart in his self-imprisonment, and more still held.

"Did you do this to yourself?" she asked.

He nodded.

Her gaze softened as she imagined him without blood, realizing he was out of time and tried to restrain himself before he hurt someone. She remembered that feeling so well, the urgency of it, needing blood so often during those first few weeks. In the beginning... she'd succumbed to the thirst. She hadn't questioned it. She hadn't missed the humanity. How many hundreds had she killed? "I'm going to help you. I'm going to get you some blood, but..." she trailed off, not wanting to let him know she didn't know how the hell she was going to do it.

Leaving him alone wasn't an option. It was only a matter of time before he broke free. She had no doubt he could bust a hole in the wall if he put his mind to it.

This was not the naïve young demon hunter she'd loved. He was... built. A solid brick of a man, he had put that gym downstairs to good use. The darkness to him was new too, and a niggling in her gut told her it wasn't only the change that had brought it on.

Daring to get close, she pulled his phone from his pocket and backed out of reach. "I'm calling your team. I'll see if someone can swing by a butcher I know."

Voice hoarse, he muttered, "Not... I need..." He clenched his jaw, refusing to say more.

Adair saw where he'd opened the garage for her, then pulled up his calls, finding her number right up top. "You were trying to call me?"

He nodded again, but wouldn't open his mouth. There was something he wasn't saying. And, she suspected, a lot he wasn't going to say.

She backed out of the closet. Logan and his wife were still in Scotland, otherwise she knew her brother could be here within the hour if he risked a few speeding tickets. But newly human, his proximity would probably make things worse.

Unsure who to call, she checked his texts. A dinner invitation from someone named Astrid. *You there?... You okay?... Please call me back.* And another from someone named Ryan... *Hey, my flight is delayed so I'm stuck in Seattle overnight before my deployment, can I crash at your place?*

Risking it, she clicked send on Ryan's name. He answered right away, a deep rumbling voice, "About fucking time. Where've you been?"

She paused, then said, "Hi. This... um, my name is Adair. I–"

"The vampire?"

A whoosh of relief filled her lungs, plus an ill-timed glimmer of thrill that her name was familiar to Bennett's friend. "Are you... part of his team?"

"Yeah. What's going on?"

"I saw your text. Are you still in town?"

"Yeah. He didn't answer me, so I'm at a hotel next to the airport."

"How quickly can you come to his loft with a few pints of blood?"

"Blood? As in..."

"Not human. It will be tough enough for him to fight the cravings. Cow or pig or something a butcher might have."

She heard him already on the move, grabbing a bag and a door slamming behind him. "You have five seconds to tell me what's going on."

"They changed him."

"As in...?" His voice went thready.

"Vampire."

"Fuck."

"Yeah. I know. I found him. He's chained himself up, but I won't be able to stop him if he gets loose. He needs blood, fast, or he's going to hurt someone."

"I'm coming. Call Astrid and Bodie. Have Astrid stop to get blood. He won't want to feed off Bodie and I'll need help if he breaks free, so have Bodie come straight over."

"Okay. Hurry." As she hung up, a niggling curiosity tickled her brain as she wondered why Bennett wouldn't want a taste of Bodie. Despite their lack of scent, there was something about demon hunter blood that appealed–Bennett's in particular, but she knew *that* was her own personal bias.

She clicked off and dialed Astrid. From the closet, a deafening crash rattled the building as iron and steel ripped apart. She inched back as she held the phone to her ear, cringing as she saw that Bennett had busted one chain. Her heart thundered in her chest, dreading the impossibility of holding him back if he got loose.

"About time you called, I was about to come knock down your door," an edgy soprano said.

"Astrid?" Adair asked hopefully.

"Who is this?" Astrid's tone was clipped at the unexpected person on the line.

"This is Adair. Yes, the vampire. Can you get blood to Bennett? Like, now?"

On the move, Astrid sounded to be getting dressed. She whispered to someone else, *Bennett needs help.* "Why does Bennett need blood?"

"They changed him. Please, hurry. He's chained up now, but it won't be long before he breaks free."

"That's not possible."

"It's not supposed to be. He needs help before he hurts someone."

Astrid seemed to catch her breath before speaking again, her feet still pounding the pavement. "We're fifteen minutes out. Can he... would my blood help? I have no idea where to get blood on short notice."

"No. If we can do this with only animal blood, that will help him control it. There's a butcher off Ninety-Nine. I can call him and see if he can have some waiting for you. Ryan is on his way and said to send Bodie straight here. Hurry."

Clicking off, she made the call, then walked back into the closet. Shit, Bennett was making headway. Head in his chained hands, he looked defeated. She dropped to her knees in front of him.

"Bennett?" she said. Something was off. He looked hungry, but something wasn't right. The rage, the desperation made sense for a fledgling, but he looked awful. Was it because he was a demon hunter, and it truly wasn't possible for him to change? It's not like she'd ever changed anyone; was this normal?

He looked up at her quiet entreaty, his eyes wild as he fought the internal battle she knew he'd lose.

"I know how hard you fought this."

He snorted, shaking his head. "Not enough."

"It was a trap."

"Think I don't fucking know that?"

"I don't know what Calloway's end goal is, but... he wanted *you*. Bennett, do you know what prophecy he might be talking about?"

He shook his head. "No idea. I don't want a part of any fucking prophecy." Pausing, she could see the confusion clouding his vision. "How did you find out?"

"I, uh, we used to be together. I wasn't always a vegetarian." She smiled with a painful etch between her eyebrows.

"I... a security guard... I couldn't resist. Wasn't strong enough. I don't know if he made it."

Her heart shattered to bits as she saw the regret taking over, battling with the hunger that would inevitably win. "Hey, it's okay. You're already doing better than I did. You're locked up in your closet, suffering to keep others safe."

Unable to resist, she reached forward and cradled his cheek with her hand. He leaned into her palm. His lips parted, his teeth bared, but he forced his lips closed again to avoid biting her.

Wincing, he pulled harder against the binding. Ducking on instinct, Adair heard another link shatter, the shrapnel blasting into the walls around them, striking her skin.

One hand free. Releasing a murderous roar, he grabbed the remaining chain with his free hand, but hesitated.

Footsteps resounded as heavy boots pounded up the stairs. She rose to her feet. "Your friends are here."

Crashing in the door, a brilliantly blue-eyed guy stormed in, smelling blatantly of human, with a lingering scent of natural wolf shading his skin that sent shivers down her spine. Nope, she absolutely did not want to get close.

His lips curled back in a growl as he sighted her, and he recoiled. Catching himself, he said, "Hi. Bodie. Where is he?"

She nodded towards the closet.

A crash resonated as iron broke free from steel. Barreling out of the closet, Bennett took off for the exit. Blocking him like a defensive tackle, Bodie wrapped his arms around Bennett and dragged him to the ground.

Bennett paused and lunged for his neck, then winced and pulled away. "Fuck, Bodie, you smell like a wet dog."

Bodie shifted to keep him pinned. "Quit struggling or I'll go feral on your vampire ass."

Bennett knocked Bodie off.

Flipping to his feet, Bodie dove onto his back and wrapped around him as if he'd die before letting Bennett out the door. "Kicked your ass once and I'll do it again," Bodie growled, straining to bring him down.

Through the open door, another guy, tall and dark with gunmetal black eyes in a Coast Guard t-shirt and cargo pants, didn't hesitate and barreled in, taking the pair out and knocking Bennett flat.

Pinned to the ground under two huge guys, Bennett's eyes were sharp as a predator and he snarled at Ryan, "Been wanting a taste of you for a long time." Tilting his head, Bennett nipped at Ryan's arm.

Flicking his wrist, Ryan growled, "Happy to duke it out sometime, but let's wait until you're not so... pasty."

Bennett writhed under them.

Ryan growled again, "Calm the fuck down. Astrid will be here with your dinner soon."

Slamming his head back into the concrete floor, Bennett whimpered, his teeth still bared, "I was in a mood and went off on my own."

Arms folded over her chest, Adair backed into the shadows. Pulse pounding in her skull in rhythm with his, she felt Bennett being torn to pieces as vampire and demon hunter battled for dominance.

Ryan didn't let up in his hold, but his chest rose and fell with a heavy sigh.

Bennett's eyes sealed shut, a single tear budding at the corner of his eyelashes. He mumbled under his breath, "You stole my life. Took my prophecy, Quinn, had my baby. I needed the fight... I walked right into their trap."

"I know. I'm so sorry."

Bennett whispered with a gravel edge to his voice, "I always fuck it up."

Bodie let up in his grip, leaning down to whisper in Bennett's ear, "Yeah, you fucked up. But don't fuck it up worse by ignoring who and what you are, or by pushing away your friends. You'll get through this. If they're willing to put up with a werewolf? No problem on a vampire."

Under his breath, Ryan said, "You started this team. From what Quinn tells me, there hasn't been a fight yet that you've backed down from, even an unwinnable one. I've seen you dive into the scariest damn shit on the planet. Now? Think any demon is going to want to fuck with us?"

Unmoving, Bennett didn't fight back. He almost looked to have a measure of control.

The moment they let their guard down, he let out a blood-curdling roar that echoed off the walls. Thrashing wildly, his veins about to bust out of his neck at the strain, he fought. Growling, snarling, he bit at Ryan again.

Slamming a fist into Bennett's face, Ryan hissed, "Stop it."

Adair ran over and dropped to the ground. She fired a glare at his friends. "He can't help it. It's all instinct." She rested her hands on his cheeks and traced her fingertips along the angle of his jaw. Again, he leaned into her touch but didn't bite. "I know you're hungry. Please, wait."

Footsteps pounded up the stairs and a willowy blond flew into the room with a paper grocery bag.

Bolting up, Adair grabbed the bag and pulled out one of the containers and popped off the lid. "Okay." She nodded to Ryan and Bodie. "Don't let go in case he books it, as this is like offering a starving person Brussels sprouts when they could have souffle, but let him sit up."

Grimacing, Bennett reached for the container, but his friends held his arms down. He flashed Ryan a pissed-off glower. "I'm not going to run." Even half-crazed, half-ill with the hunger of a fledgling, Bennett still exuded an almost aristocratic arrogance.

Hesitating, Ryan released his arm, backing away a few steps to block the door. Bodie held at his other side, ready to grab.

Bennett pulled his lips back with a disgusted sneer as he inspected the viscous brew, but she could see the hunger driving him to desperation. He took a long breath, his body relaxing as he accepted what he needed. Tipping it back, he guzzled, his Adam's apple bobbing with each gulp. After draining the last of it, he wiped the base of his thumb over the drip that pooled in the corner of his mouth. "Fuck that's terrible."

"It's better warm, but we were out of time." Adair shrugged, easing to her feet.

Arms wrapped around his knees, he turned toward Ryan. "Sorry."

Rubbing the wound that was healing as they spoke, Ryan shrugged. "No worries."

6

SHELLSHOCKED, NOBODY MOVED. BENNETT sat on the floor, surrounded, an empty container in his hand that he had the most revolting urge to lick clean. Quinn's dad walking in on him in bed with a vampire was nothing compared to the embarrassment he now found himself embroiled in.

Fuck. He'd have to tell his parents.

Eventually, the paranormal world would know that a demon hunter had been changed. That it was possible. He numbed at the thought, hating the burden he'd brought on all hunters with his recklessness.

As the blood filled his belly, he felt the soldering energy of it seep into his veins, penetrate his brain, his muscles, revitalizing his skin. He rose to his feet and brushed past Astrid in the kitchen, resting a hand on her shoulder as he paused. She squeezed his hand, her illuminating smile now heavy with sorrow. Yeah, fucking awkward and downright humiliating, but the connection reassured him that the team had his back.

Now if only he could be sure he'd have theirs. He rinsed the container before dropping it into the recycle bin. He checked the paper bag, then stuffed the spare pints in the fridge.

His friends, his former lover, all observed his every move. "I'm good. You guys can head out. They'll be here soon to finish the job, so for now I'll max out my security system and then... I'll figure it out. Adair, if you wouldn't mind leaving me the information on some butchers that won't bat an eye at someone wanting blood? Astrid, Bodie, I know you are eager to get back to Montana. Ryan, your flight must be leaving in a few hours?" Standing with his arms folded over his chest, his shirt ripped to shreds from tearing the closet apart, then from his friends trying to subdue him, he knew he looked the mess that he felt.

Still lightheaded, the blood in his veins unsettled, he knew it wasn't over. Blayk said he had time, a day or two, and the clock was ticking. As his gut churned, something in his bones demanding that he finish it, he'd nearly called Adair to come feed him. But he couldn't risk her like that. He'd rather go hunting for a vampire himself, or maybe feed from the ones that came to finish the job.

Or to see what happened if he let his body reject it. Death would be better than eternity as a monster.

Ryan shook his head. "I'll call my captain. I can board when they dock at Kodiak in a few weeks."

"No, I got this. My mistake, I'll handle it. You're already late joining the crew."

Astrid waited at the edge of the kitchen. Her honey eyes softened as she took in what a wreck he was. "We'll handle it. Together. That's what we do."

"I fucked up, going out alone. I may be bullheaded, but I won't make that mistake again." He moved closer and glanced up at his library. "Apparently there's a prophecy."

As expected, Astrid's eyes lit up at the prospect of research. "Tell me more."

Adair stepped closer, speaking up for the first time since he'd gotten ahold of the blood. "A vampire, an old partner of mine to be honest, he found it and has plans for Bennett. All he said was, '*There will be a hunter changed. Fated to crave as the vampires do.*'"

Bodie looked from Bennett to Adair and back again, suspicion deep in his glowing blue eyes. "We'll hit the books. There must be more to it."

Astrid bit her lip, then glanced to Adair. "Why Bennett?"

"Because of me." Voice flat, Adair didn't embellish. She teased her hands in her hair and looked to the windows, the waning sunlight seeping around the edges of the curtains before disappearing behind the Sound. "We need to move."

Bennett clenched his fists across his chest, looking to his team. "They're not going to let me walk away."

Astrid eyed the box of books he'd gathered before the hunger had overtaken him. Bringing it down from the loft, she looked to the others. "I think I know what book we need. The one where we found Quinn's."

Hanging back as his team moved for the door, Bennett stood back and chewed his cheek.

Stepping up, toe-to-toe with him, Adair cradled his jaw in her hands. "This is my fault. I'm sticking until I can fix this."

Leaning into her touch, Bennett closed his eyes. "There is no fixing this."

Ryan lit up the security camera next to the door. Across the street, a darkened van was tucked nearly out of sight. Ryan turned and stood tall with his shoulders back. "You up for a fight?"

Flexing his fists, the thrill filling his veins headier than human blood, the corner of Bennett's lips curved up. "Let's find out."

Stalking out of the apartment, he headed straight for the weapon rack. At his side, Ryan grabbed the biggest long-sword of the bunch and tested its weight. Astrid swung open the door of Bodie's truck and pulled out her matched short swords, swinging and warming up her grip. Bodie tossed his sweatshirt in the front seat, ready to shift to the wolf on the fly if needed.

Standing back, Adair watched the team prepping for the fight. Bennett flashed her a wink and gestured to the wall of steel. Her bow lips turned up as she crossed her arms over her sleek dress, and she rolled her eyes in amusement.

Astrid stood by the garage door opener and glanced back. "Watch out, the sun is still up."

Bennett let out a measured exhale that caught in his chest. He lowered his replacement shield, his untested sword feeling foreign in his hand. Backing up, he moved into the shadows.

Yeah. This was going great. *If* he survived, and *if* he could control the cravings, he'd always have to be watching the sky, an escape plan mapped out. Great fair-weather teammate. Maybe he'd have to invest in a fucking parasol.

Adair joined him and grazed the back of her hand down his arm. Turning, he pasted on a smile. That crease formed between her eyebrows and she mirrored his uncertain smile.

Leaning into her, he absorbed some of her warmth, the skin-to-skin contact sending the familiar rush through him. As if the dreams weren't vivid enough already.

Daylight streamed in, extending a blazing light across the concrete floor as the garage door eased open. Moving together in a protective wall, Ryan, Astrid and Bodie stalked across the street toward the van.

Tearing open the door as the vampires attempted to drive off, Ryan yanked the vampire from the driver's seat and tossed him into a patch of sun in the center of the street.

Shrieking, the vampire sprinted into the warehouse for cover.

Grinning, Bennett recognized this one. Must not have finished them all off. A taste for spicy foods, his blood had carried an unexpected heat.

As the vampire realized his mistake, his eyes widened at the sight of Bennett approaching.

"Miss me?" Bennett taunted.

Eyes darting, scanning for an escape that didn't exist, the vampire accepted the inevitable. Fists swinging, using his speed as he knew he didn't stand a chance at defeating Bennett in strength or skill, the vampire snarled and came at him.

Feeling the hum of the air vibrating over his skin, hearing boots scuffing against the concrete, each movement predictable as if he could see it before it happened, he calculated the vampire's trajectory.

He seemed to think that he could flatten Bennett with his momentum, as he might with a human or even another vampire.

Bennett tightened his grip, eager to test out his new abilities.

From behind him, a knife whizzed past and nailed the vampire in the throat. Clutching his neck as he bled out, the vampire gargled on his own blood and slumped to the ground.

Turning, Bennett saw Adair's snarky grin quickly dissipate before she masked it with her default poker face.

Shaking his head, he strolled back toward her and tipped his head up in challenge. "Come on. After the shit I've been through the last few days, you could have at least let me test this new body out."

Stepping closer, Adair cupped her hand on his jaw and stole what was probably intended to be a sarcastic kiss, but the intensity of the subtle move struck him like a critical blow to the heart. Fuck, he was such a sap. Did she have any idea what she did to him?

Pulling her keys from her purse as the others returned from the fight, she flashed him a wink and brushed past him.

Hovering at the driver's seat while Ryan and Bodie piled into the truck, Astrid hollered, "More on the way. Let's move."

Bennett aimed for his McLaren, then felt his heart break a little more at his fatal flaw.

Adair nodded to her heavily tinted Porsche. "I'll drive."

Hopping in the passenger seat, Bennett dumped his sword and shield in the backseat. Flooring it out of the garage, Adair led the way.

Bennett glanced back and ensured the garage door closed okay, then fired up the alarm from his phone. Checking back one last time, his gut churned as he realized he was never going to live there again, and would be lucky to even go back for his things, if he survived the next few days.

A darkened SUV came roaring up behind them.

Adair turned toward the freeway.

"This way." Bennett pointed toward the private airfield.

Nodding, she changed direction and gunned it.

The SUV came up beside them. Adair kept her eyes on the road, seeing everything, her reflexes ridiculously fast.

Gripping the wheel, she held her speed as their turn approached.

Shifting in his seat, Bennett grimaced as he anticipated the repercussions if they blasted past security.

As they neared, she flipped the e-brake to change direction on the fly. Cool as a cat, her gaze unfazed, she tore out of the turn and sped down an alley between two breweries.

Checking behind them, Bennett watched as the team struggled to catch up. The vampires' SUV spun out as they followed, the scent of burnt rubber filling the air.

After a series of wild turns, the SUV was gone. So was the truck. Bennett dialed Bodie's phone.

"Where the hell are you?" Bodie hollered over the sound of the engine that screamed at the intense pace.

"We'll meet you at the hangar."

"Gotcha. We've got a tail we need to shake first. See you soon."

Miles out of the way, Adair finally turned and hopped on the freeway and headed in the direction of the airport.

"I, uh, think we lost them." Bennett glanced over at Adair.

She ran her fingertips through her hair and grinned at his tease. She checked the rearview and relaxed her grip on the wheel, but her bright mood quickly faded. "They knew where you live. I don't know how long they've been tracking you."

"Not long."

"How could you know that?"

"I couldn't have said what was up, but for the past two, maybe three weeks, there's been something in the air, so I've been cautious." Rubbing a hand over his face, he braced his hand on his jaw. "Not to say it was only out of suspicion. I've been avoiding even going to Astrid's place across town, haven't been up to my place in BC in months. For... lots of reasons." Maybe it was the history, or knowing she'd understand, but he wanted to tell her why. That having every naïve hope for the future getting pulverized as grotesquely as his intestines had been, had been the real driver behind his self-isolation.

Running his tongue over a razor-sharp tooth, he reminded himself how his prior laments had been a drop in the bucket. Not just upside down now, but any hope of a future was now pulverized and hung out to dry.

Reaching across the car and resting her hand on his thigh, Adair gave a gentle squeeze. The radiant heat of her touch soothed the gnawing ache, her silent way of telling him she understood. Afraid to move, lest she get scared and stop touching him, he shifted his gaze and watched her expression. Whatever he'd been through, her heavy blue eyes, the weariness in her gaze... she was suffering too.

Neither spoke the rest of the drive. She pulled into the hangar where the others had already opened up the jet. Belly stirring as the hunger returned, Bennett let out a controlled exhale and suppressed the craving.

Bennett dropped into the copilot seat and let Astrid take charge while he leaned back and closed his eyes. Like the horny pubescent-teenager-walking-erection he'd been so many years ago, he was obsessed. Not with sex this time—although, Adair's proximity was contributing to his unpredictable mood—but his imagination ran wild as he craved a drink of savory, coppery, soothing ninety-eight-six... Sweat beaded along his brow as he fought the image. He was so fucked.

Astrid gave him a sad smile. Tying her pin-straight blond hair out of the way, she nodded toward the door, "You look terrible. I've got this, go get some rest."

Not up to arguing, he dragged himself out of the cockpit. Bodie brushed past him to join his wife up front.

Leaned forward in one of the cabin seats, Ryan scrunched his hand in his hair and dialed. Bennett overheard as he connected with his captain, explaining the emergency that would delay him at least a few days, likely more.

Stalking toward the small bedroom in the back, Bennett ran a hand over his face as he strained to remember what normal felt like, his brain and body were being torn in too many directions. Outside of the hunger, the vampire in him sensed the air itself, drawn to the subtle scent of orchid from Adair's shampoo. The demon hunter in him was planning his next move, banking on taking out a few of the assholes that did this to him with his bare hands. And the human wanted a nap.

Adair blocked his path. Arms crossed over her chest, a deep furrow between her eyebrows, she hesitated.

Dead on his feet, he halted toe-to-toe with her. Damn, she smelled good. Her gooey blue eyes were as clouded as glacial meltwater, her cheek parked between her teeth. Hip cocked out to the side, she wouldn't let him pass.

In the chaos, he hadn't exactly stopped to appreciate what she was wearing, but... damn, she looked incredible. Refreshing in the snug blue dress that hugged her sleek curves, the skirt riding high on her thighs. Decked out in club attire like the first time they'd met, her irresistible features were entirely on display in the wicked dress. Those freckles dotting her cheeks, bow-shaped pink lips, and those spectacular breasts... She was still the vampire-meets-girl-next-door in an absolute sexy-as-fuck dichotomy.

For the first time in way too long–but definitely appreciated considering his preoccupation with murder in the last few hours–his brain was wiped of everything useful and his dick declared it was done being ignored. Legs a mile long, stiletto heels that brought her height to his, she was beyond supermodel. Vampires were inherently alluring, but Adair had an edge that was unique to her alone.

His judgment had never been great around her, as his parents were fond of reminding him.

Flashing back to their last moments together, of Quentin's look of frank disappointment that had hollowed him out. And worst of all, Adair mirroring the regret. Patting his cheek so condescendingly, telling him she'd had a lovely time, but it was time for her to move on, she'd strolled out of his life without a backward glance.

Chewing on his cheek, he traced his hand along her side to brush past.

Her shoulders slumped, but she quickly righted her posture and moved to the side. "What aren't you telling me?"

He shook his head. "Nothing."

"No, it's something. That blood should have been enough to hold you over for hours, but you're pale and clammy already." Her melty blue eyes were drenched with pity.

He shook his head and slipped into the bedroom without answering. Closing himself in, he ripped off the shredded shirt and chucked it. The hunger was like nothing he'd felt before. He'd kill for it, happily. But the moment he'd heard her voice, seen her face, exactly as he remembered, sweet and irresistible with the edge that immortality had sharpened, things weren't so intense.

The feel of her hands on his skin, her crooning voice reassuring him like a song that penetrated deep to his bones, fighting to save him, filled him with a hope he didn't dare to hold. Years of dreams of her bombarded him in half a second, like a fist to the throat.

He stripped out of the rest of his clothes that were drenched from the feverish sweat, then crashed face first onto the mattress, letting exhaustion overtake him.

An hour or two later, he awoke to the searing ache in his throat. Gut wrenching, like he'd die without a tangy taste, imagining the feel of it coating his mouth and easing the burn, that feeling that would bring him halfway to heaven. Breaking out in a cold sweat, he jerked up.

Anticipating him, Adair appeared at the foot of the bed and handed him a heated mug of Brussels sprouts, as she'd described it.

Much better warm. It eased the craving but lacked the orgasmic feel of the real thing. "Fuck, that's like vegan cheese," he griped as he glared into the dark mug.

She chuckled. "Once we land, I'll find us some better stuff. More like vegan sausage."

"Oh boy, I can't wait," he teased, watching over the lip of the cup as he drained the last of it.

"It's not so bad once you get used to it." She curled up on the foot of his bed in her bare feet. As the drink soothed the burn, he followed the curve of her shoulder, his gaze trailing across her collarbone.

A shy smile blossomed on her lush lips, her cheeks pinking as he studied her. Quietly sipping from her own mug, she peered through the steam. "What?" She pulled her lower lip between her teeth, her eyes drifting down. Holding her breath, she shuddered as she looked him over.

Finding a smile for the first time in too damn long, his hands fiddled with his mug. For a woman that left him a decade ago, claiming they had nothing in common and that she wasn't capable of more than an occasional passing fuck with the innocent hunter, she was adorably shy around him now.

Unable to resist for so many reasons, he leaned close and grazed his lips along the pulse of her neck. He halted, biting his tongue between his teeth. He breathed in the scent of her skin. Up close, that orchid was laced with something more dangerous.

She whispered, "I don't think you'll enjoy that like you think."

Trailing soft kisses along her neck, the curve of her jaw, he groaned, "I don't plan on tasting you the way you think."

She really didn't know. And he wasn't about to explain what he needed. He'd been seconds away from killing Blayk, even knowing he held the answers he needed. Most of the feedings before were a blur, but he knew he'd sucked a few dry and crushed a few more as he took what he needed. Not that he regretted killing the ones that changed him, but he wouldn't risk her.

Her pulse skipped a beat and accelerated. Lips turned up in a devious grin, he stole one last kiss behind her ear, savoring the taste of her skin in an entirely non-bloodthirsty, and purely aroused desire, then pulled away and downed the last drop from his mug.

The spark left her eyes as she watched him feign strength, but she could tell this dose of blood left him less satisfied than the last, as if the blood was nothing more than a Band-Aid attempting to cover a gunshot wound. Saying nothing, she scowled and reached for his empty mug. He shook his head. "You don't have to wait on me. I got it."

Sliding his legs out of bed, he held the sheet over the goods and glanced around for pants.

She reached for the mug again. "I'm not waiting on you, I'm not ready for a show quite yet."

A wicked grin teasing at his lips, he pounced on her word choice. "Yet? So maybe later? Like, in a few minutes or a few days?"

"Nice try. We're landing soon. Get dressed."

An extra swing to her hips, she closed the door behind her. His center of gravity shifted with the hum of the engine as they began the landing sequence.

Adair had no idea what was going on in his body. He could feel it getting worse with each passing hour. The vampire was ready to take over, but the demon hunter was refusing to let go.

7

NIGHT THICK ON THE air, the wintry breeze was welcome. Her reason for being here? Not so welcome. Or not so refreshing anyway.

Stepping onto the concrete floor of the hangar, Adair looked back. As he exited the jet, Bennett rubbed a hand over his face, wiping a sheen of sweat from his brow. He'd just fed; he should look better.

Behind him, Ryan's voice was laced with gravel. "Let's move."

Bennett sniped back, "Fuck off."

Softer, Ryan asked, "Whoa, sorry man. Seriously, Bennett, are you okay?"

"I'm fine," he said, sneering.

Astrid followed behind while Bodie locked up behind them. As Bennett stepped onto the concrete, his foot stumbled beneath him. Adair reached him in a flash, wrapping her arm around his middle to steady him.

Grumbling, he righted himself and shook off the assist. Stalking toward the SUV, he dropped into the seat and leaned against the window with his hand over his face.

Astrid caught up to Adair and rested a hand on her shoulder. "I guess I don't know much about the change. Is this normal?"

"No," Adair whispered. "I don't know much about the change either. My own is a big blur. Lots of blood and sleep, then I remember coming around with a desperate thirst, but there was this strength, a power coursing through me that seems to wane in Bennett when it should grow stronger."

Expression grim, Astrid nodded. "Maybe this is why demon hunters can't be changed."

Bodie caught up to them and linked hands with Astrid. "If this guy was so sure he could change Bennett... I'm not one for prophecies, but if this is supposed to be some prophecy unfolding... We're missing something."

They were running out of time. Or maybe Calloway was wrong.

The drive along the dark coastal road was interminable. Even when they had first met, Bennett was a mountain. Tough, sweet, and had charmed her with an effortless grin.

But it seemed the more he weakened, the more he pushed her away. She didn't know what to make of him. Weak, pasty, and exhausted when he should be high on the intensity of his new abilities. As they turned down the long drive, the ocean glowing softly in the moonlight beyond, Bennett stirred.

"We're here," she whispered, grazing her fingertips over his temple, brushing his hair out of his face. He was burning up. Cringing, he pulled away.

Adair's stomach churned as they pulled into the driveway, seeing Quinn waiting on the front step, a baby monitor hooked to her belt. Apparently, Ryan was with Quinn and they had a newborn. When had that happened? Last she'd heard, Bennett and Quinn were on track to get married, set to live the life he always wanted.

As they parked, Quinn came rushing to them. She caught Bennett as he stumbled out of the car. "Oh god Bennett, I'm so sorry. Come on."

Astrid dashed ahead. "The book?" she asked as she breezed past Quinn.

"It's on the table, plus a few others."

Ryan ran to catch up, not slowing when he reached her. "Hang on. We have other priorities."

Feeling completely useless, Adair watched as the others dove into stacks of books at the kitchen table, those from Bennett's and others that Quinn had laid out, all frantically searching for answers while Bennett leaned on Quinn and stumbled into the house. Slowly, one foot in front of the other, they headed for the stairs.

Quinn murmured, "You look awful."

"I need some rest, that's all," Bennett hissed. "Keep Skye close to you. I don't think I could ever be so hungry as to hurt her, but she's human enough until she accepts the gift. I can smell her already."

Nodding, Quinn paused. "You won't. We chose you as her godfather for a reason; even at your darkest, you will always be a protector."

Checking that he made it to his room safely, Adair stood in the doorway as he ducked into the bathroom to splash cool water over his face.

"I need..." He held her gaze, a weary desperation swimming in there, but he looked down at the floor and said, "Thanks for coming for me."

She nodded, then left him to get some rest. She hated leaving him alone, but she needed answers, and sitting and waiting for a miracle wasn't going to help.

The team was already poring through a stack of books; Ryan came in from a back room with another armful of ancient texts. "The prophecy can wait. We need to figure out what's wrong with him."

Astrid added, looking to Adair, "This is entirely new territory for us."

All eyes landed on her. Adair could see the heartbreak in each of them, their expressions as lost as Bennett's had been. "I don't know what's wrong with him," she said. She glanced around and remembered she'd left her purse, her phone... everything in her hurry to get Bennett to safety. "Can I borrow a phone?"

Her brother answered with a confused voice at the unknown number calling. "Hello?"

"Logan, it's me. I need your help."

"Adair? Are you okay?"

"I'm fine. It's..." She glanced to the windows and recoiled at the faint lightening in the sky that warned of the impending sunrise. Ryan caught on to her worry and closed the curtains. "I need to know everything about the change."

Logan answered, "I don't like the sound of that."

She explained Calloway's mysterious plan, what little she knew of the prophecy, and Bennett's worsening state despite blood and rest.

"Shit. You're in a hell of a predicament. I'll be on the next flight home."

"No, stay where you are. We don't need Calloway deciding to go after you too." She cringed, hating her brother's new fragility of mortality. "We're out of time. Please. What's happening to him?"

"You never changed anyone, did you?"

"No. I never had any need to. Come on, you changed me."

"I changed a few people in the early days. Let's back up a few steps. Does blood help him?"

"Definitely, but not for long, like it's not enough. I still can't scent him, typical for a demon hunter. He craves often and uncontrolled like a new vampire, but he's getting steadily weaker."

"Did you see who changed him?"

"There were dozens of them. In a crumbling warehouse that looked to have been destroyed in the fight to take him down. From the state of things, the scent, the air, it had been days. Blayk was there."

"Fuck. Not helpful. Didn't Blayk change most of Calloway's following for him?"

She recoiled as she flashed back to the trail of blood that she and her friends had drained from Scotland to India back in the old days. Even then, changing another had required more commitment than she was willing to invest in another. But Blayk had mastered the art of it for fun. "Blayk would know what he was doing better than anyone."

"Days, huh?" Long pause. "Dozens? Was it dozens of vampires that were killed in the fight... or that died feeding him?"

Closing her eyes, she brought herself back to the scene. She loved to dabble in human occupations; detective work had been one of her favorites. She'd been forced to quit when she made waves as the only female detective in Chicago in the nineteen-thirties... and the youngest. "Hang on, I'm putting you on speaker with Quinn and some of the team. Walk us through how the change works."

Pacing to quiet the baby, Quinn stood back as Adair set the phone on the table.

"Hey guys. So, the change is rough on both the fledgling and the sire. First the sire drains the human victim until they're depleted, like critically anemic and inches from death. It takes a lot of control. Then the sire replenishes the drained human by feeding them. It's a lot for the sire, to give so much. As the fledgling's human blood is replaced by the vampire's, the demon blood innervates the tissue, restructuring the fledgling from the inside out. It's beyond exhausting for the fledgling; they're pretty much comatose through the process, barely waking enough to feed."

Bodie cleared his throat and interjected, "What if it's not enough? I mean, you take a small sire and a big human, he's probably got a good pint or two on her."

"Exactly," Logan said.

Astrid nodded, seeming to realize the implications. "More than one feeding, or perhaps more than one sire. That must be why demon hunters can't be changed. It would take so much vampire blood to overcome a demon hunter's ability to regenerate."

A sinking feeling in her gut, Adair feared the answer as she flashed back to the wreckage in the warehouse. He'd fought off dozens. Near where she'd found his sword, there had been a lot of activity that had stirred up the rubble, and a strong scent of fresh vampire blood. "A demon hunter would need a dozen sires. Maybe more."

Quinn asked the question that needed asking, even though they all knew the answer already. "And if the fledgling receives enough to start the change, but not enough to finish it?"

Long pause. "The fledgling's body will try to fight it. Like an organ transplant. Except it's every cell in their body."

Biting her lip, Quinn furiously muttered, "Bennett doesn't look like he's winning any fights."

Logan's heavy exhale silenced the room. "Once the demon blood has entered their vasculature? There's no going back. If they're interrupted before the sire can feed them enough... or the fledgling is too strong for the sire and can't get enough, they'll die within hours."

Bodie was already out of the chair and moving to the door. "Come on, let's go hunting."

Adair took a long breath, backing toward the stairs as she realized what needed to be done. Bennett was out of time.

Her brother's voice sharp through the phone, knowing exactly what she was thinking, he barked, "Adair? Don't. He won't have enough control yet. He's too strong and could kill you before he even realizes..."

"He won't," she said, hoping she was right.

Astrid's phone chirped in her pocket. She held up a hand, a desperate edge to her expression. "Vann?"

Adair heard a rich, rumbling voice laced with dread on the other end of the call. "Why is Bennett asking me to bring vampire blood, stat?"

She tore down the stairs and swallowed the burning fury that boiled in her throat. Bennett was sitting up in bed, head buried in his hands, his complexion ghost white.

"You knew." She sneered, slamming the door shut behind her.

"What?"

She lowered to the bed and moved her hair off her neck. "Come on. Now I see why you were planning to call me before calling your team, but chained yourself up instead of hitting send? You don't plan to taste me like I think?"

A weak smile teased at his lips. "I'd rather taste you in a very different way."

"Well too fucking bad. Don't die because you're too stubborn."

Snarling, he pulled back. "I can't even remember how many vampires have already died trying to change me. I can't risk you."

"Take it slow. It shouldn't take much to finish it."

His eyelashes fluttered as he struggled to stay conscious.

"Dammit Bennett. They won't get the blood to you in time."

Fingertips trailing over the angle of her jaw, he traced her skin until he landed on the pulse of her neck, gently grazing his thumb over her skin. "I'm not going to forgive myself if I hurt you."

"Have a little faith in me," she said, leaning into his touch. How many days had she laid awake, craving his touch, to feel his skin against hers one more time? Exactly why she should have left him alone to begin with; he didn't deserve this. "I've lived half a millennium. I can handle one overeager demon hunter." Her lips quirked into a smile as she goaded him, needing him to give in.

Pressing his lips to her neck, he didn't bite. "I missed you," he uttered so softly she couldn't be sure he'd said it. He smiled weakly against her skin, the heat of his lips radiating through her veins. "This whole thing is like one bad sexual innuendo."

She rolled her eyes. "I am neither tragic virgin nor one to tolerate abuse. And you're not a creep. But you are a hungry fledgling."

He looked ready to tip over, helplessly leaning into her for support. His lips turned up in a snarl, his eyes scrunched shut as he nuzzled into her neck.

"Now, Bennett, before it's too late. I trust you."

"You shouldn't," he murmured. Piercing into her skin, his teeth made two small incisions. Sipping, soft and easy, he wrapped his fingers in her hair and massaged.

Growing stronger by the second, he came to life in her arms. He wrapped his hands around her backside and hauled her onto his lap, clutching her tight against him. At first, she felt the thrall her victims had succumbed to, the drugging arousal as the vampire fed. With Bennett, it was so much more intense, as if both could finally satisfy the craving for each other she knew they'd both suffered.

Sweet morphed into urgent, and then into something much more dangerous.

Faster, the frenzy overtaking him, he gripped her tight and gulped.

Cheeks numb as she felt herself fading away, she said, "Bennett. Stop."

Withdrawing in an instant, he panted and leaned into her, then soothed the wound with a delicate kiss. His lips trailed up to her jaw. She was lightheaded from the exchange and wrapped her arms around him for support.

Unable to pull away, as if she were the one under the thrall, she shifted and pressed her mouth to his. Warm and pliant, his lips took hers as if savoring a delicacy. Deepening the kiss, he caressed her tongue, tangy and alive, equally spellbound.

Rocking against him, she held tight, already taking back what she'd given him with each kiss, with each touch.

His body relaxing, he rested his forehead on hers. "You okay?"

"I'm good," she lulled, her voice sleepier than she'd realized. "Told you."

As she opened her eyes, she found his equally heavy. He smiled softly. "Wasn't easy, stopping like that. I'm fucking exhausted."

Adair tugged her dress over her head and climbed into the bed. "You and me both."

Breath shuddering as he watched her climb into his bed with breasts uncovered, wearing nothing but a wisp of panties. Bennett gulped and climbed in next to her. "Pity I'm too sleepy to get it up. You are so beautiful."

"You know, I see where vampire legends get the whole sex-association with feeding. It's always been more of a nutritional thing, but I rather enjoyed your mouth on me. Just not the whole you-sucking-the-life-out-of-me aspect."

"Honestly, I'm going to need more. I'm so sorry. I hate this. I'd rather have my mouth on you in so many better ways." He pulled her backside up against him and wrapped the blankets around them. Tenderly, he kissed her shoulder. "Without taking. Only giving."

EVERY FEW HOURS, HE'D awoken with the same ache deep in his muscles, thirsting like nothing he'd imagined before. Each feeding had been a little easier than the one before, as her vampire blood both fed the cravings and restored the damage from his own demon blood fighting to drive out the vampire. Hours, days, all a big fucking blur, but he eventually felt complete, the vampire having fully innervated every cell in his body.

It was fucking bizarre, the sensation humming under his skin as he laid awake in bed, the sun hiding behind the dense curtains. The demon hunter was still who he was, still filled his veins, but it had become laced with a darkness. As much as he felt settled, there was an edge he couldn't tame.

Not taking too much or too hard had been a challenge every time. With the mountain of willpower it had taken to stop each time? No wonder vampires rarely sired any spawn. Like a mantra, he'd chanted her name in his mind. Only once did she have to twist his ear to get him to stop when he was too ravenous and lost control.

And she'd granted him another kiss each time he released her. And another look at her glorious body.

A soft knock on the door interrupted his lamenting. He slipped out of bed, leaving Adair to finish recovering from the last feeding. His team had been incredible, bringing in blood and food for Adair every few hours to help refuel what he'd taken.

Already, he'd become the monster he feared. Adair at least knew the risks. She knew what he was capable of. He'd have to track down that security guard and find a way to make it up to him... or to his family if he hadn't made it. Last he checked the obituaries, nothing has popped up, so he held on to the hope that he hadn't betrayed his duty as a demon hunter.

He opened the closet that was already stocked with the clothes he'd left at Quinn's apartment ages ago that she'd simply brought to the new place. Enough bedrooms for the whole team, she'd insisted they keep stuff here, so they always had a place to crash. Hell, he still had a box of her stuff at his place that he had yet to return.

He pulled on the nearest jeans and shirt and eased open the door. Padding out, his feet eerily silent on the tile floor, he found Quinn waiting in the hall.

She said softly, "You look so much better."

"Not going to say I feel better… I mean, I do. But it's not normal. I can see every speck of dirt on the floor, can hear every creak of the walls settling. I'd say your pulse is about seventy beats per minute. Fucking unreal."

"Ouch. So I don't clean well enough, and there will never be another secret around here?"

He felt a welcome lightness at her snarky response. "And I won't have to ask if you're mad at me; get that pulse fired up and I'll be able to feel it."

"Ha. As if I've ever kept my thoughts to myself. Anyway, I thought Adair looks like she wears the same size I do, so…" she trailed off and handed him a cloth grocery bag filled with clothes.

"Thanks."

"Come on up for breakfast?"

"I'm starving. Which makes no sense with the amount of blood I've consumed over the last few days. But I need a shower first." He brushed his hands through his overgrown hair. "Thanks again."

"For what?"

"Everything. I fucked up. Big-time. This is one hundred percent my fault. As it usually is. And instead of tearing me a new one, you opened your home."

"Well, now that you're feeling better, you're getting roped into the cooking and cleaning rotation."

"You must be wiped out. You've got Skye to look after, and now you've got all of us invading your space."

"I prefer it this way. Vann brought a few gallons of 'premium' animal blood for you. I think he stopped at every butcher between San Francisco and here. Apparently, there's even elk. Lana got in this morning; weather was shit in Sitka, so it took a little longer than she'd hoped. Ryan says he'll risk dishonorable discharge to stay until he knows you're okay."

"You know? Fate may have known what she was doing when it came to you and Ryan."

"Oh, that reminds me. We're making progress on your prophecy."

"I believe I made it clear, I'm prophesied out."

"Fate's a bitch that way. She doesn't really care what you want."

"Fine. I'm showering, eating, and I presume the plan is to spend the day hitting the books?"

"Astrid and Bodie are already at it." She paused before backing away, her face scrunching in sympathy. "Bennett?"

"What's up?"

"I... I like Adair."

"Me too."

"But... if she breaks your heart again, I'm cutting her head off."

He snorted, unsure if it was a laugh or choke. "Not sure she'll let me get close enough to risk it."

"But you're going to keep trying."

"Not saying I'm a smart one."

"Stop. You're smart. You're bullheaded. And a hopeless romantic."

"Neither of which have ever worked out in my favor."

She wrapped her arms around him and gave him an almost painful bearhug squeeze. "They will one of these times."

While Quinn rejoined the others upstairs, he heard their chattering relief as she informed them he was up and about. "Stable."

Huh. *Stable*. Verdict was still out on that one.

Either way, he set the bag in the open closet and ducked into the bathroom. He flicked on the bathroom fan, needing that subtle white noise to drown out the sounds of the house. Didn't completely block things, but muffled at least. Flipping on the shower, he stood under the spray, bracing his hands on the wall to let the water stream over his shoulders and down his back.

Feeling almost refreshed, he pulled on his jeans as the doorknob turned. Reaching, he pulled open the door and found Adair standing in one of his t-shirts, running a hand through her sleepy-wild hair, her eyes still hazy from... well, from spending the last three days in bed with him. Regrettably, *not* making love.

Holding his breath, he backed up to let her pass and closed the door as he left her to it. Didn't matter. He could hear her soft moan as the massaging spray of the shower washed over her skin. Could smell the lather of his soap as she ran the suds over her body.

Ignoring his deprived libido, Bennett tamped down the long-ignored lust. Making a move after sucking the life out of her? Sure, he'd been so... enthralled, he wanted her like nothing before. He'd kissed away the wounds, nothing more, knowing the feelings they had for each other still as fresh as the day she'd left, but the circumstances were still set against them.

He tugged the sheets off the bed and loaded the washing machine down the hall. Snagging a set of clean sheets from the linen closet, he made the bed, the breezy scent lifting the darkness from the room.

By the time he finished tidying, he heard the water shut off. He heard Adair open the drawer, then brush her teeth.

Pulling out the bag of clothes, he knocked on the bathroom door. Okay, this was an even dumber idea. A towel pulled around her, water dripped from her wavy hair and trailed over her skin.

Her lips were pouty and lush, skin pinked from the heat... he felt like the horny kid he'd been the day they'd met. His gaze magnetically following the stream down between her breasts.

At a club, looking for trouble, he'd stumbled upon the best kind of trouble. Dressed in a snug black dress that barely covered the good stuff, drawing him to the dance floor, she'd been looking for trouble, too. "I never got to finish that dance with you," he found himself murmuring.

Gripping the bathroom door, she lowered her eyes to his mouth. "You were too pleased to find somebody to slay."

"True. I was an idiot."

"That, I can agree with." She grinned, her lips turned up in a full tease.

Lightness bubbled in his chest, a welcome relief. "Well, I'm still an idiot. Quinn thought you two might be about the same size, so she brought some clothes for you."

She set the bag on the bathroom counter. Glaring at it, that notch furrowed between her eyebrows. "I'm not sure how I feel about wearing your ex's underwear."

"You were my ex long before she was."

"And apparently the cop that lived in 708? And I heard a rumor about you and Lana's sister. Didn't you date that reporter for a while?"

"All true. You dumped me. Not exactly going to sit home and pine away for the vampire that got away."

She winced. "I am sorry for the way I left. I never meant–"

Slap to the jugular, the memory struck him, hating that she knew what she'd done to him. "Yeah, well, it was for the best, I'm sure. Wear the clothes or don't. Walk around naked or in that skimpy club dress if you prefer. I'm hungry," he grumbled as he backed out of the bathroom, attempting to make it clear that he wasn't leaving himself open again.

"Wait. Bennett. For whatever it's worth, I still think about those nights we had together. More often than I should."

Rubbing a hand over his face, he tried to mask his snarl and murmured, "And I moved on."

Closing the bag, she pushed it aside and dropped the towel. Feet anchored in place, Bennett stopped fast, his jaw dropping to the floor. Hands on her bare hips, the corner of her lips turned up haughtily. "You know, showers are a fairly recent invention."

Breath rushing from his lungs at the fucking gorgeous sight, those perfectly rounded breasts on full display, the curve of her waist he wanted to wrap his arms around again. "I, uh..." he garbled.

"We used to go out whenever the weather was nice, the women of the clan, to the loch to bathe together." She trailed a hand over her abdomen and graced over her soft curls. "It was nice to have someone to lend a hand now and again." She bit the corner of her lip in a devious taunt.

What the hell was she doing to him? Every drop of blood in his body surging south, he struggled to find any sort of response.

"We'd inevitably get distracted and splash and play in the sun, naked and wet. Sometimes the soldiers would come back from a raid, dropping their gear and diving in while we were still out in the lake." She reached for him and yanked him closer by the waist of his jeans. A devious look of victory teased at her lips as he lost the ability to speak.

"I wasn't kidding when I said I missed you," she whispered, smiling at his apparent surrender.

Remembering the way she'd left, his heart shattering in her wake, he was brought right back to the fury that chipped away at the naivete that she'd tried to protect by leaving. If she'd had a damn clue how her exit had darkened him...

The memory flamed under his skin, entwined with so many better ones of their time together, of the last few days, fueling that damn lack of self-preservation that had gotten him into this mess to begin with. Hauling her against him, his hands gripped firm around her hips. He took her mouth and devoured, giving her more than the jaw-dropping reaction that she'd tried to provoke in him. Sliding his tongue along hers, he didn't give her an inch, but shifted a hand and burrowed into her hair as he deepened the kiss.

Not holding back, he kissed her with a furious confidence, letting her know he was no longer the eager virgin. That he hadn't sat at home alone each night, pining away for her all those years. As she sighed a desperate moan against his mouth, she slid her hands under his shirt and clung to his bare skin.

Half-mad with lust, he released her and stepped back. "Don't play me again."

She blinked, the softness in her hazy expression clearing as she realized he'd played her harder. Lips bit tight together, she stepped back and dug into the bag, the crease between her brow downright cavernous. Fury? Regret? Embarrassment?

Whatever it was... not his problem. "I'm not the naïve hunter you deflowered, thrilled to see a woman naked."

She dipped into the bag of hand-me-downs. Under her breath, she muttered, "I'm not wearing your ex's underwear."

He rubbed a hand along his jaw, roughened from days without shaving. "I don't care who's seen you naked before, but my team doesn't get a show."

8

HALFWAY UP THE STAIRS, Adair paused. She smoothed the cotton fabric of the simple t-shirt. The easy laughter, the clanking of dishes as someone set the table, the scent of scrambled eggs and bacon wafting through the air... Like nothing she'd been a part of, not in her short life as a human.

Expectations and rules, always being the proper lass, never quite understanding how to fill that role as her mother had passed away before Adair's second birthday. Then her father died of infection. Eventually Logan disappeared. And Adair was left alone to bring security to her people by marrying Richerd. In all fairness, it had been her idea. Not that there had been another choice; her clan had needed the ally. And it was all she'd had left to give.

Her husband had been years older and uninterested in anything but an heir. From her or from whatever set of tits he found appealing. His clan hadn't been much friendlier, only begrudgingly accepting the alliance with her inferior clan. Eventually she'd made a few friends, but she hadn't been allowed to leave the grounds.

It didn't take long to learn why. With their stronghold so close to Inverness, they were a popular target for the vampires that infested the area. Done with being treated like a feeble goat, she spent months planning her escape. She'd sent one of her few friends into town to find Logan, knowing in her heart that he was still alive.

When Logan found her, miles from the grounds, she was bruised, broken, and inches from death. She had a bleeding head wound from her husband, thanks to her husband's feverish response to her insolence. He'd been convinced she had gotten knocked up by his fiercest warrior.

Logan had brought her back to life, but not in a way she could ever have imagined.

As she reached the top step, Bennett's posture righted, and he gripped his coffee tighter. The corners of his mouth quirked up in a sardonic smile, the heat behind that furious kiss still burned under the dark expression. What had she been thinking, provoking him like that? Sometimes she feared she would always be a natural predator, enticing her prey before striking. No longer the naïve virgin, he delivered a surprise response... and she was the one left stunned.

They'd spent days cuddled close, her feeding him, then him trying to kiss the hurt away, his guilt heavy on the air. His restraint had been palpable, trying damn hard to only take what he needed to survive. But she'd driven an irrevocable divide between them years ago, and, apparently, her survival instincts weren't as keen as she thought.

A bubbly brunette with wild wavy hair, dressed in a denim miniskirt and cowboy boots, topped off with a chunky sweater, came sweeping over with a piping cup of coffee laced with blood. "I think I remember you enjoyed your coffee *extra* bitter?"

Accepting the mug, Adair grinned. "Thanks, Lana. How have you been? Staying out of trouble?"

"Never." Lana hooked arms with her and dragged her to the kitchen table. "I should thank Bennett for shaking things up a bit; I'd been getting restless."

Countering the sunshine-shunning curtains, the room was aglow with lamps in every corner, plus an iron and seeded-glass chandelier over the timber dining table. Bodie and Astrid were curled up on the plush couch in front of the roaring fire, each with their nose in an ancient text and comparing passages. Riling each other in the kitchen, Quinn added an extra scoop of cheese to the scrambled eggs, while Ryan snatched the bag out from behind her, claiming there was indeed such thing as too much cheese. A tall guy, must be Vann, flashed her a casual salute as he paced with Skye, the infant's eyes slowly closing as she snuggled against his chest in her fuzzy pink blanket.

Lana seemed to feel her awkwardness and distracted her with easy conversation. "I like your necklace," she remarked.

Adair looked down at the silver leaf on the leather string. "Thanks. I picked it up in a shop in the seventies and forgot all about it until I rediscovered it in my jewelry box a few months ago."

"Crap, that must be so odd. I get excited when I rediscover things from a few months ago."

"You get used to it. In another century, you'll be doing the same."

"They say everything comes back around, fashion and such."

"Sort of. I'm never going back to heavy dresses that seem designed to cover the fact that I have legs and hindered my movements."

"Ugh, the sexism you've had to live through."

"Oh it's still thick in society, but we're on the right track. I buck some of the old traditions by wearing pants and fun shoes and short dresses that would have made my husband's eyes roll back in his head with scorn."

"Husband?"

Adair bit her tongue, realizing Richerd had intruded in her memories. Bennett didn't move, but his chocolaty brown eyes melted. "Briefly. Trust me, I got my revenge in my murderous phase. I think that's the one kill that I don't feel guilty about."

"You're what, five-hundred something?"

"Uh-huh."

"And you never remarried?"

"Hell no. A human life is too fleeting and fragile, and I never met a vampire I wanted to commit to forever with. Plus, most humans don't want to hear, 'So, I will not age, I can't go out in the daylight with you unless I want an epic sunburn, I can't have children, and I will do my best to avoid eating you.'"

Baby in one arm and coffee pot in the other, Vann came around with refills before setting the carafe in the middle of the table. "And here we only have to worry about, 'By marrying me, you'll live a few hundred years and never get sick again, but I will have to leave you for weeks at a time and risk my life to save the world, as will our children one day.'"

Quinn came in with the scrambled eggs–extra cheesy–and set it on the table, while Ryan followed behind with bacon and sourdough toast on another platter. The troops quickly descended and annihilated the meal. Impeccably mannered, as usual, Bennett waited for the others to dish up.

Swallowing a salty bite of bacon, Adair asked, "How does it work? Changing your partner by marriage, I mean. It's almost like you change your mate like a vampire might change someone, but the blood exchange almost makes scientific sense to me."

Setting down her strip of bacon, Astrid said, "It's like our choice to accept the gift when we turn eighteen. Something activates within us and changes our genetic structure. Except we copy some of the demon strands and share them with our partner. It requires a focused, undoubting commitment in our mind that this person is our equal and our future, and the words enable us to share some of our abilities."

Bodie cleared his throat. "The process is the same for werewolves. The words are important because they symbolize the confirmation and the decision to proceed that starts the process. Actually, this is where the phrase, 'you may kiss the bride,' originated. It's that intention and the physical connection that officially begins the exchange. But coming together completely, makes it permanent. Which is why a marriage must be consummated before it's considered binding in most civilizations. Seals the deal, so to speak."

Holding Skye tight against her as she scooped in another bite, Quinn grinned at Bodie before turning to Adair. "Bodie is an anthropologist specializing in the paranormal. Most of us have no idea how it works, we know to say the words that have been passed down through the generations, and the rest of the good stuff is rather inevitable, as if you didn't truly feel that way, the transfer wouldn't happen."

"Kissing and sex to claim someone? Sounds more romantic that biting and sucking." Adair grinned over the rim of her coffee cup.

Bodie winked. "Those are important too."

Ripping off a chunk of bacon, Lana added, "I like to practice as often as possible, so I get it right when the time comes."

Nodding, Bodie said, "It was really weird when we got married, as we shared different gifts. I mean, we both have longevity already, but werewolves don't heal as rapidly as demon hunters. As soon as we kissed at the end of the ceremony, I could feel something in that connection; painful, like rebuilding every cell in my body, but weirder yet, was feeling Astrid bearing the bulk of the agony for me, while I was fighting back to protect her from the wolf changes in her."

Bennett leaned back in his chair and folded his arms over his chest. "I always wondered about that. Why anyone would risk bringing that pain on a mate."

Lana shook her head. "My dad's been trying to get me to settle down since my fricking eighteenth birthday, so I know way more than I care to. I got used to hearing about where babies come from, the sex talk, and the chastity belt threat at every family dinner. Dad did not take after Grandpa and hates that I do. Mom was his childhood sweetheart. Anyway, by instinct, we shoulder the pain of the change for our partner, not just to be nice, but we have the strength to handle it."

Hand rubbing the back of his neck, Bodie added, "By the time the exchange was done? I was so tempted to go out and get hurt so I could see how fast I heal. Really cool. But, you know, by that point, I was a little distracted by the consummating bit."

Astrid swallowed her bite before speaking. "Werewolves get married under the full moon, either based on suspicion or an awareness of that's when their power is at its strongest, and as we kissed, I felt the strangest energy from the moon, and I do every month now."

Ryan slid his empty plate forward and took Skye so Quinn could finish eating. "Not everything is shared though. Only what is necessary to form the lifelong partnership, and what can be shared. Longevity and healing, yes, but strength, instincts, and for werewolves the ability to shift, those aren't shared, either because they're not necessary or not possible to pass to your partner. Quinn didn't get my ability to travel across the veil to the demon realm."

She nodded as she swallowed a massive bite of eggs. "I was a little disappointed by that. But Skye has it. I mean, I can't say for sure, but I had some control while I was pregnant, and that's gone now."

After kissing the top of Skye's red fuzzy head, Ryan said, "When she's older and we can tell for sure, I'll take her to the demon realm to meet her grandfather. I visited him before she was born, and he says there's no reason she wouldn't be able to. As a direct descendant of the demon king, she would inherit his control over the veil like I did. And, like with me, the gift may not be a choice, but could come more gradually with puberty instead."

Laughing softly as she slid her empty plate forward, Adair settled back and folded her arms over her chest. "I'm old, like, really old, and this is, without a doubt, the strangest breakfast conversation I've ever had."

Bennett shrugged. "You haven't spent enough time with demon hunters." He punctuated the invitation with a wink. He gulped down a pint of Vann's unique delivery, bison blood this time, and then claimed it was his turn for Skye now that he wasn't hungry. She was awake and alert, so he sat on the couch with his legs propped up on the coffee table, the happy baby resting in the makeshift seat he'd made for her. Her dark eyes focused in on him with a knowing look. He grinned and chatted with her, tapping the tip of her nose to elicit a reflexive smile.

Adair felt the demon hunter, human and vampire in him starting to settle. His cravings were so much better controlled than hers had been this early on, either due to his stubbornness or the hunter inside him, protecting at all costs. He moved differently now, faster and smoother, but he still held that power in every movement. She'd felt the demon hunter strength still running strong when he'd fed from her. Even restrained, he exuded that untamable physicality.

A crack in the curtain creeped across the room as the sun rose high in the sky. Adair felt it for the threat it was and dodged its burn. She crossed to sit next to Bennett to smooth over the incident from earlier this morning. Before lowering to the couch, she felt the warning flame over her skin and looked down at his arm.

He caught her hovering and glanced up. "What?" His eyebrow raised at her open-mouthed concern.

"*Look.*"

He followed her gaze to the scrap of sunlight that should feel like roasting under the oven broiler.

"Oh, shit." He shifted Skye and rose to his feet, moving out of the light, then passed Skye to Adair.

Awkward and totally uncertain with the delicate package, somehow less fragile than she would have imagined, Adair wanted to refuse, but Bennett was freaked. She balanced the little one in her arms and rested her against her chest like Quinn had done through breakfast. Snuggly and cozy like a little heater, Skye burrowed into her.

The room stilled as Bennett stood stunned. Testing the water, he reached into the strip of sunlight and let the ray dance over his fingers. "Isn't that supposed to hurt?"

"Yes."

Moving to the curtain, he glanced back at her. "Stay in the shadows." With a cautious thrill, he drew back the curtain and let the golden waves wash over him.

Standing like a warrior, the sun rising over a frozen battlefield, he closed his eyes and opened his arms. Drawing in a breath of the morning sun, his lips drew into a resonant grin. Rare dimples flashed in his cheeks, the tension that had tightened over his neck and shoulders loosened.

Breath catching in her throat, Adair watched as he savored the sensation she hadn't felt in centuries. She loved her immortality, the speed, feeling her surroundings with intensity. But the sun on her face? *That* she would give up eternity for.

Turning with a dreamy smile, Bennett flashed her a wink.

Quinn chuckled and crossed the room to pull him in for a hug. "Look at you, all impressed with yourself. A few days ago, you were at death's door, and now you're all smug and showing off again."

Sinking in her gut, Adair choked on a glob of jealousy. She knew he wasn't with Quinn anymore. That they were friends. But to tease him in the full light, to have that history...

Running forward, Lana added to the hug and jumped up and down, nearly knocking Bennett over. "I don't think I've seen that ego in months. I missed that kick-ass attitude."

"I'm glad I can still fight and not have to skip out on any daytime missions."

The team moved into the light, happy and chatting and welcoming Bennett back into their fold. Standing in the shadow of the kitchen, Adair looked down at little Skye. The infant didn't have a clue how wide open her future was.

ON REALIZING ADAIR HAD been trapped in the kitchen, the excitement of the moment had faded damn fast. Bennett's thrill at the realization that he wasn't totally useless to his team was quickly subdued at her isolation.

Would she even want to join? She'd made it clear she was happy as a vampire. Hell, she had some crazy stories. She'd been offered a ride on the *Titanic* but had enough wherewithal to *not* head out on a maiden voyage; like dirigibles and old ironclads, she'd left the crazy to humans. But she'd been a force with the suffragettes, had heard Martin Luther King Jr speak, had tossed tea into Boston Harbor, and was on the cover of *Vogue*.

She'd help to take out Calloway, as she had no other choice. When they'd taken on Sonra and her cronies, Adair had made it clear it was only out of self-preservation. He'd tried to convince her she'd make a hell of a hunter, but she wasn't interested. Despite the change in circumstances, he doubted her feelings had changed.

He gulped down the last of his beer and set the glass on the table. Diffuse moonlight shined into the room, coalescing with the glow of the fire that warmed the night. "This vampire thing is brilliant." He grinned. "My eyes should be swimming from reading old texts all day, but still fresh."

Astrid glared at him. "Speaking of. I think it's break-time. I'm not finding much."

Leaning back in his chair, Bodie graced his hand over her back. "Me neither. I'm finding stuff on how vampires change—wish we'd found this book a few days ago—but no mention of a demon hunter ever being changed, or even anyone considering it."

Closing her book, Astrid pushed it away. "I was so sure I would find the prophecy in the book that we found Quinn and Ryan's. But I've read it twice in twenty-four hours, and there's hardly even mention of a prophecy that pertains to vampires."

"Hardly?" Ryan glanced at the monitor that chirped, rising to check on Skye.

Bennett shook his head. "She's falling back to sleep."

Lowering back to the chair, Ryan fisted his hand in his short hair as he settled back in. "Creepy, but thanks."

"*You* think it's creepy? I had to hear Lana's chat with her latest boyfriend this afternoon. I really didn't want to know that much about her... uh, her... Wow, I can't even say it out loud." His cheeks flushed as the vivid imagery invaded his brain.

Lana threw a piece of popcorn at him. "You were the one saying that I should try dating a guy for more than a night or two."

Adair smiled softly and flipped the page in her book. "You get used to it. At least people bathe and wear deodorant these days."

Crunching a handful of popcorn, Ryan shook his head. "Let's get back to the 'hardly.' What did you find on vampire prophecies?"

Scowling, Astrid grabbed the book and flipped the pages. "Something about a vampire cure, which sounds ridiculously complex and more likely to end in a painful death, or worse. There was another about vampire origins."

Bennett waved his hand along encouragingly. "And...?"

"Well, I don't know that it's relevant; it doesn't make much sense. Supposedly the demon that fed the first human to create the first vampire left something somewhere in our realm. The language is excessively verbose and has been translated several times over, but he either left his blood for an emergency, or it is some sort of door, or it will unleash something. It doesn't make any sense. No vampire can actually get to it, but only a vampire can get to it. It sounds like a complex gauntlet of puzzles, blocked stone passageways, leaps of faith, sunlight, and I'm pretty sure it even references a blood test."

Raising his hand, Bennett chuckled. "Like, maybe someone with vampire blood that can withstand daylight and is strong enough to move heavy rocks that might block a doorway, someone that can jump far, run fast, drink blood..."

Quinn snorted with an amused chuckle. "Yeah, like if someone merged a vampire with a demon hunter."

Astrid grinned sheepishly and threw popcorn at him.

He caught it midair and popped it into his mouth.

She left the book open and slid it to the center of the table. "And I'm calling it quits for the night."

Vann sat quietly, a scowl on his face. "This prophecy is relevant, but there's more. I want to know what Calloway found. The why of it. For now? Agreed, I'm toast. Let's sleep on it, and maybe more will come to light now that we have something to explore."

Bennett watched as the others traipsed off to bed. Adair remained at the opposite end of the table. The space between them had been cavernous since... since she'd tempted the hell out of him and simultaneously pissed him off with her little seduction that morning. Had she truly been uncertain that he was indefinitely attracted? He'd made it clear, years ago, that she was permanently imprinted in his fantasy world. Yet she had remained unmoved like they were no big thing.

Groaning, he rubbed a hand over his face as the sounds of the night were a little too clear in his superhuman hearing. "How do you stand it?" he asked Adair.

She closed her eyes and smiled. "You mean Lana and the phone sex, Astrid's little striptease, or that demon hunters heal so fast, that Quinn, and Ryan are already back at it and thoroughly enjoying themselves?"

A chuckle vibrated his ribs at her smartass quip. "Yep. Pretty much."

"I like your team. And it's apparent they really like each other."

Grumbling, he rose from the table and nodded toward the door. "Walk with me?"

Sporting her poker face, she was neither smiling nor frowning, but her pulse kicked up as she brushed past him and walked into the night. Ever the fool, he nearly reached to take her hand, but shoved his fists in his pockets instead.

Ahead of him, Adair stood on the edge of the field and scanned the long stretch of grass and patchy forests that sprawled in all directions before hitting the coast and endless nothing spanned to the horizon. Not another home in sight on the isolated Northern California coast. Taunting him, she backed up until her feet left the stone path. "Think you're pretty badass now? Still the demon hunter, plus enhanced senses? Let's see if you're fast as a pure vampire."

"Like a race?" He stalked closer and stood a few inches away. He glanced down at her bare feet, the pastel pink nail polish where she'd

worn blood red before. In borrowed jeans with more holes than denim, the plain t-shirt that wasn't meant to be sexy, yet highlighted her
spectacular curves, topped off with the makeup-less face, she didn't
look anything like a vampire. She looked like everything he'd dreamed
of since long before they'd met.

Tugging her plump lip into her teeth, she contrasted the
girl-next-door look with predatorial fangs, her blue eyes flashing with
killer instincts... and capped the look of everything he'd dreamed of
since. "To that fallen tree on the horizon." Backing up, she taunted
him to accept the challenge. "Scared?"

Tipping his head back in a subtle nod, he grinned. "Never."

"Ready? One... Two...."

Spinning, she took off full speed, like a fricking Olympic sprinter
on performance enhancement drugs.

"Cheater." He laughed as he took off after her. Arms pumping at
his sides, legs moving faster than he would have imagined possible, he
moved with the velocity of the wind off the ocean. Air flowed in and
out of his lungs smoothly, his heartbeat steady in his chest.

Laughing wholeheartedly, she soared, each footfall quicker than a
blink, her strides long as a gazelle.

Shit, she was fast. The distance between them widened, but he was
still so much faster than he'd been before.

She vaulted into the air and leaped over the log, her landing flawless.
Laughing and beaming at her victory, she had an extra second to rest
her hands on her hips before he caught up.

Not slowing, he launched over the log and grabbed her around the
waist, pulling her to the ground with him into the tall grass.

Landing atop him, she sat up, her head tilted up to the sky as she
calmed her laughter and tossed her hair out of her face. Her delight
sent him off the planet. Holding her atop him, he gripped her hips

and sat up to meet her. Sliding his hands under the hem of her top, the smooth silk of her skin warm under his touch, he craved her like nothing else.

Wrapping around his broad shoulders, she slid one hand around the back of his head and clutched her fingers in his hair. The cloudy night reflected as she searched his eyes before her gaze landed on his lips.

Uncertain after this morning, he waited. About killed him, her hesitation. His heart rate kicked up, and he could feel hers following.

His thumbs graced along her low back. While she decided if she was going to kiss him or not, the corners of his lips turned up in an ornery smile. Chuckling under her breath, her gaze met his.

There it was.

Leaning to meet him, she brushed her lips over his, tasting, tormenting him as she settled. Keeping still, he closed his eyes and savored the sensation while she seemed to debate how far to take things.

Something shifted. A decision. Instinct. Desire. Whatever it was, he was fully on board. Clutching her hands in his hair, she devoured.

Breathless at the urgency, he moved with her, needing to break down the barrier between them.

His hands shifted and slid under her bra, palming her breasts. She whimpered and leaned into his touch, then released him long enough to ditch her top.

Whispering against his mouth, she pleaded, "More."

Heart thundering under his ribs, his cock aching at the mere possibility, at the feel of her, heat radiated through him. Massaging, he squeezed enough to bring a yearning gasp, then trailed his tongue along her skin.

A soprano moan passed her lips, her hips rocking against him. Taking her breast in his mouth, he laved, her breath quickening, her pulse thundering in rhythm with his. At the scent of her desire, indescribably arousing, he took her deeper, suckling one side while massaging the other, the intensity of her reaction so vividly palpable to his heightened senses, he drove her higher, faster, her thrill perpetuating his.

Desperate, hungry for more, he released her breasts and met her lips again, her bare chest pressed against him, wondering how to ask after the roller coaster they'd been through.

Instead, he fucked it up.

As usual.

Voice saturated with too damn many emotions, he found his breath to say, "All the reasons we couldn't be together before are gone. We can be whatever we want now."

Drawing back, her brow scrunched and she cleared her throat. Easing off his lap, she rose to her feet and pulled her clothes back on. And walked away.

Rubbing his fist over the throb in his chest as his heart shattered all over again, he gritted his teeth and stared off into the night. The ocean waves pummeled against the rocky shore. The breeze didn't even ruffle the weathered branches that had grown to withstand the unyielding force.

9

HEAT WELLED BEHIND HER eyes, the regret threatening to spill out and make it that much worse. Adair returned to their room and dropped to the bed, wishing sleep would come. As the sun rose high enough to extend the house's shadow long across the field, she felt the heaviness of sleep ease the pain of her achy limbs.

The door creaked. She didn't open her eyes, but she could feel his fluid movements, his scent rugged and fresh as the ocean breeze as he tugged off his shirt and jeans. Gut rolling with nausea, she wanted to say it, but knew it would only make it worse. Once Calloway was dealt with, they would go their separate ways. Because she had to.

Slipping in behind her, Bennett didn't say a word, but wrapped his body around hers and held her close. Melting into him, she fell into sleep. All night, she'd dreamed of him. Of what could happen. Of his lips on her body under the starry sky, of him holding her close like he was now. Like he would be content to hold her forever.

Proving exactly why she wouldn't keep him.

By the time she stirred, he was coming out of the shower. In nothing but a plush towel draped loosely over his hips. The time that had passed struck her like a bullet in the vest. Filled out was an understatement; he'd been toned and undeniably strong as all demon hunters were, but now he was solid. His shoulders showed the bulk of someone who trained with sword and shield for days on end. Those abs... well, they were... epic. She hoped he didn't see her sigh.

Nope, he did. She didn't bother masking the blush as he caught her ogle. Hand in the cookie jar. Or, well, she *wished* her hand was on the goods.

He grinned. "Not looking for a show, are you? I mean, I could tell you some hot story, like last September, when the heater in the prop plane got stuck on full blast, and Vann, Bodie, Ryan, and I stripped down to the skin to cool down..."

Letting his dopey humor wash away the awkwardness of last night, she laughed and chucked a pillow at him. "No. I'm sleepy, I'm hungry, and I need a shower." And him.

"Suit yourself." He shrugged, then flicked off the towel to torment her before pulling on his jeans. Her breath whooshed from her lungs as she appreciated how he'd... developed.

How was he in such a good mood? Contagious, his humor rubbed off on her and she laughed and burrowed back into the pillow, a smile on her face as she inhaled one last breath of him before getting out of bed.

Upstairs, she found a similar scene to the previous morning, but this time Lana was in the kitchen and had just finished cleaning up breakfast dishes, and was scooping her out a bowl of cowboy oatmeal the moment Adair hit the top step.

"I was about to give up on you," Lana said as Adair poured a cup of tepid coffee and splashed a skosh of blood in the mug.

"Couldn't sleep last night."

"Sexy vampire keep you up all night?" Lana winked and helped herself to oatmeal-seconds, leaning back against the counter.

"Sort of," she pouted.

"It's okay, he's outside with Ryan." Lana motioned to the front door, keeping her voice low. "What's up? The sparks between you guys have been threatening to start something explosive."

"That's a very real, very dangerous possibility. It's just... Bennett's larger than life. He's kind and thoughtful... and sexy and built... and affectionate, and understanding and..."

Lana grinned. "And the problem is?"

The microwave beeped as her mug was done heating. "You're his teammate. I can't talk about it with you, that would be weird."

Lana set down the oatmeal and parked her hands on her hips. "I know we only got to hang out for those few days while we took out Sonra and her goons, so I know you don't know me well enough yet. But I like you. And, call it ego, but I know you like me, too. And I love Bennett too much to tell him something that would hurt him, so I can keep a secret. And you need a friend. Dish. What's up?"

"It's complicated." She crossed one arm over her chest while sipping the blood-laced coffee with the other.

"Your brother was cured."

"Yes."

"And you'll lose him one day."

"Yes."

"And we don't know if Bennett will live a typical demon hunter lifespan, or if he's gained a vampire's immortality, or somewhere in between. Even if he is immortal, well, he's Bennett, and doesn't really stop to think about whether he'll survive the fight."

Lips bit tight together, Adair nodded.

"It must be so hard, losing so many over so long. I would be afraid to get close, too. I can't convince you to risk yourself like that, but if anyone is worth the heartbreak? It's Bennett."

"I know."

The front door swung open, sunlight casting an expansive glow on the entry. Bennett strolled in, sporting a fresh haircut. His hand played with the short sides before rustling the longer bit up top.

Lana snuck out of the kitchen, leaving Adair to her pathetic ogle. Damn, he looked good all cleaned up. Slick and timeless, the cut suited him. Didn't hurt that it accented the strong angle of his jaw.

She nodded as he came closer. "Nice."

He grinned and reached around her, pulling out a coffee cup, taking advantage and leaning down to brush his lips over the pulse of her neck. "Thanks," he said. He filled the mug from a pint in the fridge and stood shoulder-to-shoulder while his drink heated.

Ryan appeared in the kitchen a minute later. "Your darkened carriage awaits." He winked.

"What?" she said as she scooted away from Bennett before she combusted.

Vann came in from outside. "All packed up." He caught her confused scowl. "You missed the morning scheming. We're traveling."

Wandering in from the bedroom, Quinn had Skye in her arms. "Everyone but Skye and me. We get to be the command center. Or at least, that's what I'm calling it, so I don't feel left out." She winked, then ruffled her hand over Bennett's hair. "I can't believe you went so long without a cut. Isn't this better?"

He smiled sheepishly, then stood at Adair's side, lacing his arm around her waist while they both sipped on their blood-laced brews. "I hinted a few times, but you were busy growing that little one."

Astrid walked by with a box of throwing knives, then ducked outside.

"Um, where are we going?" Adair asked. The commotion was nuts. Everyone was moving with a purpose or was transitioning between tasks. All grinning and thrilled, as she suspected they always were when walking into the fray.

Bodie filled up his travel mug and finally answered her question before trotting back downstairs. "Astrid and I are heading to Eastern Europe. Vann and Lana are off to Bangkok. Ryan's for Alaska and the Coast Guard. And you and Bennett get a romantic getaway to Paris."

"Okay..."

Quinn took pity on her. "Astrid re-read the passage about the demon that created vampires again this morning, and Vann remembered something he had read that may relate. There was mention of a river city. Impossible to narrow it down, but based on some of the vampire history in Bangkok and Paris, they were obvious choices. Bennett's parents have the apartment in Paris, so that made sense for you guys to start there, and it's pretty central to some other possibilities like London, Verona, Cologne. Vann dibs'd Bangkok as he's always wanted to go, and it has a solid history of vampire activity. Ryan really needs to get back to work anyway, and as we discovered last year, there was a tear in the veil off the Aleutians so it's a bit of a demon hotspot, plus there are a lot of river towns, so a good place to start. And Bodie has some werewolf family in the Urals he'd been planning on meeting soon anyway, so he and Astrid will consult with them before hitting Moscow."

"With so much burned down in the Great Paris Fire and the Hausman destruction of nearly all the medieval structures, I'm not sure we'll be able to find much prehistory."

Bennett released her long enough to rinse out his mug and put it in the dishwasher. "Notre Dame has a lot of preserved history inside, the catacombs, and some of the other older buildings may hold some secrets. Astrid and Bodie will fly with us to Paris, where they'll catch a flight east. With Calloway and Blayk likely hot on our trail, we shouldn't stay in the same place for long, so we'll have the jet and can keep moving until we find a more solid lead. We're at a standstill here."

"Wow, okay. I guess I can't exactly go home until Calloway's out of the picture anyway."

"Not even a little excited to visit Paris?" Lana asked.

Shaking her head, perhaps too vigorously, Adair nodded. "Of course, it's a favorite of mine."

Rinsing her mug, she dashed downstairs and packed her few borrowed belongings in the paper grocery bag and found Quinn waiting for her at the top of the steps. "They're all loaded up. Come on, you can go through the mudroom to the garage."

"Thanks. Really. I'm sorry to have intruded like this."

Quinn's brow tipped down and her midnight blue eyes went all melty. "Don't for once think you're not welcome here. Especially now. If you hadn't come? Bennett wouldn't have made it."

Adair's throat tightened. She breathed through the sensation and shook her head. "He's solid. He would have found a way."

"It's more than that."

What was it with these people? Why couldn't they be like other demon hunters and treat her like the demon she was? Adair cringed as the spasm clenched in her throat. "You'll let us know if you find anything else in your research?"

"I have little doubt you'll find what you need when you need to. Fate's a bitch like that."

Packing Skye in his arms, Ryan breezed in and grabbed Quinn. Sensing the change in atmosphere, Adair hoisted up her bag of clothes and walked to the garage. At the doorway, drawn to the heady scent of longing behind her, she glanced back to see the perfect little family embraced, Ryan and Quinn's lips connected as if this kiss might be their last. The life of a demon hunter. Like warriors throughout time, they risked everything, running into the fray while others took the safer path.

Wishing she could ignore the words they whispered to each other, Adair shifted her attention. The windows of the SUV were now limousine-dark. There was a curtain pinned up between the front and rest of the seats.

Astrid rolled down the driver's side window and waved her in. "Everything's packed. Climb on in."

Sliding into the backseat, Adair took the empty seat next to Bodie. He gave her a nod, then took her bag and turned to add it to the stack of supplies behind them.

The drive to the airport was quiet; Lana, Vann and Ryan turned off in their car toward the commercial flights, while they turned toward the private hangars. Bennett and Astrid chatted up front, joking about some past encounter with a group of vampires that had taken them for innocent college kids a few years back and had been unpleasantly surprised when their guests turned out to be demon hunters rather than rowdy co-eds ripe for the tasting.

They pulled into the private hangar and closed all the doors before letting a crack of light even touch her. She rolled her eyes as she climbed out into the shade. "A few minutes of sun won't hurt me. Not saying I'd enjoy it, and I'll look like I spent the week in Hawaii, but it's not a big deal."

The others smiled and shook their heads, unloading the SUV while Bennett stepped close and took her hands in his. "And it's not a big deal to keep you safe."

Tipping her head up, she bit her cheek. "I'm not human. Not a victim. I don't need protection."

"Don't I know it." Releasing her, he backed away, then moved to the rear of the SUV and unloaded his gear.

Once inside, Astrid made herself comfortable in the cockpit. Bodie leaned back and stretched out his legs in one of the cabin seats, his nose in a book. Fingers fidgeting in her pockets, Adair stood in between.

"Here." Bodie shifted forward and pulled out a dusty leather-bound text. "May as well get researching."

Sure, her eyes could handle the fine, aged script for hours, but somewhere over the Atlantic, she gave up. After setting a seventh useless book back in the box, she headed for the bedroom. Dropping onto the tidily made bed, its plush navy-blue comforter wrinkled underneath her.

The moment her head hit the pillow, the door eased open. "You okay?" Bennett's smooth voice was gratingly kind.

"I'm fine." She wrapped her arms around her middle and stared up at the ceiling.

"What's up?"

"Just a long flight, that's all."

"It is, but that's not what's bothering you." Rather than leaving her alone, he kicked off his shoes and laid on his back next to her.

And said nothing. Rubbing a hand over his face, he sighed, then rested his hands on his abdomen.

The texture of the taupe wallpapered walls created a natural feel in what should be a cold environment. Even the floors of the plane weren't bad; deep-blue carpet and faux wood. The cognac leather seats of the cabin were soft as butter, and the bedroom was a cozy retreat. "How long have you had the jet?" Her voice cracked.

"Not long."

"How long have you had your pilot's license?"

"Few years."

She released the last of her oxygen from her lungs. "Bennett?"

"Yeah?"

"I'm sorry about last night."

"I know."

"Why aren't you mad?" For the hundreds of years that she had been around humans, vampires and creatures that most people refused to believe existed, her knowledge of demon hunters was paltry. Or this one, apparently.

"Why would I be?"

"Why? Why wouldn't you be? I'm doing it to you all over again."

"Doing what?" Hearing the humor in his voice, she turned to find the dimples were out in full force.

"Are you nuts? Vampire or not, you're not the naïve young hunter I used to know or the... whatever you've become these days." She really, really didn't want to use the words of what she actually thought of him. That ego was massive enough. "I'm still me. A vampire that can't help but torture her victims, and I've foolishly fixated my efforts on you."

"Go back a step. What am I these days?" He rolled onto his side and teased his fingers at the hem of her shirt. Was he even listening?

"You know." Her cheeks flamed red.

"Hot?"

"Maybe." Redder.

"Broody and sexy and a badass demon hunter?" He bit his lip and grinned, his gaze gleaming with pure ego.

And for the first time in over five centuries, maybe ever, she giggled. Bubbling from deep in her belly and pinching her cheeks as the mirth flooded over her. "Maybe," she squeaked out.

Flipping her underneath him, he trailed his lips along the curve of her jaw as she tried to calm the delirious giggle fit.

When his lips met hers, the laughter flowed into blinding lust. Combusting on contact, completely unprepared for everything that was Bennett, she relinquished to feeling everything Bennett had become.

Breath mixing with hers, taking her mouth with that heavy intensity that was and always would be *him*, he ravaged. On fire, he devoured, tongue caressing hers, teeth tugging on her lower lip, hand splayed around her waist... as if he craved her more than blood or even life itself. Hard and tempting, he pressed against her core.

Wrapping her legs around him, she pinned him against her. A soft whimper radiated from her throat. Lacing her hand around the back of his neck, she held him close, needing every inch of him.

Halting, panting, a breath away, he glanced down at her lips, taking her lower lip between his teeth.

Frozen, the shift in altitude sucked the breath from her lungs.

Voice filled with gravel, he whispered, "You pull me in and push me away. Dumped me when I was foolish enough to believe myself in love. And you drew the line at any hope of a tomorrow yet again. I think it's well established that I lack survival instincts." He paused, then stole a lingering, sipping kiss before pulling away again.

She opened her mouth to say something, but he shook his head.

"I know you feel what I'm feeling, and I know it scares the hell out of you. I won't ask for forever, as I know you're not willing to risk it. But I'm taking today." He held her gaze, unwavering. "We'll be landing in half an hour." He stole one last kiss before pulling away. "It's nearly four Paris time, so we'll move fast to get to the apartment before sunrise."

10

DAYS AND NIGHTS COMPLETELY swapped, vampire time and jetlag working conveniently cohesively, Bennett moved silently into the kitchen and poured his coffee. As he'd learned the habit from Adair and her brother, he forwent creamer and added blood instead, the combination remarkably soothing. And masked the grassy undertones of beef blood.

He'd closed the curtains the moment they arrived at the apartment, ensuring Adair could walk freely throughout the living space. Still, she hadn't said much. Awkward as fuck, he'd had no idea which bedroom to show her. They'd cozied up the last few nights out of necessity, then out of convenience, but there were two perfectly serviceable bedrooms.

He'd made his intentions clear, but she hadn't. Hoping to hell she would refuse, he showed her the guest bedroom. So far, she'd seemed content with the sleeping arrangement.

He hadn't slept a wink all day, yet arose with history's most agonizing case of morning wood. After rolling out of bed, he pushed opened the curtains in the main bedroom to watch the Eiffel Tower in the distance, the details of the skyline remarkable with vivid detail as day turned to night, each window shadowed dramatically, each rooftop angle contrasting the one behind. Stomach already rumbling, he heard the doorbell ring as the groceries arrived. He checked the app on his phone and saw the alert confirming the delivery.

After throwing on some pants, he lumbered to the door. As he carted in the bags, Adair sauntered down the hall in his t-shirt. And nothing but his t-shirt. The crisp white tee hung loose on her but didn't hide much. Was she doing it on purpose? Thin enough that he could see the curve of her breasts—no bra—and he was fairly certain there were no panties either.

Forgetting how to breathe, his knees locked, and he stood staring like an enthralled moron.

"Hey." She smiled, teasing her fingers through her sun-kissed hair.

He rumbled, his throat closing in. "Hey."

"Plan?" She asked as she poured her coffee and added a splash of heme-creamer like he had.

Feet still rooted in place, he tried to remember what she'd said.

She raised an eyebrow. "Evil vampires to slay? You know, plan?"

"Oh, right." He blinked and leaned against the counter. "Calloway's plan seems to hinge on what he's turned me into. So, first and foremost, don't let him get his hands on me." Grinning, he added, "I mean, I want to torture him until he truly, irrevocably comprehends the meaning of the word pain. You know, like Prince Humperdinck. Except I'm going to rip out his throat and incinerate him when I'm done. But I'm not going to be stupid again, so that will have to wait until I know why. Tonight, I'm going to check old maps of the region, see where all the river has migrated, what's been dug up and what hasn't by modern humans, and try to find an entrance to this damn gauntlet."

Leaned against the opposite counter, she crossed one arm over her chest and held her coffee in the other. Not helpful. Snug against her skin, the white cotton brought everything out in brilliant color. Sure, vampires didn't have x-ray vision, but the detail was spectacular.

Adair eyed him over the steaming rim of her coffee. "And what if by searching, you walk right into another trap?"

"Sometimes setting off the trap is the only way to disable it."

"Sounds like a stupid, hungry mouse," she said.

"True. But effective."

"You have, at minimum, another two or three centuries of hunting ahead of you. With the vampire in you, it may be forever. Why would you risk losing that?"

Bennett shook his head, unsure how to convey his meaning so she would understand, hoping he wouldn't drive her away by yet another poor choice of words. His mortality, and lack of prioritizing his survival, seemed to remain a point of contention as much today as it had all those years ago. A demon hunter's actions couldn't be restricted by the fear of facing one's end. He said, "In two hundred years, I may gloriously meet my end at the hands of the fabled Ushi-Oni, or I may get crushed under a building in a freak accident tomorrow. That's life. The risk? It's what I signed on for."

"That's what you were fated to endure from birth."

"No, I had a choice. You didn't. But you do now. You don't have to come with me. You'll be safe here. Calloway will hunt you down, so please, stay close until it's done, so I can protect you."

"I don't need you to protect me. I've been fine without you for a damn long time."

"I didn't say you needed me. But please. Let me do what I do."

Adair gulped her coffee before quietly rinsing the mug and set it in the sink. "I'm going to run some errands. Back in a few hours," she said. Expression unreadable, she disappeared down the hall while he stood like the fool he was.

What errands?

Rubbing his hands over his eyes, Bennett held his breath. No wonder she didn't want forever with him. Overbearing jackass.

Wasn't that what Quinn had been trying to tell him? Yeah, they'd officially been over when they'd faced Typha the first time, but he hadn't believed it. Then when Quinn had walked in that night, missing for months... She appeared in the middle of the tavern, hollering some crude comment to a bunch of sailors, with this badass guy all over her, loving her snarky humor. So it turned out to be Ryan, her fricking soulmate. And in that moment, Bennett realized exactly why they hadn't worked.

Downing the last of his drink, he stalked down the hall and into his room. He took way too long of a shower, letting the steaming water pool in the hollow above his shoulders as he rested his hands against the tile. He tugged on a black shirt and jeans, adding black sneakers that might stand a chance at holding up if he had to run full-out.

He crashed on the couch and pulled out his phone. Always depressing, but remarkably helpful, he searched for recent deaths suspicious for vampire kills, maybe see a pattern that could be Calloway on his tail. Huh. Not much vampire activity, but definitely a feral werewolf; he'd fire off a message to a friend that lived nearby.

Nothing else out of the ordinary. He poured another cup of coffee and fired up his laptop. Damn, Paris was old. And had been destroyed and rebuilt enough that finding the entrance would be impossible. Did Calloway know where to start? Bennett opened a map program he'd found remarkably handy on more than one occasion, and lined up map over map, trying to find a pattern, something deep that hadn't been disturbed.

Fuck, he wasn't an archaeologist. This could take years of research. And Paris was a shot in the dark anyway. Rubbing a hand over his face, he leaned back into the couch. He should call his dad.

Nope. Not yet. He'd have to be pretty fucking desperate to consider making that call.

Knee ticking a mile a minute, he looked up at the door again. Checked his phone for a message from Adair. Still nothing. They should have picked up a phone for her so she could call to check in now and again.

Cheeks puffed out, he tossed his phone on the couch and shook off the paranoia. As she'd put it, she was half a damn millennium. She knew how to take care of herself.

Key jingling in the lock, she finally turned the knob. Bennett hopped to his feet, then hesitated when he remembered he wasn't worrying. Or at least, that she would be furious if she knew he was.

Fucking goddess, she strolled in on spiky heeled over-the-knee leather boots and a shimmery ice-blue dress that moved fluidly with each step she took. No bra, the girls settled comfortably as the draped neckline revealed the inner curve of each.

She set down her shopping bags and nodded back toward the door. "My purse is still at your place in Seattle, so I had to use your card. I'll pay you back later."

He swallowed his tongue.

With a smug shake of her head, she gestured toward the door. "Come on, we're going out."

Nodding stupidly, he grabbed the other set of keys from the dish as he followed her out the door.

The bass rattled the pavement, the hum of the waiting crowd teasing at the exclusivity of the club that embodied the heart of Pigalle. Adair added a swing in her hips as she led him to the front of the line, her fingers entwined with his. With her free hand, she stepped close to the bouncer and traced her fingertips along his jaw, then flashed him a fuck-me wink. With a lecherous smirk, he held the velvet gate open for them.

Despite the dim lights in the club, he could see the sweet freckles across her cheeks, her pink-lipped adoring smile. Damn, she embodied every damn fantasy in his sex-deprived imagination. Not giving a fuck that they were blocking the club entrance, he pulled her against him and dug his hands into her hair, claiming her in front of the throng of onlookers. Admittedly, he *may* have chosen the spot to stake his claim like a moody wolf.

She may not want forever, but tonight she was his. Teasing her sharp canine across his lower lip as she'd done so many times before, back then a statement of their difference, tonight... it was an invitation. And he had no doubt she knew he was hers. Always.

Once inside, she caught the bartender's eye and ordered a pair of drinks. Accepting the oddly shaped clear glass, Bennett took a testing sip and scanned the room. She absolutely knew what she was doing. The place was at least ten percent vampire.

She slipped her hand back into his and led him to the guarded stairwell to the VIP section. The guard nodded as he saw her, then looked to Bennett expectantly. Uh... like a secret handshake?

Adair turned to him and ran her tongue over the tip of a canine, flashing him a wink. He made the same gesture at the guard, hoping he didn't look as ridiculous as he felt. For a vegetarian, Adair knew the life.

He followed her up the staircase, suddenly feeling like prey. Out of place was a big fucking understatement. It had taken dozens to take him down as a hunter. Now? It would take a hell of a lot more... but he didn't care to test that theory without backup and a foolproof escape plan.

A few private nooks were occupied by small groups. Some chatting it up like close friends. A business deal closing. And... holy shit, an orgy in the darkest corner. Swallowing his tongue, he averted his eyes from the explicit view of... naked body parts entwined and grinding and...

Passing them all with little more than an amused glance, Adair led him straight to a pair of facing leather sofas. Unable to relax, every hair on the back of his neck standing on alert, he moved to the rail overlooking the club while she lowered to the sofa like she was a regular. He calmed his pulse before he gave himself away, he turned as a rear door opened and a vampire in a long silk dress glided regally into the private sitting area.

Adair rose to her feet and extended a hand. The vampire took her hand and leaned in, resting her palm on Adair's cheek and, rather than a friendly European peck on the cheek, pressed her lips to Adair's and lingered. Kissing her back, Adair finally pulled away and flashed red cheeks at Bennett.

The woman was something out of a painting, her burgundy gown ethereally flowing with each movement, her clavicle framed by tendrils of her honey-blond hair.

Adair cleared her throat and said to her friend, "Gi, this is Bennett. A dear friend of mine."

Her friend responded with a surprisingly honest, easy smile of a woman that didn't give in to pretense. "More than a friend from the jealous pulse, I would wager."

Jealousy. That was much better than the panicked-terrified-aroused that had kicked his heartbeat into erratic rhythm.

Adair laughed. "You know me too well, Gi. Bennett means a lot to me."

"Then he means a lot to me."

Adair pulled him to sit next to her. "Godgifu was a vocal *citoyen* and particular friend during the revolution, but she's been fighting authoritarianism since long before I was born and is the foremost historian in the paranormal world." Smiling at her friend, Adair said, "To me, she is Gi."

Eyebrows halfway to the ceiling, Bennett tried to calm his reaction. "It is an honor to meet you. Truly." He extended his hand and didn't hide his surprise at her firm handshake, the fire in her eye. He shouldn't be so surprised that Adair kept such high standing friends, but, he supposed, after all her years, she had done and seen it all. For all her fear of the sun, he knew she'd never been one to hide in the shadows.

"Please." She gestured for him to sit. "Adair is too kind. What she means is, I live in the past, while she flows forward with the times, always adapting as a modern woman."

Adair rolled her eyes with a shy grin.

Taking pity on her, Gi smiled. "It has been too long, Adair. I'm glad you came to see me and that you brought your young man, whatever he may be. But I sense this is not a social call. What brings you to my door?"

"I am hoping you can help us. Have you heard of Calloway, a partner of mine from my reckless days?"

Gi spat, "Monster is what he is. I won't judge others by their dietary preferences, of course, as those that choose peace are unique. But he has an excessive taste for destruction and glory. I had thought him dead for well over a century, until that hope was recently shattered."

Bile rose in Bennett's throat. "Have you heard anything about his latest scheme?"

"He fed from my territory about two months back. He spent no more than a fortnight, then he was gone." Gi rose to her feet and opened a cupboard, pulling out a rustic bottle of wine and poured three glasses of the deep red brew. Easing back into the couch, she crossed her legs and took a testing sip.

As Adair drank from her glass, Bennett did the same. The heady spice was unlike anything he'd ever tasted. Fermented blood, not human, but not like anything he'd experienced. Gi smiled at his reaction but didn't expound.

Finally, she spoke again. "I think I understand. Bennett. You are a hunter, but changed?"

He leaned forward in his seat and locked gazes with her. "What makes you think that?"

She took another sip and smiled. "I have been around the block a few times. You lack a scent and scan the room as if the enemy surrounds you, indicative of the hunter in a den of demons. Yet you move and seek like a vampire, and, of course, appreciate an excellent vintage." She held her glass at her side and let out a heavy sigh. "The rumor is that Calloway was set on creating one capable of unleashing the original vampire. Tromos."

Relaxed into the couch, one leg crossed over the other, Adair took a considering sip. "I thought Tromos was destroyed."

"Tromos?" Bennett asked.

Gi set her drink down and gazed out over the lights of the club before responding. "Terror. The founder of all vampires. The demon that was so vile, he was banished from the demon realm. A creative one, he found opportunity in his punishment. After feeding from human after human to satisfy his appetite, he grew bored and wiped out entire cities for fun. He was quickly discovered by demon hunters and was nearly defeated. Naturally, he was unwilling to accept his end and took measures to ensure he could live on forever. Where other hybrids are born of a more loving union between human and demon, Tromos found that prospect revolting. A relief for women everywhere, that for once we were not the tragic victims in this sort of scenario. Instead, he found that by replacing a human's blood with his own, he could create an immortal breed that could easily blend in with humans, and with appetites similar to his own."

"An army of vampires under his thrall."

Gi nodded knowingly. "In secret, in the safety of darkness, we thrive. But Tromos was never one to live in the shadows. Instead, he wished to imprison humans so he could live the high life and feed conveniently as if they were cattle, while his offspring catered to his whims. A few supported his plan, enticed by the power they held over humans and the endless supply of blood, but most knew that he would inevitably destroy us with his brash actions. But no vampire was strong enough to eliminate him, and by that time he had already wiped out nearly five demon hunting teams."

"That's where the prophecy came from."

"Precisely. They knew they were incapable of destroying him. A pack of vampires and a team of hunters worked together in an unprecedented truce to imprison him. He lies in an underground chamber, bound to this realm, in stasis until one capable of ending him would be able to reach and wake him."

"A changed demon hunter."

"So it would seem."

"Where is he?"

"His location has been erased from history. None alive can say."

Bennett shook his head, downing the last of his glass. "He's not in Paris, but I will find him."

Curiosity blooming on her expression, Gi raised a single eyebrow.

"I can't say how I know. Demon hunters have good instincts. But in this case? Fate hates me that much."

Adair nudged his side. "Then we run. If you don't awaken him, then he cannot rise to power."

"One other shitty thing about fate. Try to fool her? She bites you in the ass." He turned to Gi. "We have found a prophecy describing the chamber, but there is more. Something this big, chances are, it has been foretold more than once. Have you seen the version that Calloway is banking on?"

"No. After Calloway seemed to be on this path, I learned what I could, of Tromos and his intentions. From what I understand of the prophecy Calloway has found, is that you are the key to waking Tromos."

Adair asked, "Any hint as to the end?"

She shook her head and looked to Bennett. "Only that you will be the one to free Tromos. Not only that you alone have the ability to, but that you shall."

"Pure demon, huh? We've taken out a few." He rose to his feet and extended his hand to Adair. "Let's check in with my team. I'm not going in without them again."

She rose to her feet and her liquid cobalt eyes fell heavy. Hand on his chest, she shook her head. "Can you see why I'm not interested in forever?"

Grinding his molars together, he looked away and said to Gi, "Thank you. If you hear anything that may help, would you mind letting us know?"

A devious spark glimmered in her grass green eyes. "I'll do you one better. Hopefully beneficial for us both. There is an ancient one that lives in Seizième. Cambria. She has become restless and risks our peaceable existence. She and I have disagreed in our way of life for many years. Calloway would be foolish to not form an alliance with her, as I suspect she would be one of few wise and devious enough to obtain Tromos' location and presumably his reason for coming to Paris."

Catching her meaning, Bennett smiled. "I'll see to it. It was a pleasure meeting you."

She rose to her feet and kissed his cheek, lingering until her scent of spiced wine overwhelmed his senses. "Be safe. We are counting on you," she said before pulling away.

Taking Adair's hand, he nodded to Gi and headed down the stairs, past the pointy-toothed bouncer. As he turned toward the exit, Adair held him back. Against the thunderous boom of the techno base, Adair said, "We never got to finish that dance."

Looking to the door, past the murmuring crowd, he stopped to look back to her. "Now?"

"All work and no play? Makes a dull eternity."

Letting out a slow inhale, he let his gaze fall on her pouty lips. "This is how you handle it, isn't it?"

Eyelashes fluttering, she stepped closer and rested her palms on his chest. "I knew what you were, when we first met. It's worth the risk, stopping to smell the flowers now and again."

11

THE CORNER OF HIS mouth quirked up. He followed her into the rhythm of the crowd. Still in her element in the blood-sucker-owned club, Adair led the way into the pit. Blue lights, bright and dim, shifted metrically with the beat.

As she stepped into the thick of the dancers, Bennett stood back and watched as she flowed into the pumping cadence, her pulse adjusting to match, arms gracefully over her head, hips swaying in tune. The sleek fabric of her dress moved like water over her skin. Her head tipped back, and her golden-tipped mane brushed over her shoulder blades.

Sometimes it struck him, how contemporary she was. Her movements fluid as she absorbed into the radiance of the dance, he couldn't imagine how repressed she must have been in her time as a human. Living human experiences to the fullest, she flowed with the progression of time and culture.

Eyes blue as the rare moon, she beckoned him closer. Wrapping one arm around her waist, he didn't lead, but moved in the rhythm she'd set. Leaning down, he kissed the pulse of her neck and murmured, "You astonish me."

Sliding her hand under his shirt, her palm covered his skin, her fingers teased. The rumbling of the crowd, the thunder of the bass, the vibration of the floor all faded, and he could sense nothing but her. Moving with him, she embodied the seduction of the music.

Turning in his arms, she leaned into him. His palm splayed over her abdomen, he held her tight against him. "You and Gi seemed close," he said.

"Jealous?"

"Maybe."

She increased the pace. "An old flame, and now a dear friend."

"Can we trust her?" The beat pumped in tune with her pulse, and he found his slowing to match.

"She's one of the good ones. If I didn't trust her, I wouldn't have brought you here."

He gripped her waist and spun her to face him again.

Her mouth quirked up in a feisty grin, eyes sparking with intrigue. "Protecting me?"

"Even the fiercest hunter needs someone to watch his back."

In her spiked heels, her height matched his. He leaned in and took her mouth, wordlessly saying what she refused to hear.

As the song faded, he released her. "We have work to do," he murmured. Linking their hands, he led the way through the crowd and into the crisp cool of the night. Firing up the engine, he took off across the city.

Shimmering lights accented the history of the city, modern mixed with ancient, yet Adair predated most of it. Despite the late hour, the city hummed, and he wove through traffic, around the Arc de Triomphe, and hooked onto Avenue Kléber. After the glowing lights of the Place du Trocadéro, he followed Gi's directions past the Monuments aux Morts, beyond a cemetery encased in a small forest, and down narrow alleys between houses that had been there since before the village was incorporated.

Halting outside a humble townhouse, he glanced up at the simple facade. "Are you sure this is it?"

Adair reached across and eased down the window. "You're thinking like a demon hunter. Tell me what you smell."

"Dog shit."

"Smartass. What else?"

Closing his eyes, he inhaled deeply. "Fresh blood. Human."

"Good. Not easy to pick up, so deep within the house and surrounded by the normal scents of life. Now listen. How many?"

Scowling, he shut off the engine. Through the nearest window, he heard a trio by the upstairs window, chatting about who's turn it was to order dinner. Rustling in another room. "Some upstairs. A few more down. Maybe a basement."

"We're outnumbered."

"I'm always outnumbered. Come on, let's go." Bennett flashed her a wink before reaching for the door.

"Wait for your team. I've avoided Cambria for good reason. She's powerful, and she's ruthless."

"Perfect. I've been wanting to stretch these wings."

Grinding her teeth, Adair hissed, "This is exactly how Calloway got ahold of you. From the sound of things, this is how you lost Quinn, and I'm not talking about the break-up. You can't go barging in without a plan against one of the oldest vampires on the planet. We need better reconnaissance first."

Shifting into neutral and taking his foot off the brake, Bennett released a heavy exhale. "Yeah. You're right. But without my boorish recklessness, we would never have found Ryan, and Typha would have unleashed the demon realm on Earth. Feral werewolves would have torn me to shreds. Without it... you wouldn't be back in my life." He trailed off at the end, realizing he'd yet again said exactly the words to drive her away again.

Chewing her cheek, Adair shook her head. She opened her mouth to speak, but shut it again and stared out the window at the empty street. "You're not even armed. We weren't planning on this tonight. Let's come back tomorrow night after we've had time to prepare."

"It's only a matter of time before Calloway tracks me to Paris. Head back to the apartment and I'll take a train back when I'm done here."

"Fine," she mumbled. "I'll wait out here in case you need backup. Just be back by sunrise; I don't care to cook in the trunk of this thing until you decide you're done having fun."

Leaning across, he smacked a teasing kiss on her cheek and opened the door. "If I'm not out in time, head back and I'll meet you at the apartment."

Rolling his shoulders, Bennett hopped up the steps and rang the doorbell. Murmuring on the other side of the door, his hosts debated who might be visiting at this hour. *Didn't smell like a human or a vampire*, they argued, *but it's windy out.*

Finally, the door eased open and two big guys formed a wall between him and the house, their beefy arms folded over their barrel chests. "*Oui?*" the bigger one asked. Solid muscle, these guys were like Schwarzenegger and Stallone had gone vampire, but seemed much less friendly than the pair appeared in interviews.

"*Bonne nuit. Je cherche pour Cambria?*" He could practically hear Adair's disgusted sigh at his ill-conceived plan from where she waited, parked out of sight around the corner.

Knuckles grinding as the bigger of the two popped each in sequence, he stepped closer and clutched his fingers into Bennett's shirt and hauled him inside.

Feet dangling in the air as he was lifted off the ground, Bennett went with the flow and listened. Nope, at least twenty in the building. Including five humans who may or may not have bled out yet.

With a growl, the big guy tossed him across the foyer.

The dense parlor door shattered as his back crashed into it. Bennett grimaced at the impact. A sharp pain in his back, he reached around and pulled out a massive sliver, tossing it onto the billiard-green carpet. This asshole wasn't messing around.

Behind him, Bennett heard more knuckles cracking... the trio that had been chatting it up in the parlor before he busted in. Grin spread from ear to ear, he raised his eyebrows playfully at the Italian Stallion that had thrown him and popped up to his feet.

Slamming a backward fist into the vampire that thundered from behind him, he crunched her nose. Turning, he looped his arm around her neck and snapped. The vampire dropped at his feet and lay lifeless.

Damn, he should have brought his sword and shield. But this speed was pretty fantastic. He could feel their movements, and could respond with twice his former speed.

The next pair dove at him together. Jamming his elbow backward at one, Bennett knocked it out before it could get close enough to bite, then spun around and plowed a blunt fist into the other.

One of the doormen snarled and ran into the parlor, the other close on his heels.

In a full-out spring, Bennett leaped and parkoured off the first, encircling his arm around the other and spun to pull them both to the ground.

He sat atop the greeter, pinning him down. The other leapt back to his feet and ran at him. Bennett caught him by the throat and squeezed until the vampire weakened, then dropped him.

He glared down at the big guy underneath him. "I said, I'm looking for Cambria."

"Fuck you," the moron growled.

Rolling his eyes, Bennett finished him off.

Bennett popped to his feet and dusted off his jeans, scowling down at yet another ruined shirt.

On the move, he crossed the black and white checked entry. Not a peep from the darkened hall, so he aimed for the billiard-green carpet that blanketed the path up the worn steps. Above, he could hear rustling from a group of vampires coming to see what the commotion was. He halted, waiting.

Six pairs of boots came tearing down the stairs. One was wiping human blood from her chin, another pulling his shirt on. Clearly, he was interrupting something.

Bennett barreled up the stairs. As he snapped the neck of the last of them, he achingly felt the lack of sword and shield. Speed and strength were one thing, but it was like a part of him was... missing. And this would be a lot less messy with his gear. And efficient.

At the landing, he turned into the first room and found the humans. Abandoned in the urgency, they sat stunned, three bleeding from the neck, the other two on the far side of the room seeming to realize this wasn't the party they thought it would be. "*Allez-vous,*" he urged them to hurry out.

Room by room, he cleared the upper floors. Fuck. Where was this ancient?

Feet silent on the steps, he moved on, taking out two more vampires that dined on a midnight snack of ice cream and cookies in the kitchen.

But no ancient. He checked his watch. Nearly two. If he wasn't out of there by sunrise, Adair was going to flip. He already didn't stand a chance at convincing her to give them a try, and losing her trust sure as hell wasn't going to help.

Basement. Opening the narrow door, he stepped into the pitch dark, keeping his footfalls silent despite the wood threatening to creak under his weight. Like the start of a damn horror movie, he moved into the darkness, chuckling under his breath as he realized he was a legendary villain now. Predator, not prey. Hopefully.

His eyes swiftly adjusted to the darkness, only to be blinded as an overhead bulb flashed on. Releasing the light switch, a petite woman in snug jeans and a chunky sweater smirked at him, her blood red lips twisted in a delighted smile as she clapped her hands in a taunting rhythm. "Well done, hunter. Calloway implied you would be tough to take down... but he's often wrong."

Ten massive arms from fucking nowhere encompassed him and tightened around his throat. Apparently, friends of the doormen upstairs.

Kicking back, he caught one in the balls. Biting down, he sliced the arm of another. Nothing he couldn't handle.

As he snapped his head back to smack another in the face, they heaved him thirty fricking feet across the basement. Skidding across the cobbled floor, his head cracked against the concrete wall and stars flickered in his vision. As he flipped back to his feet, the mob flooded into the... cell. Dammit. This wasn't a cellar but a fricking dungeon. Chains and all.

As his captors surrounded him, packing into the cell, leaving little more than standing room only, he lashed out with every move he had, fast as fuck, but they were ready for him.

Too late, too damn fast, a cluster got behind him and clipped cool steel around one of his wrists.

Spinning, he grabbed the nearest throat with his free hand. Letting her neck crunch in his grip, he dropped her and kicked out for the next.

In the fray, his other hand was swiftly cuffed into another steel binding.

Erupting with a feral roar, he tried to fire back, but his wrists were bound fast.

The remaining vampires grabbed their dead and dragged them from the cell.

The petite woman raised an eyebrow and slammed the prison door shut. "I hope he's not wrong about what you can do for us."

"Cambria?"

"Lovely to meet you. Not to worry, I'll have food sent down shortly. You'll need to keep your strength up if you're to unleash Tromos for us."

"Where is he?"

"I'll let you know when the time is right. Nighty-night." She waved and strolled out of sight, laughing it up with her crew.

Tugging at his chains, he strained to break free.

WHERE THE HELL WAS he? Typical. Adair checked the time. Three-thirty. Great. He was cutting it closer than she was comfortable with.

Stepping out of the car, she eyed the front door, but thought better of it. There had clearly been quite the scuffle, a few actually, but the humans that had stumbled out the door had made her think Bennett had the situation under control.

Stalking to the side of the house, she found a cellar entrance. Pulling the keys from her purse, she opened a small tool and picked the lock, then swung open the door.

Passing a wine cellar and pantry, she caught the scent for fresh blood down the hall. All vampire.

Metal grinding against metal, feet shuffling on the cobbled floor... Cringing, she knew before she saw him.

Alone in a cell, Bennett strained at his bindings. When he caught sight of her, he smiled sheepishly. "I'm on it. Just a minor setback."

"Your shirt is ripped up again," she tsked.

"I miss my shield."

Scouring the room, she searched for a key. There was a lone credenza next to the stairs. Opening the top drawer, she found what she was looking for.

Stalking closer, keeping the click of her heels silent, she eased the key into the lock of his cell. Twisting, the lock wouldn't budge.

Turning, she aimed to check the credenza for another key. As she looked up, a cluster of massive vampires flooded the basement. The first lifted her by the neck. The cell door hinges squeaked open behind her and she flew backward through the air.

Instead of the painful crash onto the hard floor she'd expected, strong arms caught her. Still chained, Bennett's reach was limited, and they fell to the floor, but he shifted so she landed on him rather than the stone.

The door slammed shut, and their jailors enjoyed a few jokes at their expense as they left to grab some dinner before sunrise.

Easing off Bennett, Adair rose to her feet and straightened her dress. Fury boiling in her throat, still sore from that asshole's grip, she opened her mouth to tear into Bennett for getting them into this mess.

Instead, he sat on the floor, rubbing his hands over his face. "Sorry," he murmured. "My fault." The corner of his mouth raised with a satirical snort. "It's easier, being faster and being able to sense the enemy more acutely, but these guys were... they were ready for me."

"There's a reason an ancient one is ancient." Searching, she realized her new purse had flown from her grip and rested against the far wall, keys and all. Dropping to the ground next to him, Adair wrapped her arms around her knees. "You manage to get into trouble often. How do you intend to get out of it this time?"

He raised his chained wrist and put a finger over his lips to silence her, shaking his head.

She heard it too.

Cambria strolled down the stairs, carrying a tray of pastries, fruits, cheeses, and two huge mugs of steaming hot goat blood. With an easy smile like she was his best friend, she said, "My apologies at the simple fare, but my chef is bleeding out on the kitchen floor. It's being cleaned up, but terribly inconvenient. I will have to order takeout instead. I haven't indulged on a delivery boy in years. Perhaps I'll try jalapenos on my pizza. I hear it adds an intriguing flavor."

Cambria set the tray on the ground, staying outside of reach. She flashed a wink at Adair and said, "Our hero here needs to keep up his strength."

Adair glared back at Bennett as Cambria disappeared upstairs. "What were you saying about setting off traps? Is this what you had in mind?"

Unable to reach the tray thanks to his chains, he nodded. "Mind passing me blood and some brie? And those raspberries look amazing. How do you think they found them so fresh this time of year?"

She reached through the bars and slid the tray closer to load up a plate for him. Cambria had a point. She handed him the meal before dishing up her own.

He settled, leaned against the concrete wall and took a testing sip. "Not bad. Like vegan sausage." He grinned at her.

Adair sat next to him, trying a strawberry. "I haven't had a garden in years; I may have to look into buying a home again."

"I've never seen where you live."

"I have an apartment in Seattle, but I haven't spent much time there the last few years. Lately, I've been staying at Logan's house in the mountains."

"But no garden."

"No time. I was working."

"Working?"

"Yes. I like to work."

"As in, a human job?" His eyes softened as he studied her, clearly realizing he didn't know her as well as he'd thought.

She nodded. "I was working as a radiology tech. A favorite sort of job, as there's no risk for sun exposure, and the people I got to meet were so full of stories. Anyway, that's how Logan met his wife; she worked with me and we became friends."

"Why don't you have a house of your own?"

"I don't know. I like the pace of living downtown, but it might be time to settle more remotely again."

"My parents signed over their place on Vancouver Island to me a few months ago. I'd planned to be there the night I was changed. It's gorgeous and... relaxing. Like the rest of the world doesn't exist. But I was too irritable for serenity."

"You seem awfully perky now. Despite the... circumstances." She snagged a raspberry from his plate and popped it in her mouth, the succulence contrasting the bitter drink. "Those are good."

"Self-medicating with violence is, unfortunately, a popular outlet among demon hunters. Something in the DNA I suppose." He finished the blood, then sampled a piece of cheese. "So, Logan's cured and married now, huh?"

She nodded. "I'm so happy for him."

Bennett traced the back of his hand down her bare arm. "You must feel so alone."

Biting her lips together, she nodded. Her heart had shattered the day he'd been cured, but he'd been so miserable, had been seeking a way out for so long, that any grief for her anticipated loss of him was out shadowed by her complete happiness for him.

"I know why you won't let me in."

She nodded again, not wanting to let him know how much she ached to hold on to him as long as she could. After clearing her throat, she blinked away the threatening moisture behind her eyes. "So. Plan?"

Bennett finished the last of his meal and stood. "Sun's rising. Do you mind riding home in the trunk? I should have had the windows tinted before risking staying out so late."

"I'd rather ride in the trunk than wait in here."

After examining the steel chains that were fastened into plates and bolted into the concrete wall, he smiled. "Back up."

Adair moved to the far corner of the cell.

He gripped the base of the first chain and wound it around his fist, then braced his foot against the wall. Every muscle in his body strained at the effort.

The concrete gave way and the steel plate wrenched out of the wall, debris flying from the force of it. He did the same with the other chain.

A frown drawing his brow, he wrapped the loose chain around his wrists to avoid dragging the steel plates on the floor. At the steel gate, he inspected the lock.

He stepped back and slammed his foot into the lock with a blunt kick.

With a resonating clamor, the gate swung open, the steel bar that had locked it snapped in half.

Cringing, Adair strained to hear upstairs. "They'll have heard that."

He shook his head. "I hope so, but these walls are pretty thick."

Adair ran for the credenza and grabbed her purse from under it. The creak of wooden steps rattled in her ears. "They're coming."

Bennett nodded. "Not to be bossy, but would you mind backing out of the way again?"

She shook her head, watching as he swung his chains like lassos.

The moment one of Cambria's crew appeared in the doorway, Bennett released a chain and it cracked into the first of them. With his new weapons, he slammed the steel of one into the next vampire while wrapping the other chain around the next.

The next pair ran straight for her. Adair spun out of their grip and lowered to kick the legs out from the nearest. Dodging another, she readied to pounce. As another ran for her, she sprang up and wrapped her leg around his neck, spinning them to the ground and twisting until he collapsed. The last of them dove for her again, but Bennett's chain launched and struck it in the back of the skull.

He flashed her a devious wink as he stood over the pile of bodies at his feet. "Come on."

She nodded toward the cellar door she'd come in through.

Bennett said, "I'm getting what I came for."

Glancing to the exit and back at him, she ground her teeth and let the acid of too many raspberries burn the back of her throat. "You're crazy."

Footsteps silent, they eased up the stairs, and found the main floor dead quiet. She followed him up the next flight of stairs, seeing the destruction from his last trip through.

Without a word, she nodded to the far door at the end of the upstairs hall. He sniffed the air and nodded in agreement. On seeing the padlock over the door, she reached into her purse and pulled out her tool.

Only a faint squeak of metal against metal, she clicked open the lock with a few easy twists. Bennett smiled knowingly.

She followed him into Cambria's bedroom. Soundly asleep in an ornate canopy bed as old as she was, the ancient one didn't seem to notice their approach. At the round table near the fireplace, a collection of books waited, a more recent map folded as a bookmark in the book on top. Bennett silently stacked them.

The ancient one had left her clothes in a pile on the floor next to the bed. Adair slipped her hand into the pocket of her pants and found the key to Bennett's chains. Adair grinned as she held it up in satisfaction, eliciting an adorable double-dimple smile from Bennett.

Without a sound, she snuck toward the door, but heard movement from the bed.

Cambria's voice broke the silence. "Take the key, but leave my books please." She bolted up out of bed and was across the room so fast, they didn't have time to react.

With rapid fire fists, elbows, swift kicks, the ancient lashed out and knocked Bennett back against the far wall.

Ducking, not quite matched in speed, Adair spun with a helicopter kick and knocked Cambria's feet out from under her. Cambria popped back up and growled, aiming straight for Adair.

Bennett leapt to his feet and threw a steel plate at her.

Too fast, Cambria dropped to the ground, dodging the blow.

Anticipating the miss, Bennett already had the other chain flying. Cambria caught it and dragged him closer, expecting to use her momentum to knock him back again.

Bennett ripped the chain from her hand and yanked her close like she'd tried to reel him in; her speed was no match for his strength.

Releasing the chain, she fell forward.

Catching her with an uppercut worthy of a champion boxer, Bennett slammed into her abdomen. Cambria flew straight up into the air. As she fell, Bennett spun and kicked her like a soccer ball straight into the fireplace.

Flames engulfing her, she screamed and rolled on the ground to snuff out the flames.

Adair scanned the room and ran for the far wall. She ripped a framed print off the wall. The glass shattered as it hit the floor. Picking up the largest piece, she ran for Cambria as she rose to her feet. Bennett positioned himself behind and shoved Cambria toward Adair.

Driving the glass into her neck, Adair winced as she gouged the sharp edge into Cambria's throat. The crunch as she punctured the trachea pierced her ears like fingernails on a chalkboard. Adair pushed further until the job was finished. "So gross," she muttered, squinting and wishing she could look away from the gruesome scene.

"Let's get the hell out of here." Bennett let out a breath he'd clearly been holding in, not so confident in their escape as he'd let on.

"Wait." Adair reached into her purse and pulled out the key she'd stashed, releasing his wrists with a flick of metal against metal. She dumped the chains and key on the floor.

He rubbed his wrists and looked down at the pile of chains. "Actually, we could keep those..."

She rolled her eyes and shook her head.

Grin spread ear to ear, Bennett grabbed the pile of books, checked the map was intact, and they tore down the stairs. Cambria's goons must be sound asleep in fricking coffins or something to have not heard the commotion... or they disliked her enough to leave her to her fate. Either way, Adair didn't question it; they were due for a lucky break.

At the door, Bennett pulled back the curtain and checked the bright street. He held out his hand for the car keys. "I'll pull up close and open the trunk. You run like hell."

She nodded and handed them over. "It's been a few years since I've gotten a tan. Although, knowing me, I'll burn and freckle instead."

Easing open the door, he slipped outside and took off.

On the count of twenty, she peeked out the window and saw him pulling the car out front. Heart thundering in her chest, she swung open the door and ran full-out. Ten seconds. That's all it was. Heat penetrated her skin, brilliantly warm and comforting for a fraction of a second, then turned to a prickly burning sensation.

She leaped into the trunk, and Bennett slammed it shut just as fast.

The drive home was... unpleasant. He took extra turns in case they were followed, last-minute jukes onto narrow alleys to ensure no one could follow.

At last, he parked. Voice muffled, he spoke to her through the trunk. "We're parked in the garage, then the walk to the entrance is mostly covered. About ten feet of direct sunlight between you and the apartment."

With a click of the lock, he released the trunk. Brow scrunched in a scowl, she dragged herself out. "You need to invest in a bigger car. Felt like a damn coffin."

"I thought vampires liked coffins," he teased, pure smartass in his grin.

Slamming the trunk shut behind her, she shook her head. "As foolish of a myth as vampires bursting into flames in the sun or turning to dust when they run into pointy wooden objects."

She slipped her hand into his for the last run to safety, giving in to the moment. His pulse kicked up at the contact and a rush of second wind flooded her veins.

12

BENNETT COULDN'T SEEM TO find the right words as they entered the apartment. Without a doubt, the moment he opened his mouth, he'd say something foolish and drive her away again. He dropped the stolen books onto the entry table and turned to see Adair leaned against the apartment door, exhaling a sigh of relief. The bright highlights to her hair had lightened in those few moments of sun, her cheeks dappled with a few more freckles than before.

She glared at his adoring examination, then smoothed her hair and tugged her dress back into place. "What?" On one foot, she unzipped her boots one at a time.

Biting his cheek, he tried to control his wicked grin that formed, as control of his brain flooded south.

Hand teasing in her hair, she exuded that walking fantasy that tormented him for so long. "Don't tell me you're expecting to get laid after getting us into that mess?" That adorable notch formed between her eyebrows, but the amused twitch of her lips betrayed the scowl.

"You are so beautiful," he blurted out as he stepped closer. He traced his fingertips along her sides. "You've haunted my dreams for so long."

"And you're going to haunt mine for the next eternity. Don't you see why I can't keep you? You are crazy. Immortality doesn't mean a damn thing if you get yourself killed." She slammed her hands on her hips and huffed.

"We don't even know that I am immortal. I'm a messed-up anomaly that shouldn't exist." He trailed his thumb over her chin, cradling her jaw.

"When this is done, I'm out. I can't spend the rest of my life worrying about whether you're coming home."

"Then come with me. Always."

"Don't ask it." She rested her hand over his heart and her lashes fluttered as her gaze swept to his lips.

"Today, tomorrow, however long you'll have me," he whispered, a hoarse desperation in his voice. "What were you saying about all work and no play?"

Gripping her hand around the back of his neck, she tugged him close and kissed him, flying right past any testing or sweetness, she seemed to be riding on the same wave of adrenaline from the night that he was. He clutched his hand in her hair, keeping pace, and parried thrust for thrust. His knees weak at the onslaught, he strained to keep up with her.

Sliding his hands down her sides, he lifted the edge of her dress up and wrapped his fingers around her thighs. Breath warm and lips pliant against his, she sighed into his mouth. Body pressed against his, she nipped his lower lip.

Her skin like satin under his fingertips, he shifted and slid the lace of her panties out of his way. One hand holding her up against him, the other slid along her slick heat. Pulse accelerating at his touch, she murmured a soft plea, pressing her cheek against his. Teasing his fingers against her core, he rubbed and massaged until she cried out with a hungry release.

As her pulse crested, he dropped to his knees and ripped her panties out of the way. Shifting her dress above her hips, he pressed his mouth to her core.

She gasped and leaned into him, her hands braced on his shoulders.

Absorbed in her, needing to send her higher, he licked along her honeyed silk, half-mad with desire.

"Bennett," she panted as he increased the pace.

Driving his fingers into her, he cupped and massaged until her breath came fast and thready and desperate. Vibrating his tongue against her until she could no longer sense anything but him, he upped the pace until she clenched tight around him. Heady, new and familiar and achingly his, he needed to taste her, touch her, claim her.

Feeling her orgasm as acutely as if it were his own, his heart beating to match hers, he clutched his other hand on her hip to hold her steady and sucked until she screamed out his name.

Unsteady, but sailing on air, he rose to his feet and he slipped her dress over her head. He craved her, beyond any thirst, beyond any thrill of the fight. Scooping her into his arms, he laid her on the dining table. She fastened her legs around his waist and pinned him to her. Plunging into her, painful, thrilling after how long he'd dreamed of her, his vision blackened darker than the night sky on impact.

She gripped him tight against her, her soprano moans drove him faster, harder in a rhythm he'd never thought possible. Breath coming fast, she held him tight inside her, her pulse soaring with his as they rode the wave together.

Grounding him, she whispered his name, easing him down from a dizzying climax. Vision clearing, he looked down to see the corner of her mouth quirk up at his delirium. Withdrawing, he offered a hand and pulled her up.

Fucking hot, naked and flushed as she leaned against the table edge, she ran her hand over his pecs and down his abdomen, full-on grin brightening her expression. "Sturdy table; I can't believe it held up. Looks pretty new. You should post a review."

Surprised laughter bubbled up in his chest and echoed across the room. "Don't move, I'll attach a picture. Their sales will soar." Imprinting the image indefinitely to his brain, he grinned. "You'd think an immortal could get stuck in the past, but you stay up with the latest. Centuries older than my parents, and they just mastered the art of texting."

"It's much more interesting to go with the flow." Fingers teasing at his waist, she smiled and asked, "As I recall, demon hunter stamina is incomparable."

Already rock hard as he mentally relived what they'd done, the taunting glimmer in her eyes, he scooped her up and she wrapped her legs around him. "Even better with vampire senses and speed."

CASTING A WARMING GLOW on the ceiling above the curtain, the sunlight hinted at midday. Bennett's eyes eased open, no gritty sleepiness blocking his view as he'd woken to every morning for the last few years. Utterly at peace, or so it appeared, Adair snuggled into him, her lips turned up in a subtle smile, her hair splayed out in carefree disarray over the pillow.

Burning brewed at the back of his throat, the thirst warning him he needed to feed soon. Overwhelmed with the need for her above anything else, again, he pressed his lips to hers, entreating her to wake. Her mouth curled into a richer smile, her eyes fluttering open as she eased atop him and sat up to welcome the day in the best possible way. With minimal preamble, she slid over him and began an aching, familiar rhythm. He couldn't imagine how she could even consider not continuing *this* for as long as their lives would allow.

In the shadowy afternoon haze, he traced his fingertips over the silk of her thighs, watching her take her lower lip between her teeth as her breath quickened and her hips rocked over his. Every sensation of their connection exquisitely vivid, completely filling him, she was everything. Taking her hips in his grip, he shifted her faster, harder against him until she cried out and crested the wave with him.

Melting over him, she released him only long enough to lie chest-to-chest, driving him wild again with delicate, tasting kisses.

Until his morning was ruined.

He knew before seeing.

Heard their voices the moment they stepped inside, laughing about their spontaneous, but long-overdue vacation.

In the seconds between their arrival and the interruption, he was too stunned to react. Adair sensed them as he did, stiffening and closing her eyes. As their voices drew closer, he stilled, too frozen to move.

Smiling and laughing together, his parents barged into the bedroom. Lizzy's eyes widened, the chocolate-brown crystallizing in shock. Jonathan's jaw tightened in frank disappointment and Bennett was pretty sure that steam puffed out his ears.

Shifting off him in slow motion, Adair held the sheet over herself and exhaled stiffly at his side, resigned.

Sitting up, watching the blankets so they could maintain a flimsy shred of decency, he ran a hand over his face and gritted his teeth. "Mom. Dad. I wasn't aware that you were traveling."

Lizzy tightened her grip on her suitcase. "It was a last-minute decision. We hadn't realized that you were... in Paris. With..."

"Last minute decision," he sniped back, already knowing exactly where this conversation was heading. Hunger pressed against his skull like a caffeine headache on steroids. Motioning to the door with a nod, he asked, "Can we speak in the living room after I've had a chance to... freshen up a bit?"

With a curt nod, his blushing father escorted his stunned mother out. A seasoned demon hunter, Lizzy would have recognized the nature of his bed partner. If she were paying enough attention, she might realize Bennett's movements were similar, but she would see him as she wanted to.

Adair shifted her hands in her hair. "I think I'll pass on the family squabble."

For which he could already hear them planning their opening arguments. Responsibility. Setting an example. Decency. Not playing with fire.

"Wish I could do the same." He flipped off the sheets and lowered his feet to the velvety carpet.

Letting his parents argue it out with each other before braving the assault, he stepped into the shower and pressed his palms to the wall, letting the steam flow over his body. Maybe he could jump out the window and kick some ass before facing them, and burn off his own opening arguments that comprised of nothing polite. In lieu of what he'd rather be doing, he tried to remind himself that they were good parents. They wanted the best for him. And catching their responsible son in bed with a vampire was insupportable.

Fuck, he needed to feed. Closing his eyes, he tried to shake the craving. Not a good time.

Shutting off the water, he dried and tugged on jeans and a t-shirt, skipping shoes and socks, ready to get it over with. When he came out of the bathroom, Adair was sitting on the side of the bed, sporting that determined crease between her eyebrows that he knew only too well. "Don't even say it." He shook his head.

"But we're back to exactly where we began. Fool me once..."

"We're so far and gone from where we began. Maybe only a blink in your lifetime, but a hell of a lot's happened in my life since then. I'm only still alive because fate hates me." He huffed, his jaw ticking, fists clenched in his pockets. "*Alive*. Undead or more demon or something so much further from the naïve hunter that fell in love with you. Look, if you want a fuck-buddy while we solve this mess, fine. If you want to help bring down Calloway so you can get back to your routine, great. But don't pretend I'm some human plaything, ready to roll over and take what he can get. Shower's all yours." Not leaving room for her to react, he stormed out to face the music.

Ignoring his restless parents sitting painfully politely on the sofa, he turned into the kitchen and poured his coffee, forgoing his new favorite coppery creamer. "Coffee?" he offered.

"I've prepared some tea already, thank you." His mother raised the delicate cup, quite the lady she was raised to be in early twentieth-century England.

Seated on one of the plush white facing sofas with a cloud blue linen ottoman in between, his mother poured a warmup in her tea and set the silver pot back on a hand-carved wooden tray he knew she had bought from a local street vendor a decade back. A massive impressionist piece hung over the retired fireplace, candles nestled in the bricked recess in its place.

They had opened all the curtains, as was their habit, so he quickly closed them in case Adair graced them with her presence. His father scowled, but didn't question him. "Would you care to explain yourself?"

Bennett sat in the center of the facing couch. "Not particularly."

Resting her teacup on her knee, Lizzy attempted her calm posture. "Is she... is this the same vampire Quentin found you with?"

"Yes."

"Bennett, dear. Vampires cannot be trusted. I know you believe her when she claims she hasn't tasted human blood in centuries, and perhaps it is true, but she is still one of them and vampires are notoriously manipulative."

"If you say so." He leaned back and sipped the bitter brew, his throat tightening as his gut realized he wasn't going to get a taste of his new favorite additive. Fuck, when had he fed last? His head pounded as the craving intensified, fueling his temper off the charts. Clenching his jaw, he kept his mouth shut before he said something he'd regret later.

Jonathan popped up from the sofa and paced the room, rubbing a hand over his mouth before speaking. "I know we've had this talk before. I'd rather have it without your mother present, but we have no other option at this junction. Your mother knows vampires, as I would expect you would by now as well. But I know foolish young men, as I was one before I met your mother." He rested his hands on the back of the couch and his brow dropped, his head a hint away from shaking as if Bennett were still the teenage driver that had flown past the stop sign. "Barely out of the house, and you *hooked up*..." He sneered as if the phrase was as callous as it sounded. "With a vampire taking advantage of you to clear her territory for her. Then what, from what I hear, you *hooked up* with Lana's sister, who had chosen a human life rather than the life of a hunter? I still can't believe you'd consider bringing this life on her. This life isn't what I was born into, but I can tell you, the life of a demon hunter's spouse isn't an easy one."

Not the time to mention that neither Missy nor he had ever had any intention of getting married. That they fell more into the friends-with-benefits category, at least, whenever the team congregated at Lana's. Bennett held his expression, sipping now and again while his father continued one of his notorious lectures.

Maybe by the time the next century rolled over, they'd accept that he wasn't the gentlemen they intended. Or, better yet, if they'd get around to having another child to take some of the damn pressure off. Especially as it was solidly out of the realm of possibility for him to pass along the Ward name now.

As the story went, Jonathan had been delivering a verbose lesson as a geology professor when his mother fell head over heels for him. And he continued. Bennett settled in for the long haul. "And then, that reporter? The police officer? The Australian actress? Who knows how many others we didn't hear about? Finally, when you settled with Quinn, we thought you had figured it out and would end this reckless behavior–"

His mother interrupted, "But that, that…" she waved her hand as she pooh-poohed, "That Ryan stole her from you while you were at death's door. Really, losing her to the son of a different demon-sire? And don't get me started on the werewolf joining your team. I love you and you have wonderful, supportive friends that mean well, but you've all bucked tradition so callously."

Jonathan nodded. "And we're back to the beginning. You're right back where you started with the vampire. Does she need you for your abilities again?"

The corner of his mouth quirked up as he considered how to let them know what a true disappointment he was. "She does appreciate my skills, but that's not why we're fucking again."

Beet red blush heating her cheeks, his mother huffed, "Bennett. I've never heard you speak so... so..."

"Sorry. I guess I've been spending too much time with werewolves and demon-spawn and vampires."

Not a sound on the air, Adair sauntered from the bedroom in her bare feet. He could smell her orchid-laced spice, could feel her accelerated pulse contrasting the calm she exuded. Ignoring the glowers from his furious parents, she poured her coffee and theatrically added a splash of blood. No longer in Quinn's hand-me-downs, she wore dark blue jeans with a cashmere top that brought out the natural blush of her skin, thanks to her time in the sun yesterday.

Feigning comfort, she eased on the couch next to him and placed a lingering kiss to the pulse point of his neck, smiled, then settled tight against him. He knew she wouldn't be able to resist the rebellion. Like the sexy outfits and clubs, the slick cars she drove, she used her innocent appearance to her advantage when it suited, but lived up the edge when she could. She smiled with pure vampire-innocent-sweet he knew had worked on so many of her victims in the past. "What were you saying about vampires? Was it that we can't be trusted, or that I'm taking advantage of Bennett's... *attributes*? Or was I teaching him naughty language?"

Before they could fling the attack at Adair, Bennett set down his coffee and rested his elbows on his knees, leaned forward to get down to business. "I'm in town working on something big that I need Adair's help with. We will be happy to find a hotel so you can have the apartment to yourselves."

His mother's brown eyes melted as she seemed to recall that he was the warrior she had trained him to be. Or at least that he was her son and a decent guy. "I'm sorry, you know I would never wish to interrupt your work. Is the team nearby?"

"Not yet. We're still in the recon stage. Although Quinn's home with Skye."

Hand over her chest, Lizzy smiled, a bubble in her throat as she said, "Oh, I haven't gotten to see her yet. Is she as precious as Quentin and Fiona have been glowing about?"

Taking pity on his parents, knowing his foul mood was driven by the craving, topped with his dread of explaining why he was in Paris, he laid off the attitude. "Adorable. A perfect little mix of her parents."

Jonathan blew out a long breath he'd been withholding and eased around the couch to sit again. "I'm sorry. That must have ripped your heart out, Quinn falling for someone else and settling so happily."

Whatever they thought of Adair, of the evil vampire that had taken advantage of his innocence—yeah, he'd been a late bloomer, but he'd been twenty-fricking-years old when he'd met Adair—they'd be fools to deny that she was everything they would want in a daughter-in-law. Well-mannered when she wanted to be, but tough as nails and un-afraid to speak her mind. Sipping her coffee, ankles crossed gingerly, she held a companionable posture at his side. Vampire thing or Adair thing; didn't matter, she was a force, of peace or war, whichever she was in the mood for.

"Somewhat, but not in the way I would have thought. I know you think ill of Ryan because you're angry at how things turned out, and, admittedly, I wasn't exactly welcoming at first, but he's the best. Glad to have him on my team and he's a good friend, better than I deserve. And the werewolf; he's probably the most balanced of all of us. Certainly has his shit together better than I do. I make a lot of mistakes, regularly, in fact, but I know what I'm about. I would actually appreciate your input on a few things."

Lizzy smiled and linked hands with his father. "We really didn't mean to barge in on you. We were planning to indulge in an impromptu holiday. Perhaps we could talk more over lunch before we leave you to focus on your work?" She glanced to Adair and seemed to remember her manners. "Or let's wait until dark and we can all head out to dinner instead? I believe we haven't been properly introduced."

Bennett slipped his hand into Adair's. "This is Adair. She's originally from the highlands, a Fenton by birth. She and her brother were invaluable in helping Quinn, Lana, and I to clear some nasties out of Seattle."

Adair smiled shyly and extended her hand across the ottoman and shook both their hands.

His mother softened her expression. "Jonathan and Elizabeth Ward. Jonathan actually hails from Inverness."

"One of my favorite places in all the world. My brother and his wife are not fifty miles from there now."

Settling back into the couch, his mother asked, "Bennett, what is it I can help with? I miss the days when we used to talk shop, but you've been independent, studying and training with your team, so we haven't chatted as hunters in too long."

A knot wrenched in his gut as he realized he shouldn't put it off any longer. "How much research have you done into some of the old prophecies?"

"Every few decades, I feel like I'm scouring the ancient texts for answers on a prophecy coming to light. The banshee war of 1996 was foretold ages ago. And I suppose that is how little Skye came to be."

"How about anything related to demon hunters, specifically on changing them?"

"Demon hunters can't be changed. We heal too quickly."

"Yeah, but what if a vampire knows what they're doing? One who has changed hundreds? That would have the intelligence and numbers to make it happen?"

At his side, Adair, rested her hand on his knee, silently letting him know she was here with him.

"I guess I don't know enough about how the change works. Your uncle is one of the foremost experts on vampires; we could call him."

"Uncle Edwin? He has an excessive hatred toward vampires. I'd rather keep him out of this."

Glancing to Adair and back, his mother nodded. "I suppose you're right. He lost a teammate to vampires a number of years ago and has had a bit of a chip on his shoulder."

Jonathan rubbed his hand over his mouth and leaned forward. "Bennett? What are you getting at?"

Now or never. Rip off the damn Band-Aid. Let them see how messed up their son truly was. As the dread of admitting his recklessness ripped through him, he could feel the sweat beading on his brow, the scent of the human coming up the stairs and strolling into the neighboring apartment. Fuck, he should have fed hours ago.

Pulling his lips back, he traced his tongue over a vampire canine, pricking a drop of blood, healing over just as fast.

Gasping, pulse pounding in fear and fury and regret, his mother jumped from her seat and backed away, eyes scanning both Adair and him in suspicion. His father's jaw dropped open, his complexion paled.

Chest heaving, her teeth grinding as his mother showed her true colors as the hunter she was, she shifted her sights on Adair and balled her fists, ready to attack.

"I…" his father looked from Adair to Bennett then back again. "I don't understand."

Raising his eyebrows with a careless shrug, Bennett rose from the couch and moved into the kitchen. He filled his mug with the rest of the pint from the refrigerator. Standing in the middle of the kitchen, he guzzled, his Adam's apple bobbing up and down as he soothed the craving he should have addressed before taking Adair again this morning. Afternoon. His sense of time was a disaster these days.

"I don't either," he said as he caught his breath, then rinsed the mug before setting it in the sink. Strolling back around the edge of the kitchen, he leaned against the edge of the island and folded his arms over his chest. "I was in a mood. Too wound up to wait for help, so I stormed into a warehouse with eight vampires feeding not far from my place in Seattle. Nothing I couldn't handle."

His mother shook her head. "Eight vampires? No one should attempt that alone."

"I know. But since the boost from our demon ancestor last year to defeat Typha, all the damn training while I tried *not* to think about the shitshow my life had become, I took care of them without a problem. But it was a trap. Dozens more flooded in. Drained me. Fed me. Changed me." His gaze fell on Adair, unsure how to react to the watery regret in her eyes, her lower lip turned down as she watched him describe it. "I would have killed someone if Adair hadn't found me. And I most certainly would have died." Under his breath, he added, "Maybe should have."

Adair cleared her throat, her voice thick as she said, "I saw what was left of the building. I can't imagine another hunter surviving what he endured. And he resisted when he should have been completely uncontrolled and enthralled."

Lizzy loosened her fists and braced her hands on the back of the sofa. "This can't be. You are our son. A promising demon hunter. You have at least two centuries of fight ahead of you."

Resting his hand on Lizzy's, Jonathan kept his voice low. "I'm so sorry, Bennett."

Bennett gave a somber nod. "This isn't what I had in mind." Crossing one foot over the other, he said, "I'm a freak mix of vampire, hunter, and human."

Adair set down her empty mug and rested her hands on her knees. "Most vampires are content to keep to the shadows, either feeding discreetly or, like me, choosing to feed only from animals and to live quietly alongside humans. But there are those that crave power nearly as much as they do blood. Bennett was changed by a group I used to run with, Calloway and his idiots that accept his hairbrained ideas. They found a prophecy that tells of a changed demon hunter. From our research, and I can only imagine this correlates with their plan, a changed demon hunter is the only one that has the power to free Tromos."

Jonathan raised an eyebrow. "Tromos?"

Nodding, Bennett said, "The monster I've become, supposedly an impossibility, but it happened all the same, it may enable me to free the original demon that created vampires. Banished from the demon realm for his unseemly tastes, he developed a particular fondness for human blood and for the power he can wield in our realm. If he roams free, he will overrun this world, making humans his cattle."

Lizzy crossed her arms over her chest. "So we fight back. I'll call in my team, you call in yours, and we will hunt down this Calloway and those that will come for you, and we can squash this prophecy before it fully unfolds."

Bennett shook his head. "I'm going after Tromos."

"You must be joking. Unleashing such a powerful demon carries too much risk. I cannot permit you to attempt it."

"Not your choice. It's mine." His jaw clenched painfully, but he had known this would be the response. Which was why he hadn't intended to tell her until *after*. "Imagine if word gets out that a demon hunter has been changed? Already, it's inevitable. I can only hope that vampires like Calloway will realize this has zero benefit for them. He had to have been pissed to realize I had no attachment to my sires; I got the hell out of his grasp as soon as I woke up. But Calloway won't be the only one with this idea, and they'll learn from Calloway's mistakes. The only way to prevent someone else from trying to fulfill this prophecy is to take out Tromos myself."

Lizzy's feet planted to the ground, her pulse firing as her speech pressured. "But you don't even know what sort of prophecy this is. Does it tell of victory or of the world's end? You cannot risk the fate of the world on your own ego."

"I'm not taking him alone. But the fight is going to happen. I choose now. It's not ego. I *know* we're the team best suited to take him out. You said it yourself, although less complimentary, we're an unconventional team."

She opened her mouth to speak, but he was still too pissed off. They'd insulted his team, and as much as he knew that was out of generations of bias and ill-taught bigotry, he couldn't let it slide.

"Come on, let's find an empty warehouse and spar right now. I will win." He closed his eyes and backtracked. "Your team is great; I'm not saying they're not one of the best. But they're like all that have come before. Proud demon hunters set on freeing the world from evil. Yeah, your team is not like some that kill monsters for the sake of killing.

"But if you met Adair the way I did? Would you have *listened* when she told you she hadn't killed in hundreds of years and had sworn to never take another human life? Or would you have believed her to be the murderer she was changed to be, and slain her without batting an eye?" Rubbing a hand over his face, he shook off the tooth-grinding sneer. "Ryan's not merely from a different demon-sire, he's the fricking prince of the demon realm. Bodie isn't some feral that's mindlessly terrorizing—and now I'm regretting telling you about him, even though it was his idea to begin to spread the word of their true existence in the hopes of one day being treated as equals. This is exactly why werewolves live in secret, and none of us knew their true nature as shifters, rather than the rabid monsters we know them to be."

Lizzy didn't budge, soaking up what he'd said.

Jonathan rubbed his hand over his jaw. "You would risk the fate of the world on your faith in your unique team."

Bennett shook his head. "Doesn't matter that the team was granted enhanced abilities when we faced Typha. Or that we defeated the largest feral army that has ever walked this earth. Or that I can run a four-minute mile without breaking a sweat, in broad daylight. The fight is now. I can't leave it for someone else, because this prophecy is going to come to pass. One way or another. Maybe we can wipe out Calloway and bury the prophecy. But in two hundred years from now, when some less-equipped team attempts what must be done, and fails?"

Adair shook her head. "You haven't seen Bennett fight. It's incredible. Like nothing you've ever seen." She crossed to him and cradled her hands around his jaw, tracing her thumb along his cheekbones. She raised to her toes and pressed her lips to his. "Don't forget, you have a vampire on that eclectic team of yours this time."

Heart in his throat, Bennett rested his forehead on hers, too terrified to ask for how long.

Lizzy cleared her throat, her chocolate eyes laced with cream. "I always worried that you would stubbornly walk into a fight without a care for your own safety. I worried you lacked some crucial instinct at self-preservation. Yet each time you get knocked down, you seem to come out stronger. Clearly nothing I've done right, as I have tried to keep you on the straight and narrow path. My team will back you up. We'll see to rooting out Calloway's followers, and any others that are tempted to follow in his footsteps."

Uneasy in his seat, jaw clenched, Jonathan shook his head. "I agree. If you survive this, you will forever be feared by your enemies and their target both. We'll back you up. Whatever you need."

"I need you far away and safe." He glanced to the bag he'd set by the front door, the books, and maps they'd taken from Cambria. "And I'd love to bounce ideas off you. Dad? I've found some maps that may point us to Tromos. If you wouldn't mind taking a look?"

Nodding, Jonathan's shoulders relaxed, and a smile softened his expression. "Of course."

13

CROSSING THE ROOM WITH an unnatural swiftness, no longer slowing his movements for the sake of secrecy, Bennett grabbed the books and map they'd taken from Cambria. His parents followed him to the dining table. Adair hung back and watched as the tension eased.

As Lizzy lowered to her chair, she bumped the table, and it rattled at the light touch. "Jonathan? Let's remember to tighten these screws down, the legs are loose already."

Cheeks flaming red, Adair caught Bennett's eye and bit her tongue.

He winked at her and said to his parents, "You just bought it, too. You should leave a review."

Blushing brighter, Adair looked away and took the empty seat, trying to blink away the penetrating image of precisely how they'd loosened those screws. She drew her eyebrows into a scowl and unfolded the map, shadowing her fingertips over the faded ink. "We obtained this from an ancient that was collaborating with Calloway."

At her side, Jonathan traced over the legend, then along the coastline.

Crossing his arms, Bennett leaned against the wall and watched. "We had read the location was in a river town, but I don't see any rivers on that map."

Jonathan shook his head as he continued to study the contours. "What language was the text where you found the prophecy?"

Bennett shook his head, glaring at the lack of rivers on the map. "It's a compilation of prophecies, likely translated several times over and could have been mistranslated or inaccurately transcribed if that's what you're getting at. I know the text well, and it's filled with riddles and convolutions."

"I wonder..." Jonathan squinted as he studied the contours. "This is clearly a caldera. Santorini, if I am not mistaken."

Adair nodded. "I agree. This is Santorini. Lethe is a river in Greek mythology that separates the underworld and Elysian, and it was also a word used to mean forget or conceal. Hiding a demon wouldn't be easy. Burying him under a volcano could disguise his activity as eruptions."

"Trapping him between worlds. Forgotten." Lizzy eased open one of the books. "Demon hunter journals. These could be devastating in the hands of a vampire."

Adair grimaced. "They were."

She found Bennett's laptop on the side table. She pulled up a map of Santorini, but it wasn't a perfect match. Searching the history, she layered past maps. "The Minoan Eruption, roughly 1610 BC, would have been too early. The next major eruption was in 197 BC. That's right around when vampires are said to have come into existence. Either their efforts to conceal Tromos caused this eruption, or they took advantage of the recent activity and chose this location because of it."

"Either way," Bennett said as he came to stand behind her, reading the eruption history. He nuzzled his cheek at her temple, his breath warm against her skin. "It's been pretty active since. I think we can assume he's not sleeping beauty down there."

Adair looked up at him, the sharp angle of his jaw shadowed by the dark edge of beard. "I think it's time to call in your team."

Bennett leaned down and pressed his lips to the pulse point of her neck, lingering long enough to stir her yearning that wouldn't quit. Backing away, he pulled out his phone and made the call.

Jonathan rose to his feet and snapped a picture of the map. "You've got work to do. As do we. I'll see if I can narrow down possible entrances based on the geomorphology, or if I can discover any unnatural features."

A soft smile on her face, Lizzy glanced to the window and back. "A demon hunter that cannot read the terrain doesn't last long. Adair, please accept my apologies for judging you so contemptuously before. If you are agreeable, let's have that dinner before we part ways?"

Blush flaming her cheeks, Adair nodded. "I'd like that."

Dinner was more pleasant than she had expected. They arranged for a private corner in a local restaurant they frequented often so they could talk almost freely. Although Lizzy insisted they keep it light.

"I confess, we haven't gotten to meet any of Bennett's girlfriends. Well, aside from Quinn of course, but we have known her since she was born." Lizzy grinned as she chewed her roast duck over mixed greens.

Jonathan chuckled. "Excellent point. Okay, let's see." He rubbed his hand over his jaw and grinned. "Got it. My favorite embarrassing story." He flashed Bennett a deviously charming wink. "Humor me, I have never been granted the opportunity and have longed to for nearly a century."

The resemblance knocked the wind from Adair's lungs. And officially took her breath away as he kissed the back of his wife's hand and beamed. A sappy lover even after a century.

"Anyway," he continued. "Bennett can't have been more than four at that time. Lizzy's team was hunkered down in our BC home, about to drive against a horde of vampires. Things were incredibly tense. Their chances of succeeding, of even surviving this mission, were against them. While they were loading up their gear, the air was heavy with a shroud of portent. Not a word shared between them, nothing but heavy sighs as they accepted their fate. I stood leaned against the pillar at the front door, watching my wife and friends working together in what I hoped wouldn't be the last time. The life of a hunter's spouse isn't for the fainthearted. Anyway, I digress. In the thick of all this, here comes Bennett sprinting and leaping out the front door, ready to join the fight."

Lizzy tipped her head back and laughed out loud, more animated than Adair had seen. Well, happier-animated anyway. She'd been violently animated when Bennett had shown his teeth, and had clearly been trying to make up for her initial reaction until she began to relax at dinner. Adair was relieved to see Bennett's mother was great company when she wasn't worrying after her son.

Jonathan calmed his laughter enough to continue. "All he had on was a leather belt cinched around his waist, a dagger sheathed at his hip, and he carried the biggest sword he could lift, swinging it over his head, hollering how he was coming to save the day."

Downright cackling and nearly unladylike, Lizzy finished the story. "I can't believe I almost forgot about that. It was a struggle to get that kid to wear clothes, lord knows why. His little penis was jiggling about as he ran, and he was growling the most fearsome battle cry, insisting that he was 'unstoppable.'"

"Okay, okay." Bennett's dimples were deep as he fought between laughing and defending himself. "I was ready to be a hunter long before my DNA let me accept the gift."

Nudging his side, Adair grinned. She leaned back and said so only he could hear, "I hope you haven't outgrown the look. Call me old fashioned, but I gotta say, I'd love to see you in nothing but leather and steel."

Biting his lip, he splayed his hand over her thigh and squeezed. His breath a warm rush, a whisper over her skin, he murmured in her ear, "Be careful what you wish for. I was determined to show those vampires who's boss."

After a few more stories, her abdomen sore from laughing so much, Adair poured another round of wine for the table.

"You were born in the sixteenth century? You must have so many stories," Lizzy said.

"Immortality is not for everyone. Seeing firsthand when history repeats itself, or when it is remembered incorrectly, can be incredibly disheartening. It's like my hands are tied."

"Even in my hundred years, I have observed as much. It would be easy to give up."

Adair let an easy smile pass her lips. "I suppose. But with a hint of patience, it can be a journey. Always a new adventure to be had."

Bennett drained the last of his wine and linked his hand with Adair's under the table. "Adair seems to find a thrill in even the smallest of details, which is why I think she never tires of this life. Someday, maybe she'll tell me about all the occupations she's worked."

She shrugged. "Not as many as I'd like. Nothing that risks my discovery, nor anything that involves sunlight."

Before his mother could respond, Bennett said, "Wait a sec. Mom? You haven't touched your wine. Isn't this from one of your favorite vineyards?"

Lizzy and Jonathan leaned into each other and beamed. Jonathan spoke up, "Actually, we came to Paris to celebrate. We have been trying for nearly a decade and are finally expecting a sibling for you. Two, actually."

Grin spread from ear to ear, Bennett raised his glass. "Why didn't you say so? And twins? Holy shit, that's practically unheard of for hunters. Congratulations."

Her smile weak as the others toasted, Lizzy sighed before speaking. "I wanted to say sooner, but, when I realized you were changed, and you won't be able to..."

Bennett chewed his cheek. "Don't. This is not what I planned, but I am accepting. I'm going to be a big brother, what could be better? I am so thrilled for you. I am godfather to little Skye. However long I have on this planet, the average lifespan of a demon hunter, a vampire's eternity of loneliness, or a few days until I'm squashed by Tromos, I have plenty of life and love around me."

Heart shattering for him, Adair's breath caught in her throat. Her eyes welled with heat and she rubbed her hand over his thigh, leaning in and placing a light kiss on his jaw where his muscle tensed in contrast to his words and smile. He laced his fingers with hers and kissed the back of her hand.

Quiet, but calm, plates empty, cozy from wine and memories shared, they eased out of the restaurant and into the night. A frigid gust chilled her to the bone, but she needed it. A wake-up call. Or something. As he had a decade ago, he was making her yearn.

Tires squealed behind them. In front of them. From the side.

A snarl from the alley.

The street, moments ago blissfully empty on the winter night, was now flooded with her estranged brethren.

"Fancy meeting you here," Blayk snickered as he stepped into the light. He snuffed out a cigarette under his boot, the smoke huffing from his nostrils like a furious dragon as he exhaled.

Bennett stepped out in front of the others, pushed his shoulders back and smirked. "Missed me?"

"Actually, I'm here for her." He glanced to Adair.

At Bennett's side, Adair cocked her hip out and rolled her eyes. "Since when did you stoop to becoming Calloway's errand boy?"

Lizzy moved to her side and snarled, "You're not taking her."

A dozen vampires filled in behind Blayk, another dozen circled them, more filtering out of the cars. Adair scanned the street for an escape, but knew the fight was inevitable.

Reaching for the nearest of them, in a blink, Bennett snatched a vampire by the shirt and tugged him close, then snapped his neck and theatrically dusted off his hands as the vampire dropped to the ground.

No one moved.

Bennett tilted his head to the side, the corner of his mouth quirked up. "Don't make it so easy on me. Who's next?"

Blayk shrugged. "Strict orders. We're not to touch you."

Pulse thundering as he feared where his son lacked the obvious instinct, Jonathan sneered, "What, you're waiting for him to do your dirty work for you?"

Eyebrow raised arrogantly, Blayk said, "I don't give a flying fuck about Calloway's plan. But in for a penny, you know?" He glanced to the crowd of vampires surrounding them. "Let's go."

Blayk ducked into the shadow.

Furious, Bennett sifted through the vampires, knocking out one, stomping on the neck of another.

His mother was as cold of a killer as he was. Movements strong and precise, Lizzy didn't hesitate. Jonathan was no hunter, but he was also no lightweight in a fight.

Despite a few familiar faces, from the club, from her past, Adair didn't give an inch.

With a series of handsprings, she nailed a pair on landing, swinging and knocking out another with a roundhouse kick.

Ducking, she dodged the grip of a goliath.

She swerved and knocked the feet out of another and plowed a fist into his throat before leaping back to her feet.

Bennett tossed four vampires out of his way to reach her. "Stay close," he hissed.

Behind them, Jonathan bellowed a pained roar.

Miles away, Lizzy struggled to reach her husband, but kept getting washed back into the thick of it.

Like a juggernaut, Bennett was furious. Barreling through the crowd, he made for his father. Sprinting past him, Adair breezed through the mass of vampires, knowing even she couldn't reach him in time.

Three of them lifted Jonathan from the sidewalk and tossed him into the back of an SUV, and took off into the night.

Arms pumping at her sides, the soles of her boots burning over the frozen concrete, Adair followed. If they lost him...

The SUV turned. Shit. Another few blocks, and they would be out in the open.

Knowing she wouldn't make it in time, she turned down the alley to catch them at the next street.

A dark van slammed to a halt seconds before she reached the edge of the alley, blocking her path. Two vampires stepped out in front of her, the SUV carrying Jonathan disappearing from sight.

"Okay," she muttered. "Let's go." Without pause, she climbed into the van and buckled up, knowing she had no other choice. Hopefully, she could find the upper hand and get Jonathan out there. "I suppose two hostages are better than one."

As they tore off into the night, she looked out the back window. Bennett was hot on their heels, but he wasn't fast enough.

Bennett stopped and rubbed a hand over his face before dropping his hands to his hips, turning back, already planning his next steps.

14

Blinker politely indicating their turn, the van pulled into a dilapidated warehouse on the outskirts of Paris where there seemed to be more steel buildings and railroad tracks than humans, but night was still heavy on the air. Adair let out a long breath when she saw the SUV coming to a stop in the center of a warehouse. Blayk seemed to have developed a predilection for large, far-from-screaming-distance buildings.

Jonathan stepped out of the car, his bruises already healed thanks to the rapid healing of demon hunter spouses, but his rumpled hair and clothes showed signs of the fight it had taken to bring him down. Finding a surprising smile, Adair recognized the bullheadedness he shared with Bennett, from the stubborn set of his jaw to his broad shoulders, and his fists squeezed tight in preparation to go down fighting.

Adair smoothed her top as she eased out of the van.

Blayk strolled up to her, hips steady in his confident gait, with the relaxed posture of a man that wasn't easily rattled. "You have always been a pain in my ass."

"You haven't exactly made my life any easier." She rolled her eyes.

His impish smile delivered a pang like a stake to the chest. Lovers for fifty years, she thought leaving Calloway would be tough. Yet she hardly had given him a second thought. Well, not any nice thoughts anyway. But leaving Blayk had been heartbreaking.

He teased his hands in his short hair, assessing the room. Nodding to Jonathan, he commanded. "Tie him up in the supply room. He's the best leverage we've got, so don't touch him or he won't be of any use."

The vampires guarding Jonathan pouted, the woman in front snarling, "Not even a bite? A drop of demon hunter spouse blood should give a hell of a rush."

"An undamaged dad is much more persuasive than half-dead father." He nodded toward a sectioned-off room on the far side of the warehouse. Adair had always thought him handsome. Dark eyelashes and dark hair contrasting his smooth skin, accented by the light dusting of freckles across his cheeks and the creases at the edges of his eyes that hinted at his rough history.

Like recognized like, and having endured a violent history himself, and he had always been her confidante. Friends from the start, she had never desired him as more. But she could easily see why so many women of the clan had. And why her husband had accused her of fucking him.

The familiar rush of panic clenched in her chest, recalling Richerd's fist slamming into her abdomen as he railed on her for accepting the seed of another man before providing him with an heir. Joke was on him; their unborn child didn't survive that fight. But she did.

"Hey," Blayk murmured, bringing her back to the moment, as he had so many times before. His eyes flashed with the darkness she'd known even then.

"Hey."

His troops were on the move, setting up a perimeter in case Bennett found them. The corner of her mouth quirked up as she sensed the fear quaking through them. And enjoyed the idea of telling Bennett about the impact his very name struck on his enemies. He'd appreciate it. "What's the plan? Manipulate Bennett into releasing Tromos? Weak, but I suppose you have little choice."

Hands resting on his hips, the corners of Blayk's lips twitched up. "Calloway thinks sentiment is the only way to get to him."

"And you disagree?" She glanced to the clock on the far wall. "I'd say you have about an hour before he arrives. Oh, and don't forget that his mother will come too; she seems to really like her husband. Others of Bennett's team can be here within hours, so he might wait, but so far, I haven't witnessed him having a shred of patience. Or mercy."

Glancing around, Blayk took a breath and silently shook his head and nodded to the stairs. His brow was furrowed, but he exuded a calm defiance as usual. He cleared his throat and pasted on an awkwardly lecherous expression. "I've got a better idea."

What was he getting at? She drew her eyebrows together and shook her head. "You've seen him. He's changed, and I'm not just talking about the fangs. Bennett is the ruthless killer you wanted him to be."

"That may be, but he's still a sap," he hissed, the derisiveness unnatural.

"And you think he'll roll over and do Calloway's bidding? That he'll risk the fate of the world to save his father?"

"What about you?" Blayk's voice lowered. "He won't fight for you?"

Her gaze softened, a sappy smile taking over before she could mask it. Quickly adjusting her expression, she said, "He's gotten what he needed from me. Trust me, he'll be glad to be rid of the baggage."

Blayk knocked his knuckle gently down the slope of her nose and grinned, "Trust me. He'll come for you." He abruptly shifted his hands in her hair and tugged her close. Tongue down her throat, he gripped his hands around her arms as he made his point. Breathless, seething, he fumed in a raised voice, "I knew he wasn't the hero you claimed. But you might be a romantic after all. Upstairs, or I'll rough up the bait a bit."

"Leave him alone."

Hand clutching firm around her arm, his fingers dug so tight her arm went numb. He dragged her upstairs to the main office. Blayk glared at the vampire inside and gestured toward the door. "Out."

"But Calloway said–"

"*I* said out." Adair had never heard the terse ferocity in his voice before. The sound was unnatural, wrenching her gut at the change. It had been a few centuries, but can his personality have veered so far from the man she knew?

As the woman slammed the door and tromped down the steps, Blayk said loud enough for others to hear, "On your knees. You owe me." He moved to the desk and blasted music from the stereo. Moving close, his gaze softened, and he whispered, "I'm so sorry about that."

Adair shook her head. "You had me going there. I was trying to decide when to drive that letter opener into your eye."

"Really, you know I would never treat you–"

"I know. You got me out of Richerd's reach and delivered me to my brother all those years ago. I will always be grateful."

"And you saved me right back when Richerd was stringing me up for it."

"I wish things were different."

"Me too. You were right all along. I should have seen Calloway's crazy sooner." He exhaled and dug his hands into his pockets. "Not going to pretend I didn't have a hell of a time. But when you left us? I was pissed at first. But I settled, went off on my own, and until Calloway returned a few years ago, I was enjoying the quiet life. On top of the world, having the ultimate plan, he promised excitement and glory like the old days, plus all the human you could drink."

"I had no idea. If you'd said something sooner–"

"Look, Adair. I'm not going to pretend I wasn't thrilled to get back in the thick of things. The challenge of changing a demon hunter? Fucking epic. Had I known he was yours... well..." he chuckled, "I might have at least had an inkling of remorse about it."

Her brow drew together, trying to read him. "What now?"

"Calloway's off his fucking rocker. He'd led all of us to believe his plan was more... traditional. I am terribly sorry for bringing so much pain on you."

"I–"

He shook his head, grinning at her. "You can lie to everyone else, but it's never worked on me." Before she could respond, he continued, "Calloway didn't even mention Tromos until a few days ago. I'm to give Bennett some motivation, as he's not the bloodsucking puppet Calloway had hoped for. Apparently, he misread the prophecy in that regard. More likely, Calloway assumed Bennett would be filled with thrall for him, as so many others are."

"You don't want Tromos unleashed?"

"Fuck no. Vampire or not, I started out in this world as the lowest form of servant, and I am not going back, and I am not forcing that life on anyone else. Calloway, you and me, we were equals. This time around? Calloway thinks he's earned the right to be in charge. Delusions of fucking grandeur. He is under the impression that Tromos will bow to him, or at least name him his second in command as a thank you for freeing him."

Visions of Blayk as the warrior flashed across her mind, one of the strongest and smartest of the clan. But he hadn't always been like that. As the ladies would tell it, he'd been a scrawny lad, but the moment he'd hit puberty, he grew into the man he was. And had been much more useful as a raider, and eventually, the top warrior in the clan, never backing down as he knew what the bottom felt like.

"Calloway is a fool. A powerful demon will never bow to a hybrid."

"My thoughts exactly. Besides, what fun is having your dinner brought to you when you could hunt for it?"

"You're talking to a woman that buys it by the pint from the local butcher."

He smirked. "Fair point. Anyway. We need to keep your boyfriend from going anywhere near Tromos."

Her ears pricked up as footsteps scraped over the steel stairs. Raising her voice, she chanted a few *oh*s and *you're-a-stallion*s.

Blayk cringed but added a few grunts for good measure.

The footsteps faded back down the stairs.

Lowering her voice, Adair said, "Not going to happen. He's going to find him so he can kill him."

Hissing under his breath, Blayk said, "What? He can't be that stupid."

"Not stupid, no, but uncompromising." She smiled, biting her lip as she envisioned the warrior he'd been all his life, never fearing for himself. A vampire wouldn't understand anything so selfless. "And if he doesn't stop this now? That prophecy won't die with Calloway."

Breath forced in slow and steady inhales, Blayk shook his head. "Okay. Then we need to be sure he succeeds. And that Calloway is nowhere near him when it happens."

Adair scowled, considering. "We need Calloway as dead as Tromos. For good this time. If he finds out Tromos has been defeated? It may be another few centuries before he surfaces again, and with a more dangerous plan."

Blayk folded his arms over his chest and raised the corner of his lips. "What do you need?"

Adair smacked him a kiss on the cheek and stepped back, her nose scrunched with her giddy grin. "Good to have you back."

He shook his head and smiled with her. "You're crazy as ever."

15

WEIRDEST TEXT HE'D EVER received. Simply an address. Nothing more.

Could be a trap. Probably was. Not much other choice.

Bennett fired up the engine, waiting for his mom to buckle, then took off across town. Stopping at every sign, keeping it legal, he flew under the radar to the edge of the city. Lizzy's knee was vibrating at a rapid frequency, her pulse thundering so hard his eardrums hurt. "Mom, he's going to be fine."

"I know." She nodded, eyes glued to the road.

"Trust me. They need me to free Tromos. If they hurt Dad–" or Adair "–I won't be so cooperative."

While his mother pulled up directions, he called the team.

Astrid answered, "We're at the airport. Are you on the road?"

"A quick stop to make first. Can you book us a boat? Once we rescue my dad, he's going to scan the map in detail to find the entrance, but I'm sure it's not easy to access by land."

"On it. I'll send you the info."

"Cool. And, Astrid? Blayk has my dad and Adair. We're on our way to get them, but I wouldn't put it past Calloway to try to take you guys out as well. Alone, I'm not as much of a threat. Be on guard for whatever he may have planned."

"Near Oia, you think?"

"Yeah. A good place to start anyway."

"Perfect. Lana and Vann should land in Istanbul within the hour. They'll probably beat you there."

He heard Bodie teasing Astrid. "Sounds like you're finally getting that fancy European vacation."

"Ha," she snorted. "When I asked for culture and beaches, I didn't mean overlying the original vampire sire."

"Be careful what you wish for," Bennett teased. "I wanted my own prophecy, and look where that got me."

"Don't pass judgment too soon."

He tried to object, but she talked over him.

"Nope. Don't think on it yet."

"K. Shit, I've got another call. Talk to you soon." He checked the number. 206 area code. Seattle. He knew exactly who it was. He clicked over.

"It's so good to talk with you at last, my progeny."

Bennett snorted and turned onto a side road, taking an indirect path. "This must be Calloway. I suppose I should be thanking you for making me stronger and faster. It will be much easier to hunt you down now."

Calloway laughed derisively. "You are a delight. I can see why Adair fancies you."

"And I can see that you are one of those long-winded assholes that thinks he's in charge. And I have no doubt you have a truly awe-inspiring plan. Let's make it simple. You release my father and Adair. And then I'll kill you after I take care of Tromos."

"Feisty too. Even you will be no match for our great founder, and certainly won't have access to me."

"Of course," he muttered as he took the next turn. "Your droves of fools will protect you, as usual. You know, if you were hoping for a thrall, you might have considered changing me yourself. And I'm sure this demon will bow before you for finding someone else to free him."

More derisive laughter. What did Adair ever see in this guy? "You haven't read the prophecy yet? I presumed you were smarter than that, having taken out Cambria so efficiently for me."

"I haven't had time to finish the assigned reading yet. I was a little busy fucking your ex-girlfriend. Great job with your vengeance plan. I have been thoroughly enjoying the time to reconnect with her."

Calloway's tone soured, his laugh even phonier. "Did I say feisty? I meant foolish. She and your father will be far from the fight. Blayk will see that they are unharmed, so far, but on my command, he won't hesitate to run them both through. If you don't cooperate."

Whoever sent the mysterious text was no friend to Calloway.

"I confess, I don't have much experience with hostage situations. At some point, are you going to tell me we'll meet in Santorini at the entrance, and be quick or you'll start cutting off fingers?"

"Oh my. No, I don't think we'll need to resort to that. I suspect your father will be easier to change than you were, and less right-eous. And Adair? A few tastes of human blood, and I can bring her right back to the bloodsucker she was. Before her brother saw to her detox, she was more devious than I am."

Lizzy gripped her hands on the seat, about to give Calloway the lecture of a lifetime. Half the demons she hunted probably dropped at her feet when she gave them that look. His future sibling was in for it.

He stilled her hand. The address from the text was approaching, another abandoned warehouse. These guys were awfully creative. "Sorry, but I've got a flight to catch. See you soon."

Bennett clicked off the call and scanned the area. Parking out of sight, he stepped out of the car and scanned the area, sniffing, listening, as Adair had taught him.

He popped open the trunk and strapped on his replacement shield, gripping the sword that was actually pretty well balanced.

Lizzy met him at the trunk and grabbed her war axe. She strapped a pair of daggers into her boots and let out a heavy exhale. "We wait until sunrise, then come blazing in. As you said, Adair is a survivor. She'll know to stay out of sight."

Glancing to the sky, a pale blue on the horizon, Bennett nodded. Without a sound, he paced down the sidewalk.

His mother watched, hesitating, but finally followed.

The light eased across the sky, casting shadows over the empty street. A pair on the roof ducked out of sight as daylight threatened.

Bennett halted at the edge of the building. Lizzy waited at his side.

A voice echoed from inside the building. "Calloway says that in forty-eight hours, we will no longer be hiding in the shadows." Blayk. Asshole. Bennett gripped his sword, ready to launch it straight for his throat.

A few whoops and hollers.

Bennett moved to slip in the backdoor. Easing inside, he found a crowd gathered around Blayk, the dickwad standing above them on the steel stairs. Adair was unchained, casually leaning over the banister at the top of the stairs. What the fuck?

Blayk shushed the cheers, his gaze landing on Bennett for only a blink, then casting back onto the crowd. "Our future lies in the balance. We can't lose hold of our hope for the future. Lay your lives on the line for the cause... and don't let Bennett out of here with our hostages."

Across the crowd, Blayk flashed a grinning wink at Bennett. Shit, this wasn't going to be an easy one. His mother moved to his side and gripped her axe, ready to start swinging.

Two dozen vampires caught his meaning and turned in place, snarling and ready to pounce as they caught sight of the hunters that joined the party.

He glanced up at Adair, unsure what to expect. She beamed; a massive grin spread across her lips as she stood at Blayk's side. He'd figured they knew each other, but she looked a little too comfortable next to the enemy.

His mother roared at his side and rushed for the crowd. Fuck, she was furious. Bennett ran to catch up.

Bashing his shield into the first, he sliced his sword through the next.

One leaped onto his back. Jerking his head back, he slammed into its nose. Spinning, he drove his sword into the hollow above her collarbone and wrenched until she dropped to the ground.

His mother quickly discharged her third kill as Bennett sliced his sword through the throat of another.

Out of the corner of his eye, he saw Blayk flashing through the mob, taking out his own guys without remorse.

In the opposite corner, Adair gracefully took out another batch of them. Across the room, she flashed a grin at Blayk. And he raised his eyebrows back as if they were having the time of their lives.

Furious, Bennett thrashed through the final few.

Bennett lowered his sword but tightened his shield.

Across the warehouse, the corner of Blayk's lips turned up, his eyes crinkling in appreciation. Strolling confidently over the scattered bodies, he moved to greet him.

Raising his sword, Bennett beckoned him close. "Ready to finish this, now that we're not so sleepy?"

Seeing one of the vampires twitching at his feet, Blayk leaned down and snapped his neck.

What the fuck was going on? Bennett held his breath and looked to Adair. She grinned at him and then watched as Blayk motioned to a meeting room at the opposite end of the warehouse and waved Lizzy over. "He's fine. He's in here."

Lizzy didn't loosen her grip on her sword, but followed. With a guarded gait, she kept her distance. On seeing Jonathan was okay, alone in a supply room, she dropped her axe and fussed over him.

Bennett sheathed his sword and hooked his shield onto his back. Adair came sprinting down the stairs, aimed straight for Bennett. As she looked ready to leap into his arms, Bennett folded his arms over his chest.

Adair stopped inches from him and her brow drew together. Fuck, he could smell the confusion on her, but not half as strong as the scent of Blayk all over her. And vice versa. As if she didn't know what he was pissed about? Yeah, she appeared so... tame, so normal, but his parents were right. She was a purebred vampire.

"Bennett? You okay?" She glanced back to see Blayk keeping his distance, a deep scowl between his eyebrows as he watched Bennett's cold reception.

"I should be asking you that, but clearly you're unharmed. We never committed to each other, no, and you made it damn clear that you had no interest in a tomorrow with me. But I'm not getting played. Again. And I sure as fuck don't share." His fists clenched so tight his fingernails broke the skin of his palms; his jaw gritted so tight his teeth squealed in defense.

She ran her fingers through her hair and stepped back. "Of course. Why would you trust me?"

Blayk came dashing over. "Hey, Bennett. I won't pretend I couldn't hear all that. And I won't pretend I don't know Adair well enough to know she's too damn stubborn to explain."

Adair shifted her glare to Blayk. "Stay out of it."

"No." He lightly punched her in the arm, then shoved his hands in his pockets and looked back to Bennett. "Can we talk?"

Shoving her hand against Blayk's sternum, Adair pushed him away. "Shove off. This is between Bennett and me."

Backing away, Bennett moved to check on his dad, but found him looking remarkably healthy and hale. Dammit. Well, not dammit that he was okay, but Bennett needed to get the hell out of here. Yeah, allies were a good thing... but, fuck, she'd shattered him enough times. He wasn't about to let her rub it in, and not in front of his parents or the asshole responsible for his situation. "Look, Adair wherever you stand on this whole thing, stay out of it. I've got work to do."

Adair pursed her lips together, her scowl forming a deep crease between her eyebrows. "As if you'd accept help anyway."

Bennett caught his parents' attention and met them outside.

Close behind, his dad asked, "Adair isn't coming?"

He crossed the street and unstrapped his gear. "Nope."

Lizzy stormed behind them. "I can't believe you're letting that fellow live."

Jaw clenched tight, Bennett refused to answer. Something was up, and his instincts were screaming that Blayk was involved. Killing him might be premature. His father was alive and well. He wouldn't kill Blayk today. But he wouldn't make any promises about tomorrow.

More? He really, really didn't want to see how deeply Adair's feelings for the guy ran. His parents kept quiet on the drive to the airport.

To stay under the radar, he booked the next available commercial flight.

At the terminal, his mother grabbed him before they went their separate ways. With a fierce hug, his mother's voice warbled, "You be careful. We'll be ready... in case you need backup. I have faith in you."

Letting out a long sigh, Bennett squeezed her back. "This is what you trained me for since before I was old enough to hold a sword."

She released him and wiped a cluster of tears from her cheek, Lizzy nodded. "Please don't push us away again. We're here for you. No matter what."

"I won't."

The flight was miserably long. He'd flown coach to keep under the radar, knowing Calloway was probably watching for his jet. As much as Calloway would know his destination, a hint of a head start would be helpful. For a spell, he'd tried to close his eyes and work in a quick nap, but even the banter of high schoolers behind him couldn't drown out the image of Adair and Blayk making out in front of his father and a couple dozen vampires while agreeing how happy they were to get back together.

Bleary eyed as he deplaned, he trudged through customs. He slid one of his rarely used passports across, describing how happy he was to be meeting some old friends for a wedding. The customs agent smiled and nodded, then regaled him with a few stories of his daughter's wedding last year and the sites few knew about.

Straightening his posture, Bennett said, "It has been my dream to come here. I've heard such incredible stories about Oia. Can you recommend any unique stops around the caldera? Anything off the beaten path?"

The agent grinned, looking around as if it were the best secret. "If you have access to a boat, jet across the way and to the outer edge.

There's this spot that looks like a hull-crusher so most folks won't risk it, but once you get around the rocks, the beach is snow white and completely empty."

Bennett tapped his passport against the counter and grinned, "I'll check it out, thanks."

"Keep it to yourself, right?" The customs agent winked with a conspiratorial smile.

"Of course." Bennett flashed a friendly wink back and picked up his bags. "Have a nice day."

He adjusted his backpack, wishing he'd been able to fly with his sword and shield, he felt naked without the gear. Yeah, he'd enjoyed brawling with his newfound speed and senses, but hell, he was old fashioned. Apparently, too old fashioned for a modern-day vampire.

From out of thin-fucking-air, scaring the shit out of him, a bodyless hand grasped him by the shoulder, and in an instant, static electricity prickled over his skin. Like being sucked through an underwater wormhole, he gasped to find air, blindly lashing out at his captor.

Suddenly back in the world, salty wind rushed over him. Dropped to his knees, he pulled air into his lungs and held his gut so he didn't lose his poor excuse for a breakfast.

Ryan stood in front of him, chuckling with that massive ego. He teased his hand in his hair, he grinned, "Sorry about that. I was going to warn you first, but I thought I saw one of Calloway's goons."

Bennett rose to his feet, swallowing the lump of nausea as he steadied himself. He shook his head. "Fuck, Ryan. I was about to break your neck."

"I was more worried about you puking on me."

Finding his first smile all damn day, Bennett rubbed his hands over his face. "I, uh, I guess I didn't know you could do that. Pull someone through the veil like that."

"I've been thinking on it for a while, how the creepy things pulled Quinn through the veil to Typha. Pulling myself through is one thing, but to bring someone that wouldn't survive if I took you too far across? Honestly, we're lucky you didn't end up a melted pile of hybrid in the demon realm."

"Lucky." He adjusted his bag on his shoulder and looked around. This must be the boat Astrid found for them. They were standing in the middle of a sitting area, a dining area was attached, and there was a door to a galley behind them. There were huge windows that overlooked the mystically blue ocean, Oia barely visible in the distance, and with his vampire sight, he could make out white and blue dome-shaped buildings. "How'd you find me? I know you can find Quinn through the veil, but I didn't think that extended to anyone else."

Ryan cleared his throat and shifted his weight on his feet. "That day Adair called and said you needed help, and we almost didn't make it in time, I, uh, well... I can reach you now."

Bennett's chest plummeted under the weight as he grasped the meaning. Ryan could find Quinn anywhere in the world and pull himself straight to her through the veil that separated the human and demon realms, but it took a hell of a strong motivator to blindly travel like that. And a big fat L-word he would not embarrass himself by saying out loud. The bromance they'd been flirting at since deciding they didn't hate each other was obvious enough.

Feet shifting equally awkwardly, Bennett said, "I'm really sorry for the stuff I said before, and, you know, biting you."

"I know. It should have been you. You got the short end of that prophecy stick."

"But it worked out the way it was supposed to. I'm good with it. Really."

"Please tell me this prophecy is going better for you."

"Not so far." Bennett scanned the room for an exit. "Anyone else here yet?"

"Lana and Vann are on board. Fiona pulled a few strings to get the boat for us, quietly. Vann's taking us far enough out that we won't be seen by curious eyes." Ryan headed for a closed door next to the galley. As he reached for the knob, the bubbly bounciness that was Lana busted in.

Speak of the devil. "You found him." She beamed at Ryan. She crossed the room and laced her arms around Bennett and leaned on his shoulder, rocking as she hugged him like she knew how shitty he was feeling. "Are you doing okay?"

"Fine. Is there someplace I can crash? I haven't slept in days." Dead on his feet, he was ready to take a nap right on that couch.

"This place is awesome. Come on, I picked out everyone's rooms." Lana led the way down the hallway, pointing to stairs down the hall to some of the rooms and led him down a ladder to the lower rooms. "I just got off the phone with your dad. He analyzed the maps, and he is emailing a few possibilities for us."

She flicked on the light to a suite with an over-fluffed bed in the center and two club chairs around a side table. High on the far wall, there was a wall of windows covered by thick curtains.

"Perfect. I'll look it over in the morning."

He dumped his bags on the floor and started peeling off his clothes as Lana left him to it. Sleep didn't come easy, his dreams mocking him for the naïve romanticism he'd indulged in for far too long.

16

"AT THIS POINT IN your life, I would expect you to have learned that honesty works a hell of a lot better than obstinacy."

Adair fired a glower at Blayk. "So says the guy that just told Calloway a pretty string of lies. Really? It made sense to tell him the hostages were secure, but to request that he save at least one of those troublesome demon hunters for you to snack on?" For all his pestering, the relief at being able to joke with her friend again made everything feel almost normal. Almost.

Sporting a snarky grin, Blayk relaxed into his seat in the charter plane and closed his eyes. "I have a ruse to keep up. Besides, I didn't specify my intentions. I wouldn't mind a taste of the short curvy one." He bit his cheek as he considered. "I've always been curious about demon hunter endurance."

Curling into her seat, Adair took a sip of her heated cow blood. "Lana wouldn't touch a bloodsucker."

Sniffing the air, Blayk scowled and opened his eyes. He reached across and took her mug. Nose scrunched, he took a testing sip. "That's nasty. How do you live on that?"

"Try it for a few weeks, and you won't even miss human."

Raising an eyebrow, he laughed under his breath and took another sip.

She rolled her eyes. "Okay, fine, you'll miss human, but it's worth it."

With a shrug, he handed her back her emptied mug and uttered, "Maybe." After a solid three minutes of silence, he brought it right back to the elephant on the plane. "What are you going to do about Bennett?"

"Nothing. You and I will stay in a hotel and find Calloway and take him out while Bennett goes after Tromos."

"Ha. You have a remarkable lack of self-awareness for an old-as-dirt woman."

"And you're an expert? Tell me, when's the last time you were in a serious relationship?"

"Last year."

"Really?"

"No, but I had you going there."

She kicked across the aisle and nailed him in the shin with her pointy boot. He rubbed at the bruise, but didn't lose his smile.

The second they landed, he heaved a heavy bag over his shoulder and thanked the crew that had transported them. Metal clanked in his bags. Adair eyed him suspiciously.

He winked.

Damn, she'd forgotten how infuriating he could be. She didn't let him see her grin.

Within the hour, under the cool glow of the moon, the wind rushed over the bow of the boat, tangling in Adair's hair. Bracing the steering wheel with her knee, she tugged her hair into a knot and then re-aimed for the yacht ahead. "How did you get ahold of such a big boat on short notice?"

Blayk ran his fingers through his hair and blushed. "Um... friend of a friend."

She slowed the engine of their boat and docked at the back of the yacht. Hopping out at the last second, Blayk secured the line. "Come on." He nodded. "You first."

Hesitating at the lip of the rental boat, Adair scrunched her brow. "Thanks to the wind, I can't smell a damn thing. Where have you taken us?"

She could hear laughter, voices, arguing. But the sea breeze was too dense and muffled her senses.

"Don't trust me?" When she glared at him, he shrugged, "I could go first, but I'm not exactly welcome in there."

"I am probably a gigantic fool for trusting you."

Knocking her gently on the arm with a light punch, he winked, "Probably."

She went for it. As she reached the top, she still couldn't scent anyone aside from the light scent of human laced with wolf. The corners of her mouth quirked up as she realized what that meant.

Bodie's laugh echoed down the hall as Lana regaled the team with a story about Vann's rare misstep in questioning a recluse hunter outside of Bangkok. A deep rumble from Vann as he said, "Fuck off," but she heard the lightness in his tone at the friendly retort.

Sensing Blayk following cautiously behind, Adair pushed her shoulders back, refusing to be nervous. She wasn't the one who misread the situation. Bennett was the asshole here.

And he was pissed.

And he'd sensed her the moment she came aboard. His jaw was clenched, his eyes were already on the doorway before she came into view, waiting. Gaze unwavering, he silently dared her to defend herself. Or to pretend nothing was wrong.

Behind her, Blayk shoved her forward a step and moved into the room like he owned the place. Aside from Quinn, the team was all here, plotting and joking.

Bolting out of their seats, the team looked ready to end him.

"Wait–" Adair moved to stand at his side.

He raised his hands in casual defense and cleared his throat. "My associate here..." he began, flashing her a playful wink, "would say that she's not here to defend herself. Stubborn ass didn't want to come in the first place."

Tapping her foot on the teak, she scowled, refusing to argue. "And my associate is too stupid to let you all know that he comes in peace."

The team eased, not as eager to attack, but none sat back down. Astrid asked, "How did you find us?"

Adair answered, "Lizzy was grateful to have her husband back, unharmed, plus a few tips as to where she could find bloodsucking vampires to slay. She's already gathering her team and going for Calloway's friends in Seattle."

Flinching, Bennett held her gaze, but didn't drop the menacing glare.

"I don't know what Bennett has told you, or what he gleaned from the unusual scene at the warehouse. Blayk will side with us because he is like many other vampires, perhaps most, and doesn't want to see Tromos rise any more than you do."

Jaw clenched, Bennett feigned a lightness to his voice. "And we should trust him why?"

Crossing her arms, Adair huffed, "Oh, of course. Never trust a vampire. Even one that is on your side."

"Oh, I'm sorry, I guess I don't move with the times as fast as some. First time I saw this guy, he turned me into a vampire. Next time, after he'd abducted my father, he was all over my I-refuse-to-commit, it's-complicated girlfriend. Please forgive my thickheadedness."

Lana cleared her throat and teased her hands in her dark hair. "We'll leave you two to talk this over."

Still fired up, Adair stepped up and took an empty seat across from Bennett in the living area. "Oh no, you should all stay. Who knows what deviance I'll consider if left unsupervised?"

Letting out a long exhale, Blayk parked on the couch between Ryan and Vann and rested his elbows on his knees. The team slowly lowered back to sit. Blayk looked from Bennett to Adair, landing his gaze back on Bennett again. "You have no reason to trust me, but you do her. She's exactly the woman you knew yesterday. And she's the reason I am alive today. What has she told you of her husband?"

"Not much." Bennett chewed his cheek, not letting on what he was thinking. Adair wanted to smack him upside the head. Or crawl onto his lap and tell him what an idiot he was.

Curling into the seat and scooting closer to Adair, Lana said, "He was abusive."

Adair didn't say anything.

Blayk nodded. "He was a pathetic excuse for a human. I tried to stand up for Adair when he... proved how brutally insecure he was. He took my defense of her to mean that she and I were lovers. I managed to get her out of there, eventually, but it took time to arrange. I tracked down her brother and met him on the road to Inverness. Her injuries too severe from his latest outrage, she was dying in my arms. Thinking her dead, I left her with her brother and returned home, refusing to let Richerd get away with it. Foolishly, I'd hoped the clan would stand against him. My mistake."

Swallowing a salty knot that had wedged in the back of her throat, Adair murmured, "As soon as I recovered, Logan and I went back for Blayk."

Vann's expression was dark, knowing already when he asked, "And your husband?"

She nodded. "I took care of my husband, my first human victim, while Logan saw to Blayk, who was in no better shape than I had been. As he had with me, Logan changed him to save his life."

Bennett's posture eased, but Adair knew they were far from returning to the fragile safe space they had found together.

Blayk must have seen it too. Tone sharp as his canine teeth, his gaze bore into Bennett. "You don't deserve to be in the same room as her. One misleading moment–my idea, to be able to speak in private to a woman I have known centuries longer than you have–and you're accusing her of exactly the deceit her husband did. She and I have *never* been more than friends. And, despite my many mistakes since Calloway returned, she has accepted me. You can treat her with respect, or you and I can finish what we started in Seattle."

Voice full of gravel, Bennett looked to Adair. That damn salty knot sunk deep into her belly and pushed against her lungs at his weary look. He murmured, "Can we talk? Alone?"

She managed a nod and rose to her feet. A hesitance to her step that she knew he wouldn't miss, she pushed her shoulders back and powered down the hall to the back of the yacht, while he followed close behind.

He kept his distance, but she could feel him and couldn't help but wish he'd reach for her, but she'd sock him if he tried. The cool night air washed over her as she opened the door and stepped outside. She inhaled every molecule of the salty breeze before sitting at the edge of a lounge chair under the light of the moon. She nodded for Bennett to sit on the other.

He dropped into the opposite chair and leaned forward, resting his elbows on his knees. Inches from touching her, he rubbed his hands over his face. "Why didn't you say something?"

"You were dead set on believing that I was exactly what you had been taught."

He scooted closer and trailed his fingertips over her forearms, gently, hesitantly, seeming to need the connections as much as she did. "It was more a matter of not trusting myself, more than you. Fuck, that sounds like a feeble excuse. As I've said before, I am a thickheaded idiot."

The corner of her mouth twitched. "As you have proven many times over."

"Please. Accept my apologies. When I walked into that room and found you smiling in the midst of Calloway's followers? While I could sense my father alive but fresh from the fight nearby? You stood beside the guy that brought this curse on me, and I could smell you all over each other. I... not to make excuses, but I guess I've been waiting for you to break my heart again."

"You are a hopeless romantic. Emphasis on the word *hopeless*."

"Never said I was good at this stuff. Hell, there's a reason Quinn dumped me. And that I haven't been able to maintain a steady relationship for long." He laughed mirthlessly under his breath. "Fuck, no wonder my dad enjoys lecturing me about women. Perhaps I should have listened."

Teasing her fingertips across his hands, she said, "You are not the first one to mistake Blayk and I for lovers. Even Calloway went on a killing rampage once, after he'd found us living it up one wild night in Rome."

"But you've really never–"

"No. Seriously, he's as much a brother to me as Logan. And if you ever even imply–"

"Hell no," he laughed, his shoulders relaxing. "You scare me too much." He tugged her across and pulled her onto his lap. Under the hem of her shirt, he traced his thumbs over her skin.

Tipping her head to the sky, she let out a long breath before easing in to straddle him, keeping out of reach when he tried to kiss her. "Not half as much as you scare me." Locked onto his gaze, searching, she murmured, "I'm sorry too. I'm overwhelmed by you. Like a confused magnet, torn between north and south, I sabotage and do my utmost to push you away while I try to put you under the thrall you hold me in."

Reaching to kiss her again, he smiled when she taunted him. "We are a hell of a pair."

Tugging her tighter against him, he took her mouth with his. And she let him. Igniting on impact, she wrapped her hands around his broad shoulders, holding him close.

Rhythmic waves lapped against the hull. Wind rushed through her hair, whipping the strands to form a curtain around them. With every kiss, every breath shared, she felt his apology, his longing for more. Hating how easy it was to drive them apart, so many times, she rested her hand on his cheek as she kissed him softly, tenderly, needing him to understand her. Hoping to understand him.

Easing her shirt over her head, he trailed his lips over her collarbone, pressing an open-mouthed kiss over the curve of her breast. Silently urging him on, she leaned into him.

Aware of his senses, that he could feel her accelerating pulse, her need for him thundering out of control, she felt the last trail of doubt between them melt away. Sliding her bra strap over her shoulder, he followed the fabric with the tip of his tongue, the sensual trail sending shivers over her skin.

Freed from the satin, the chill wind brushed over her sensitive buds, tightening in contrast to the heat blazing in her veins. Hands grasped over her breasts, he teased his thumbs over her, then took her deep in his mouth, thrill rushing straight to her core at the exquisite sensation.

Reading her response, he pulled harder when she craved it, then eased and trailed his tongue over her skin again.

Her hunger for him rose higher with each touch, each kiss.

He paused long enough to meet her gaze, silently asking for more.

Taking her lower lip between her teeth, she rose long enough to strip off the rest of her clothes. In half a heartbeat, vampire speed coming in remarkably handy, he was deliciously undressed and ready for her.

She lowered to straddle him and reached between them, gripping his cock in her hand, tormenting, massaging until he hissed in desperate response and thrust his tongue over hers while he pulled her over him.

Driving inside her, he groaned with a long-awaited satisfaction.

Exquisite heat coursed through her as he filled her, the stirring connection more vivid, more... vital.

Moving together, fluid, intense, he trailed his fingertips up her sides and cupped her breasts, his eyes never leaving hers as he drove her past the point of no return. Nearing her climax, his name on her lips, she drove their pace higher, faster. Meeting her stroke for stroke, his grip tightened over her hips as they crested together.

Riding the wave, easing, slowing, the throbbing heat lingering, she rested her forehead on his, breath coming fast and heavy.

All the words needing to be said filled her throat, forming an impenetrable blockage.

Bennett's hands rested on her thighs as they sat frozen together. "Thanks for not giving up on me," he whispered.

"Never," she said, terrified he'd ask what she meant.

17

Sipping from a blood-laced mug of coffee, handing her a matching cup, Blayk winked at Adair and said, "See you two made up okay."

Lana strolled into the galley and winked, "Don't need vampire senses to have heard how thorough their make-up was. And the second round. And the third. And–"

"Okay." Adair shushed her as the blush flamed her cheeks. "You're one to talk, Miss 'Tell me how you want to lick my–'"

"Okay." Lana nudged her and moved around Blayk to grab a coffee cup for herself. "We can exchange tips later."

Adair cradled her coffee in her hands and leaned against the counter. "What does your boyfriend think of you being off the grid for a while?" She glanced to Blayk, curious if he'd be disappointed.

He shrugged, as if to say, *easy come, easy go*. Okay, so maybe not Lana. But now that she had her friend back, finding him a non-vampire mate, even a demon hunter, might be the perfect way to keep him around and out of the crosshairs of demon hunters. Already, he wasn't complaining at his non-human drink.

The sun was rising over the horizon, the curtains brightening as the darkness faded. She could hear the team up and about, none acknowledging the day ahead.

Poking his head in the fridge, Blayk asked, "So Bennett can walk in the day, huh?"

Adair nodded, filling up a mug for Bennett as she heard him coming up the steps. "You didn't know?"

He shook his head. "Nope. And Calloway doesn't either."

Reaching the top step, Bennett's short hair was deliciously tousled from the shower. Dressed in black cargos, athletic shirt and sturdy boots, he was primed for the mission. The corners of his lips turned up as she brought him a mug, more blood than coffee, knowing he'd need the extra fuel today.

He slipped his arm around her and pulled her against him, nuzzling his rough beard against her neck as he stole a kiss over the pulse point of her neck. Releasing her only to make room for the others, he splayed his hand around her middle. Bennett asked, "I read and re-read that prophecy in the book we found at Cambria's. There is nothing about what I can and can't do."

Phone to his ear, Ryan came in, dressed to kill like the rest of them were. "No one thinks you're abandoning them... Yes, I promise I will get you and bring you here if we need you..." He winked and made his way for the coffee pot in the cramped galley. Finally, he ended the call and scooped a few dozen eggs from the fridge while Lana ripped open some packages of bacon.

Bennett said, "Quinn hates missing out."

Ryan nodded. "She's doing better than I thought, but my mom's there in case she's needed in a hurry. We've already got a fricking stockpile of pumped milk in the freezer for emergencies."

Adair leaned into Bennett. "She's a good mom."

Leaping back when the bacon spat, Lana shoved her burnt fingertip in her mouth before shaking it off. "Crazy woman, that's what she is. But, well, Skye's pretty worth it, so we can go without her this time." She glanced to Blayk and winked, "Besides, we've got this guy to take her place."

Cringing, Blayk snagged a piece of undercooked bacon from the pan and wolfed it down. "Hell no. I mean, I'll be happy to take down Calloway, but don't ever imply I'm even close to a hunter." He shivered in disgust.

Bodie came in behind Astrid, rubbing a hand over the back of his neck and grinning as he said, "Famous last words."

They ate breakfast in peace, teasing and joking like today was going to be like any other. Although, Adair had to laugh, she supposed it was for them.

Keeping to the shadows with Adair while the others loaded up the boats, Blayk reappeared from the common area where he'd crashed on the sofa last night, carting the clanking bag he'd carted from Paris. "Bennett."

"Yeah?" Bennett answered as he strolled into the common area after loading up the boats.

Blayk pulled a dented shield from the bag and passed it to him. Without a word, his gaze darkened as Bennett accepted it.

Strapping it onto his arm like it belonged there, Bennett's movements were slow, hesitant, as he accepted it back. Cheeks heavy, the corner of his mouth quirked up in a curious smile. "I thought it had been lost in the fight."

Blayk nodded. "Can't say why I took it. Souvenir or something." He cleared his throat and moved down the hall, keeping to the shadows.

A pit of worry brewing in her gut, Adair hollered to him, "Be careful, okay?"

Blayk saluted. "Back at you. Stay out of sight." Taking a long inhale, he grabbed the door and sprinted out to his boat, immediately ducking out of the light.

She turned back to Bennett and watched while he tested out the shield and strapped his sword to his back. His gaze finally sweeping up to hers, he grinned. Hooking his free hand in her belt, he tugged her close and enfolded her into his arms, his shield blocking any imaginary foes that threatened behind her. Pressing his lips to hers, he lingered, savoring. Heat licking through her veins, she melted into him.

Releasing her, he rested his forehead against hers. "Not going to ask me to be careful?"

She snorted. "No."

"What?" he teased, yanking her tighter against him.

"I would hate for you to have to lie to me," she taunted.

Nipping at her lip, he grinned. "Never."

Framing his face with her hands, she met his gaze, shared his smile, and kissed him again. "But I will ask you to please try to come back to me."

"Always," he said, deepening the kiss.

Ending it long before she was ready, he stepped back, flashed her a wink, then hopped in the boat with Blayk. Studying his movements, his swiftness, his strength, his absolute lack of fear, she watched him duck out of sight while Ryan fired up the engine and pulled away.

The rest of the team piled into the other boat, keeping a clear path for her. Moving swiftly through the light, she felt the golden burn singe her skin, goosebumps prickling in response. With a swift hop over the water, she landed in the boat and dove into the cabin, out of sight. In the distance, Bennett, Blayk and Ryan's boat was already fading from sight, the penetrating sun blinding her from watching through the narrow window.

At the driver's seat of her boat, Astrid stood with Bodie as they whispered private affection to each other. Envy tugged at Adair as she thought of how many times Bennett had looked at her with his rich chocolaty eyes, trailed his lips along her collarbone, or said the words he knew she'd never say in return, not worrying that he'd never hear them back. Vann rechecked their weapons, his focus unshakable. Lana leaned back into the seat and absorbed the moment, her hair whipping about in the wind.

"Think Calloway will wait for me to reach Tromos, or he will want to nip at my heels every step of the way?" Bennett asked as he peered through the porthole, while Ryan drove the boat through the rocky graveyard after hours of navigating the area, checking for spies.

The pristine white beach the customs agent had described came into view, exactly the location his father had pinpointed. Damn, this would be a great spot to take Adair, bring a picnic, make love on the warm sand. Just the two of them. In the moonlight, of course. Well, and if it weren't the doorway to Tromos. And if Calloway weren't lurking about somewhere.

Answering from his seat at the microscopic galley table, Blayk shrugged. "I've never known him to be patient, so he won't stay in the shadows for long." Pausing, he glared out the tinted window and said, "But he also will want to save his own hide, so he'll keep his distance if there is any potential risk to life or limb."

Bracing his gait as they pulled onto the beach, Bennett smirked. "Which is why he put you in charge of changing me."

"It's a dangerous business, and he's far too chickenshit to change anyone himself. Not saying I didn't mind the task. I mean, there's an inherent thrill in the risk of it, but I got pretty good at it, thanks to his cowardice."

"Pegged you as the sidekick, huh?"

Huffing a derisive laugh under his breath, Blayk said, "He came back from his journey of self-discovery with an even bigger ego than before, plus a grossly distorted reality. He'd like to think of us as Batman and Robin, but I look a hell of a lot better in black, and he is absolutely the yellow tights guy."

After beaching the boat on the sand, Ryan knocked on the door to the cabin.

Bennett scanned the horizon while Blayk checked the rocks. Voice at a graveled whisper, Blayk said, "He'll want to ensure you're past the point of no return before he shows his face. And when you least expect him. I don't know what's in that prophecy, but he's afraid of you."

"And when he realizes you're not where you're supposed to be?"

"I can't wait to see the look on his face. Narcissistic asshole." Blayk ducked back out of the way, tossing a pillow onto the bed and pulling out a book.

Bennett swung open the door and booked it to the far overhang as if the sun nipped at his heels, in case Calloway was already watching.

Deep in the shadow, the overhang was more of a shallow cave. Bennett traced his hands over the wall. Like an inverse lava dome. Cool under his hand, the rock was completely unaffected by ambient temperature.

Ryan jogged up behind and scanned for signs of an entrance. "Nothing out of the ordinary."

Nodding, Bennett followed the rings to the center where the magma had heated and cooled, the weakness causing sloughing. But reversed from what it should be. One of the curves was more jagged. His finger pricked on a shell. "Huh," he mumbled out loud.

"What?" Ryan came over to look. "Cool. Fossil."

"This is volcanic rock. This fossil shouldn't be here."

"Um, what?" Hands on his hips, Ryan stepped back and squinted.

"My dad's a geologist as old as the rocks he studies, and eternally a verbose educator. If you ever want to hear about how much the fossil record of eroding Cenozoic turbidites can teach us about ancient sea life, I have the entire lecture memorized."

"I'll call you next time I can't sleep."

"Call my dad; you'll make his year." Stepping back, staying inside the shadow, Bennett searched for more inconsistencies. At the edge of the curves, another layer of sandy, rippled rocks, and a cluster of fossilized oysters jutted out. "Hey, this did used to be a river, well, an estuary, and not a natural one."

As he manipulated a prominent cluster of oysters, the ground beneath them quaked. Rattling so heavy he had to clench his jaw, or his teeth would vibrate out of his skull, the circle in the center of the rock wall involuted, rock grinding against rock as it twisted in on itself until an opening formed, just big enough to crawl through.

Inhaling as he stared into the midnight blackness, the wintry breeze chilled his skin. Turning, he nodded to Ryan. "You're on lookout."

At his side, Ryan pressed his hand to the edge of the doorway. "Hell no. You're not doing this alone."

"Designed for me, remember? Chances are pretty damn good there are traps in there that you won't be able to survive."

"Probably. How about I go in as far as I can, and I'll turn back if things get dicey?"

Bennett's gut clenched as he imagined the consequences. "I know I've fucked up enough, going out on my own. Hell, you know I hate admitting it, but this prophecy is why. I'm fated to go alone."

Scrunching his hand in his hair, Ryan cussed and stepped back. His fists balled at his sides and he paced up and down the beach before returning. "I can't pull through the veil, so close to a demon, or he may sense something and try to follow. You go in there, and you need help? I have to go after you the old-fashioned way."

"I know. I swear, I'll call for you if I need help."

"Even a damn paper-cut."

"If I stub my toe, I'll cry for you to come kiss the booboo."

"Jackass," Ryan ribbed and stepped back. "Hang on," he said as he disappeared into the boat. A few seconds later, he returned with a spare line. "Here."

Bennett shrugged and adjusted his sword and shield on his back. "I'm not stupid though. I'll come get you before waking Tromos."

Checking his watch, Ryan scowled. "You'd better. If you're not out by dawn, I'm coming after you."

"See you in the morning." Ducking into the opening, he crawled over the subzero rock into the darkness.

Challenge number one, apparently. Few could resist such frigid temperatures. Ice prickling into his fingertips, he grimaced; the cold wasn't exactly pleasant.

As if passing into space, the air was thin, the cave endlessly black. Pausing as the light from the entrance waned, he inhaled slow and steady. The scent of rust tickled his nares. A dim light glowed in the distance.

Crawling faster, the ground beneath him growing colder the deeper he drew, threatening to turn him into a popsicle, he followed the tunnel, hoping for a break while his fingers still had adequate circulation.

The ground beneath his hand disappeared. Jolting back, he crawled a few paces back into the tunnel, but the ice was so damn cold, his skin blistered.

He moved on, no fucking clue if this was some leap of faith or a fool's trap.

Either way, he didn't have a choice, needing to move before he froze solid. Launching into the unknown, he hoped to hell he landed on his feet.

18

Hiding in the cabin of a motorboat wasn't Adair's idea of a good time. Nor was pulling on a lava-red wig and disguising herself as Quinn. But Calloway had to believe she was still Blayk's captive, at least until Bennett took the upper hand.

The team seemed to be enjoying themselves. Astrid drove the boat around the edges of the caldera, scanning the hillsides. The sun was still high in the sky, so there was no way they would see a sign of Calloway yet. They'd stopped to check out a few boats anchored around the edges, but nothing appeared out of the ordinary.

They drove to dock after dock, inquiring about Calloway's whereabouts. Nothing. It was like he wasn't even in town yet.

Which she absolutely knew wasn't true. Blayk would make the call soon, and she needed to be there when he did, or Calloway would know something was up.

Ryan had called to check in a few times. No sign of Calloway anywhere near the entrance. Nor anything from Bennett. He'd gone inside hours ago.

After five hundred years, Adair assumed she'd have some measure of patience. Apparently, she didn't.

Knuckles rapped gently on her door. Giving her a second to get out of the way, Vann popped in and closed the door behind him. "You hanging in there okay?"

Doing a double take, Adair realized she had to strain to read him, as his pulse, his posture, showed that he was remarkably calm considering the stakes. "Calloway?"

"Rumor has it, there's a big party of night owls holed up in a beach house around the bend. Quinn found the lead following local police reports. No one's gone missing, but a few calls have gone out over some tourists having too good of a time," his deep voice rumbled, the lilt of amusement mirroring Bennett's enjoyment of walking into the middle of the fight.

"How can you be sure it's Calloway?"

"Just a hunch."

"You demon hunters and your hunches. Any word about Bennett yet?"

Expression grim, he shook his head.

Grabbing a sword that probably weighed as much as she did, Vann slipped back out to keep watch. Lana strapped a war axe to her back, Astrid strapped on a pair of streamlined swords that moved with her.

Adair grinned at Bodie from her shadowed corner as he steered them through the moored boats while the others geared up. He shrugged and glanced down at her. "Ever seen a werewolf change?"

She shook her head.

"Hope you're not shy." He flashed a wink, then stripped off his shirt.

Lana strapped a few throwing knives in her boots. "What he means is, the clothes don't shift with him. Honestly, my favorite is when he changes back from the wolf to the man and has to find his clothes." She flashed a wink at him.

With a shrug, Bodie said, "Not much privacy on the ranch, but with these guys? Even less."

Vann pulled out a pair of daggers from his box of pointy things. "I didn't see that you brought any weapons?"

She accepted the simple leather and steel knives and strapped them to her belt. "Thanks. These are perfect."

In the distance, the sun cast an orange glow over the horizon, a dark haze blocking its final glow from the sky. About damn time.

An expansive home came into view as they docked. White adobe surrounded by greener than green shrubs and a stone patio overlooking the ocean. Not a soul out yet, and the windows were all darkened. Astrid pulled the boat into a cove out of sight.

"I'll hang out here," Adair said as she leaned against the doorway, willing the sun to set faster, or for the fight to come to her. Although, as soon as she could be on the move, so would Calloway. "Wait," she hissed before they moved out. Something wasn't right. The wind was intense, but she caught a whiff of dozens of vampires on a waft from the direction of the house.

Lana turned and shrugged. "It's a trap. We know."

"And you're going in anyway? Are you all as crazy as Bennett?"

"Sometimes you need to spring the trap to root it out. Calloway might be in there, or maybe not. But we need to root out those that would follow in his plan."

Voice heavy, Vann added, "And any that would stand with Tromos, should we fail to end him."

Adair nodded and backed into the shadows. She dropped to the bench and waited for the troops to invade. They were a force. Slicing, shredding, they moved through the vampires as they raided the house, cleaning up Calloway's mess. And, like Bennett, they didn't hinge their decisions on whether or not they succeeded. Failure wasn't an option. How different from a vampire, that would sooner run and hide than risk their immortality.

Watching, she waited. Not patiently, just waited. Her knee rattled, her jaw clenched, and she knew she dug the notch between her eyebrows deeper. And the last film of raw daylight finally faded.

As evening took over, she rose from the bow. The hunters had busted in like a SWAT team, the scent of vampire blood heavy on the air. Trap or not, the hunters didn't seem slowed by the numbers and shadows set starkly against them, thus proving again that vampire immortality didn't extend past a run-in with demon hunters, no matter their skill or the foolproofness of their plan.

Out of the corner of her eye, she saw a familiar face sticking to the shadows and ducking into the boathouse. Smirking, Adair moved into the dusky light, strolling confidently like a hunter on the prowl, hair from her lava-red wig sticking out from her hood, presumably Quinn to maintain her apparent hostage status. She had another two hours until Blayk's daily check in.

Startling as she wiggled the rusted key to unlock the boathouse, the vampire about leaped out of her wedge sandals as she scented Adair approaching. The woman from the club. Still slutty, still reeking of Calloway, Milan's sneer turned into a playful grin. As if that covered her fear. Pulse pounding through her carotids, breath coming fast, she placed her hands on her hips and leaned against the wall casually. "Look what the cat dragged in. Regretting which side you chose?"

Kicking down the boathouse door, Adair shoved the other woman inside. Milan stumbled over her impractical heels. "Pardon?"

Flipping her beachy-curled hair out of her face as she rose back to her mile-high heels and adjusted her matching red leather purse, the vampire was... annoying. "Outnumbered. Outmatched. When Tromos awakens, do you really want to be flattened under his boot?"

"Okay, we can play this game. Or you can save us both the time and point me to Calloway. As you're clearly either on your way to join him, or running to save your own skin." Adair looked her up and down. "Judging by the outfit, I'd say the latter."

"You can't have him back."

Stepping up, Adair stood disgustingly close to the annoying bitch. A solid four inches shorter, the woman glared up.

Adair leaned down to whisper, her mouth a breath away. "Calloway will drop you as fast as he did Sonra, and you know what happened to her."

Eyes darting side to side, the slut muttered, "At least he'll avenge me like he did her."

"Call it what you like. It makes him feel bigger to pretend he does any of this out of love. For Sonra, for me. But Calloway doesn't understand the concept. When he rules this realm, do you really think he'll pick *you* to stand by his side? The coward that hid from the fight, waiting for him to claim you once it was safe for your little preciousness to come out to play?" Doubt radiating off the poor thing, Adair pushed on, "Tell me, in the last few hundred years, has he figured out how to make a woman feel respected? Or to send you straight to heaven with his touch? Or does he still hold his sexist beliefs and think women should leave the toilet seat up?"

Milan's gaze dropped, her jaw pushing forward as she doubted.

"I mean, seriously. Can't we all just close the toilet seat lid out of respect for each other? No one wants to see inside the toilet when brushing their teeth."

Honey eyes rising and suddenly watery clear, Milan growled, "I know what you're trying to do. It won't work."

"If you think our plan revolved around you giving up Calloway's location, you're a bigger fool than I thought. But as I have found you running away with your tail between your legs, I thought it worth asking. I will find him and I will finish him, as I should have done centuries ago. Right now, the man I love is fighting for *all* of us. But I won't stand by and watch him risk himself alone. Last chance. Tell me where Calloway is, or I'll see if you can survive a knife to the jugular like he did."

Speech rapid as she scooted away, she squealed and pulled her purse tighter against her. "Calloway trusts me alone with his secrets. He's been studying the entrance for years; he has every turn inside the labyrinth memorized. He will wait until Bennett is at death's door and sweep in from behind. The final challenge isn't meant to be won, only to awaken. And when Calloway meets Tromos, he will guide him to the surface where they will set fire to this earth."

Urgency building, imagining Bennett already struggling, fighting a fight he wouldn't win, Adair slammed her fist into Milan's smug face and grabbed her purse as she hit the ground.

TEETERING ON THE LEDGE, his shoulders aching as he strained to hang on, Bennett's vision came into focus in the midnight blackness of the cave. Gripping his fingertips into the slick granite, he heaved himself up and over the edge, collapsing flat on his back. Letting out a groan, he rubbed his hands over his face. Gauntlet was right. What kind of monster built this absurdity?

After the first pit he'd fallen into, he'd crawled back far enough to holler to Ryan to bring more rope for a fun day of fricking spelunking. He'd tried to clear the path however he could for the team to follow.

Moving through the cavern, an amber glow like waning streetlights lit the way, as the darkness had otherwise become so thick that not even a vampire would have been able to make out the path.

The ledge narrowed to no thicker than a thumb. Pinning himself to the wall, he edged along the flimsy outcrop, one slip away from an infinite fall.

A whiff of rotting vampire struck him as the wind coursed through the pit. Okay, not infinite. And he wasn't the first one in here. Calloway must have convinced a few idiots to try the fool's errand before realizing he needed a... whatever Bennett was.

At long fucking last, he felt an opening in the wall and hooked into an arched hallway. The ground steady for a moment, he stretched his neck and took a swig of blood from his water bottle. After a few hundred meters, the path widened and he entered another poorly lit, echoing, ominous cavern, this one offering a new challenge.

Great. Even better. Parkour was way more Vann's thing than his. Ahead awaited twenty, maybe thirty narrow pillars of doom in a non-forward path to relative safety. On the other side, a jagged arched doorway, this one leading into another tunnel.

Here goes nothing. Bennett hopped to the first.

As if it hovered above the ground in timid defiance of gravity, the pillar descended in a lethargic plunge under his added weight. Fuck, Bennett quickly assessed the layout and leapt to the next.

He missed the landing and slid off, gripping the sinking rock with his fingertips.

Hauling ass to get to his feet, he propelled to the next before the pillar sank any further.

Moving fast, not pausing for more than a second, he leaped from stone to stone, each pillar jutting askew from the force of his leap.

The last jump was a flipping monster; he dove across and grasped the ledge with his fingertips, dangling one-handed like a thrill-seeking climber. He may not mind diving headfirst into the fight, but that's when he was guaranteed the relief of landing a few punches. This... danger for the sake of the adrenaline rush was less gratifying.

Swinging up, he grabbed hold with his other hand and pulled himself to the ledge and into the hall. May as well add a gigantic boulder rushing down the tunnel, or maybe some guillotines dropping from the ceiling to slice through him. Seriously, this place was like something out of Indiana Jones. A fingerprint reader or blood test would have been a lot simpler.

At the end of the hall, a solid obsidian boulder blocked the doorway. Bracing himself on one side, he pushed. Nothing. Sucking in a lungful of air, he tried again. Took every scrap of muscle from head to toe. His jaw gritted tight as if every part of him was needed. Grinding, stone against stone, it shifted. Heaving with the last bit of strength he had, he shoved it out of the way.

Let's see a vampire try that. Or, hell, even an ordinary demon hunter. Yeah, fate had been grooming *him* for precisely this mission. Dusting off his hands, he admired his handiwork while suppressing the urge to drop to his ass and take a break.

Wiping a sheen of sweat from his brow, Bennett looked ahead to the next challenge. Might have to design something like this in his warehouse, if Calloway's minions hadn't trashed the place. Fuck; he'd have to clear out of the Seattle area, Adair too, in case some of Calloway's followers slipped through both his mother's and his own team's attacks today. Dammit, dead or alive, preferably dead, Calloway was going to haunt him long after today.

At the end of the next series of bends, a fork. Okay. Great. Pulling a knife from his boot, he etched an arrow to the left to guide the team.

After a fucking hour of twists and turns, he was utterly convinced that this was the wrong path. Dammit. He ran back the way he'd come, not caring that his lungs were burning from a long night and day of maximum exertion. When this was over, he was crashing at his place in BC. Hopefully Adair would want to join him, at least for a vacation, and they could relax in the hot tub for a month.

Finding his way back to the first fork, he stopped. Closing his eyes, he inhaled slowly, sensing every nuance on the air. Dumbass; he'd been thinking like a hunter again. To the right, he caught the subtle scent of blood. Centuries old, not human, not vampire, but unmistakable.

Rubbing out the first mark, he drew a new arrow to the right.

A few more forks, a few more arrows etched into the rock, and he reached another door.

No scent to pick up. Shoving with all the force he could muster, he tried to open it demon-hunter style, but no luck.

He stepped back and scanned the doorway, the surrounding walls. Markings.

Fuck, this was Astrid's area of expertise. He was no code-breaker.

The markings didn't match any runes or ancient language he could recognize. He was about to turn back, accepting he had gone as far as he could, when he looked up and saw a sunshine carved into the ceiling.

He stepped back and matched the markings on the wall to the pattern on the ceiling. Pushing on the first symbol, the rock warm as a bath, it depressed and locked into place.

Nailed it. In sequence to match the sun, he finished the pattern.

Grinding over stone floor that screeched under its weight, the squealing gears from an ancient pulley system, the door edged open.

Bennett shielded his eyes as the light in the next cavern was so bright he couldn't see.

Condensing in an instant, the light tightened. Fast as a lightning blast, a ball of pure, blinding, blazing sunlight burst through the doorway.

Raising his shield, he tried to protect himself from the explosion.

Like a rocket, the rush of luminous energy sent him flying back.

Crashing against the wall behind him, his skull cracked against the solid stone.

Head throbbing, he reached back and felt blood oozing from a head wound.

He struggled to stand, tried to move, to see... to do *anything*, but his eyelids fluttered closed, too heavy to stay open, and a wave of nausea wafted over his stomach. Turning, he wretched until his gut ached with emptiness.

Consciousness fluttered out of reach.

19

JARRING FORWARD, ADAIR'S HEAD struck the corner of the windshield as they landed hard against the beach next to the other boat. Grabbing her forehead, she didn't pause, but leaped out. Astrid shoved off the engine, apologizing for the crappy landing, but equally rushed to get to Bennett.

Ryan came rushing out from the overhang. "Please tell me you took care of Calloway."

Adair checked her lava-red wig hadn't budged, hoping Calloway believed she was Quinn. "We got most of his followers, but he's waiting. Probably watching right now." She hoped to hell he was far enough away that he would mistake her for Quinn. "He won't show his face until... until the last minute."

Leaning in, Ryan whispered, "Your friend has fielded a few calls, but Calloway's getting suspicious."

Leaving the cave entrance, she stalked into the other boat and tore open the door to the bow. Blayk sat comfortably on the sofa, feet up, reading a piece of fluff fiction. He flashed her a one-sided smile and set his book down. "Have a nice day at work, dear?"

She rolled her eyes. "Let's get this over with. When was your last call?"

Lowering his feet to the ground, Blayk pulled out his phone and checked the time. "I'm to call hourly until it's over. If he doesn't answer, it's because he's gone in. Gotta say, I do a damn good impression of you, but I think I miss the nuances of your huffiness."

"I'm not huffy."

"Sure. Anyway, we've got another fifteen before I'm due to check in."

She grabbed his phone and hit redial. Three rings in, Calloway's smug voice slimed through the speaker. "You're early. You know I've got bigger priorities than your–"

"I should have finished you off when I had the chance," she snarked back.

"There she is. With more to say than pathetic whimpering. Tell me, how does it feel, having all of your friends turn against you?"

"You're a monster."

Blayk folded his arms over his chest and raised an eyebrow.

"What a delight to see you so improved from our prior calls. Much more like you."

"If you run into any of Bennett's friends, let them know I get to be the one to finish you off."

"Tromos will take care of your friends before they get the chance."

"How will you get past them?"

"Tromos will be awfully hungry when he wakes. Why would I approach a hungry demon myself, when he can feast on an entire team of hunters?"

"You'd better watch your back. If Bennett doesn't make it out of that cave alive, I'm coming after you."

Blayk accepted the phone as she handed it over and talked over Calloway's clever retort. "Yeah, whatever. You do what you have to do. I'm done listening to her whining. Bennett's probably already at Tromos anyway. I'm feeding her some human to see if I can find the old Adair in there somewhere."

Laughing delightedly, Calloway said, "Excellent plan. Our new world could use a devious brain like hers."

"Good luck with your fight and everything." Blayk smirked and leaned back in his seat, adding, "Snap a few pics of those nasty hunters as they die." Before Calloway could respond, he ended the call. "It's done."

"Off to the quiet life again?"

"Guess so."

Aching as if she were losing him again, Adair said, "See you around." She tossed him the red leather purse.

"Not my style."

"Mine either. Some interesting reading anyway."

Vann and Ryan waited outside the entrance, armed to the teeth and loaded with ropes and flashlights.

"Ready?" Vann asked.

She nodded. "We need to get to Bennett. The last door..."

Ryan's expression dropped. "I'll go. He promised to leave a trail."

"You still haven't heard from him?"

Ryan murmured, "No. I promised I would wait until sunrise. I'm not waiting any longer." Ryan motioned to the cave entrance. "Be careful, it's cold."

She held her hand over the cave walls, recoiling at the instant frostbite. "I'll say. A human would freeze solid like being coated with liquid nitrogen."

The rest of the team waited inside, Lana's flashlight illuminating the room, ricocheting off the walls as if daylight were upon them.

Seeing her flinch as the light reflected so intensely, brighter than the sun off the cavern walls, Lana flicked it off. The light lingered unnaturally, gradually fading as they crossed into a tunnel and an amber glow from afar guided them further in.

She sniffed the air as they moved deeper in. "Damn you demon hunters and your tricky lack of scent; I can't find a trace of Bennett."

Bodie stood at her side, "Demon hunter scent is subtle and fleeting. I'm getting better at tracking them, but I can't pick him up either."

Coming up behind them, Ryan said, "He's been in nearly eighteen hours."

Something foul held stagnant and dusty in the air. She couldn't say what, but it wasn't friendly. "I'll see you guys at the end."

Astrid rested her hand on her shoulder. "Go get him. But be careful."

Pausing for a second, Adair shook her head as she took off. "Not this time."

The path was crazy. Bennett had left clues along the way, had left doors open that he'd unlocked with brains and brawn. The first step of a parkour course was pushed down, making the rest nearly unreachable, the others jagged, pushed away as he must have crossed. Leaping from pillar to pillar, she followed his path.

Now and again, she heard an echo of the team following far behind, but she didn't slow. Aching in the pit of her stomach, fluttering under her chest, she knew Bennett was running out of time.

BENNETT HAD SUFFERED PRECISELY one hangover in his lifetime. A few nights before the big ceremony, one of his last nights before his demon blood activated in his veins, he got trashed. All alone. Experimenting with his dad's scotch.

His head had throbbed, his brain had swelled and pummeled against the inside of his skull. The thirst had been unquenchable.

That was nothing compared to the concussion raging in his head now. Sitting on the stone floor, head in his hands, he tried to clear his vision. To shake his thoughts back on track. But it hurt too fucking bad to move. His external wounds had healed, but his brain was a long way off.

Not that he wanted anything on his fragile stomach, but he needed to feed if he was going to heal. Risking reaching for his supplies, he found the aluminum bottle of blood shattered, its contents caked into the floor.

Bracing his hands on the ground, he rose to his knees, righting himself as he teetered, finally rising to his feet. Wobbly as a newborn foal, he rocked to the side and his shoulder slammed into the wall.

One hundred percent pure sunshine. Hotter than an August wedding, brighter than the midday sun reflecting off a glacier. The blast would have fried a vampire on sight. How the hell had they stored up a sun bomb?

Staggering one foot in front of the other, he advanced down the hall. The light was dim now, thank fuck, nothing more than the eerie orange glow that had illuminated his path now and again. Crossing through the archway, he moved into a massive cavern.

In the center, a small pedestal stood fresh and cool like a drinking fountain, gently illuminated with a beckoning light overhead. Bracing his hands on the sides before he toppled over, Bennett inhaled and found the scent coppery crisp, tempting him with everything he needed to soothe the burning hollow in his gut. The scent was irresistible, like a steak grilled exactly right after a long week in the field.

Under the surface was pure menace. Evil of the darkest kind. Like an aged wine from the finest grapes, untouched, untarnished, promising to bite him back.

A drenching sweat coated his pores. His throat was desiccated like he'd swallowed a bucket of sawdust. His hands trembled, the quake of withdrawal sucking him dry.

Glaring at the dark liquid, he clenched his jaw, knowing what he had to do.

Or not do.

Fuck, he preferred the treacherous parkour or the Tarzan leaps, or even the rocket-propelled sun bomb to this. As if that hadn't been enough to prove he was both vampire and hunter.

The craving lurched in his gut, like hitting the brick wall of indecision. Didn't matter if the challenge was to resist... he couldn't refuse the drink any more than he could have sat at home while the rest of the team took on Tromos. Desperate, knowing he was too far gone with hunger, he dipped his hands into the fountain.

Perfectly warmed, viscous blood trailed down his cupped hands, trickled out of the corner of his mouth, and down his chin as he consumed.

Fire brewing in his belly, he stumbled back. Uselessly blinking away the fatigue that washed over him like a tsunami, he dropped to the ground. Underneath him, the ground shook, vibrating his aching skull.

A PEACEFUL DAPPLING OF rain tapped in the distance, echoing down the granite halls, but the floor underneath her was bone dry. The walls were scorched, as if a wildfire had rocketed through here, two, maybe three hours ago. No charred body. He'd made it this far.

As she moved along the burnt hall, she caught the scent of blood. Glancing down, she found his supplies scattered across the floor.

Another earthquake shifted under her feet, rattling the cave. She braced her hand against the wall to stay on her feet. And then it eased again.

Tromos was stirring.

Looking ahead, she saw an amber glow casting shadows in a cavern. As she neared, she saw an illuminated vessel. Fat drops of rain fell from the domed ceiling. Beneath...

Bennett.

Another quake sent rocks dropping from the ceiling. She ran to reach him, to drag him to safety, but the opening to the cavern collapsed before she could reach it.

Utter darkness. Silence as the dust settled.

The boulders covering the entrance were too heavy to even budge as she strained to clear the path. He was unreachable.

Closing her eyes, she inhaled slow and steady. The ominous scent singed her nares, but behind her, another, familiar, evil scent.

Calloway.

In the distance, she could hear the team progressing through the labyrinth, closing in and running full-out since the quake. Scraping her knife into the ground, she signaled Bennett's location. Only the hunters would be strong enough to reach him now.

Making her way back into the maze, she followed the path from the map. If Calloway reached Tromos, if Milan was right, he could transport him to the surface before the team could stop them.

Turning fast, she rounded another bend.

Skidding to a halt, she stared ahead.

Calloway sauntered toward her. He clapped his hands together, his smile wide and toothy. "You're not where you're supposed to be. I guess I have some housekeeping to do. But that can wait. I should thank you."

"Be careful, you may get crushed under the weight of that massive ego. Are you thanking me for escaping, or for finding you?"

"I suppose in part, for finding such an ideal hunter for me. Apparently, your selfless lover was bent on risking himself even without bait. Unexpected. I had known this one to be foolishly noble, but I had not anticipated he would be so arrogant." A small tremor shook the room. Calloway smiled wider. "And it appears he has succeeded. Tromos is rising from his slumber."

"And Bennett will kill him before you can reach him."

"Slim chance. According to the prophecy, he is already dead."

An aching hollow filled her chest. Bennett had been lying there, lifeless, out of reach, with the scent of Tromos' blood radiating off him. His cheeks had been flushed with fever. Not dead, but on his way. Standing straight, she cocked out her hip and flicked her tongue over her sharp canine. "Sure about that?"

He glanced down the hall behind her. "If you will excuse me, I have work to do."

"Can't you hear? They will reach him soon."

"I had hoped at least a few would be taken care of at the house. No matter. Tromos will walk over them as he did so many before the demon hunters imprisoned him." Calloway shrugged carelessly.

"Vampires imprisoned him," Adair fired back.

A familiar voice vibrated down the hall. Strutting in like he owned the place, fearless as usual, Blayk grinned. "Actually, they worked together."

Calloway's head turned sharply toward him. "You were supposed to bleed her the moment he entered the cave." Under his breath, Calloway muttered, "Can't trust anyone these days."

"Oops." Blayk shrugged. "I guess I'm not very obedient."

RUMBLING BENEATH HIM, THE cavern threatened to collapse around him. Eyes slamming open, Bennett rolled out of the way as a chunk of rock fell from the ceiling. Heat blazed under his skin, rapidly cooling under heavy beads of rain that fell from the ceiling.

Licking his lips, he tasted seawater.

Roaring, stomping... not an earthquake.

How long had he been out? The fever should have swallowed him, but he'd survived far worse.

He felt... different was an understatement.

Fight after fight. Evisceration. The surge of enhanced power from his demon ancestor and the thrill of an impossible victory. Heartache. Training for days on end until his knuckles bled and he could feel something. Face-to-face with his own end, again. Vampire blood infusing him with sharpened senses and speed. All had built up to this moment.

This? This was something else entirely. Like the vampire, hunter, and human inside him fused into one. He rose to his feet and tensed his fists, his arms, the speed of the vampire no longer awkward in the hands of a hunter, the heart of a human no longer muted.

Senses on full alert, as if he could slow the scene with his mind, he watched a beast rising from a stony grave. Tromos was pure demon. Humanoid like Ryan's demon-king father, yet his fangs were massive, his eyes pale as the moon. And he was... huge, probably had a solid five hundred pounds on Bennett.

Snarling, he seemed to smile, but it was tough to tell, as his over-sized canines were threatening no matter his expression. With the raspy breath of one that hadn't spoken in centuries, Tromos growled at Bennett, his heavy brow furrowed in confusion as Bennett lifted his shield and tightened it down. "Impossible... You shouldn't exist. Shouldn't have... survived."

The corner of his lips rising, Bennett shrugged. "You're telling me." Drawing his sword, he waited, knowing he needed to draw this out. "So you speak? I figured you were one of those rage-spewing demons that didn't care for the humans you trampled."

"A predator must know his quarry. I speak in all the whiny tongues of this realm."

"Impressive." Bennett nodded. Too bad that little trait wasn't passed in his demon blood.

On the other side of the rock pile that had sealed him in, he heard the muffled sounds of his team making their way to him. Heat boiled behind his eyes, feeling their desperation to get to him, and knowing he couldn't do this without them. Clearing his throat, he looked to Tromos. "Fascinating though, isn't it? I've spent my life dreaming of embodying some great prophecy. Until it was the last thing I wanted."

Tromos took a step toward him, the ground shuddering under his weight.

"I'll bet you were looking forward to this day, too. The day you rise to power." Rolling his shoulders, Bennett stood tall. "I hate to break it to you, as I know you've been waiting a long time for this moment, but I was not designed simply to wake you. I've waited my whole life to destroy you."

Stomping his foot, Tromos roared and sent an impaling stalactite tumbling from the ceiling. Bennett held his ground, shifting his shoulder an inch to dodge it.

Snarling, Tromos picked up a boulder bigger than his head and hurled it at Bennett.

Raising his shield with a speed that would impress Adair, the boulder shattered against the steel and sent shrapnel flying off in every direction.

Tromos rumbled, "But you are also a puny human. Weak. Alone. Doomed."

"Nothing new." He shrugged. Ears perking up, Bennett heard his team drawing closer. Through the thinning rubble, he could scent Bodie, could hear Astrid insisting that Bennett couldn't think he was alone, not even for a moment. "Hasn't stopped me so far."

"You were to hunger as I do."

"Funny thing. I do hunger. Fuck, I'd give about anything to taste a human, to savor until my belly was full. But I am also a stubborn son-of-a-bitch and nothing like *you*."

"Ah, but you are me. You drank from my vessel, or I would still be incarcerated in slumber."

"Thanks for that, by the way. But I've also had an infusion, so to speak, from the mother of all demon hunters. So, well, the two rather balance out remarkably well."

The earth quaking at his fury, Tromos held out his hands and roared to the ceiling. Rock came crashing down around him. The rain accelerated, as the ceiling separating them from the sea thinned.

Fast despite his size, powerful on long legs, Tromos shook the room as he ran for Bennett.

Anticipating the massive fist before it slammed into his head, Bennett stopped the blow with his shield. The force of it should have sent him flying, but Bennett held strong.

When the next blow came, Bennett juked to the side and drove his sword into Tromos' side.

Spinning, Tromos slammed his fist into Bennett and sent him flying across the room.

20

"You let her go, didn't you?"

"I did. You came back a fucking nutcase." The corner of Blayk's lips quirked up as he added, "Maybe you always were, but it was in a direction that suited me."

The ground shook again, harder this time. The vampire trio flinched as gravel rained from the ceiling, blocking the falling debris.

As it let up, Calloway strolled toward Adair... and Tromos. "If you don't mind, I have work to do."

Adair moved her hand to the hilt of the knife at her hip. To Calloway, she winked.

His smile widened as Adair sprinted at him full speed.

From behind him, Blayk was on the move.

As Calloway drew close, Adair swung her knife and gouged into Calloway's side. Calloway recoiled and turned away from the attack. Blayk anticipated the move and knocked Calloway in the jaw with a blunt fist, sending him back toward Adair. She swung again and sliced across his cheek.

"And you mocked me for training with that blacksmith rather than eating her," she said. With a flourish, she tossed her knife in the air. "Some humans are worth keeping around."

Swinging, slicing, she lashed at Calloway. Matched in speed, but he couldn't anticipate her rhythm and he couldn't get close enough to stop her. In a feeble attempt to back away, Calloway ran into Blayk. Knocking an elbow into Calloway's throat, following with a few martial arts moves that were new since Adair had seen him last, he dropped Calloway to the ground.

Rolling away and leaping back to his feet, Calloway grinned with pure malice, delight and something nastier. Those blows should have at least slowed him, if not left him weeping on the ground.

Adair glared at him, the uncertainty plaguing her. "What have you done to yourself?"

Sneering, he boasted with a puffed-up chest, "Your boyfriend isn't the only one who's been modified. Have you ever tasted a hunter? Invigorating. The hunter I stole the prophecy from? He heals so beautifully. Or, he did until I finished him off this evening. Like he was made simply to feed me and make me stronger."

Hatred boiling in her throat, Adair shook her head. "I should have finished you off all those years ago."

She caught Blayk's eye, and they lashed at Calloway from either side. The trio fought two-on-one, their energy, their speed stirring the air in the maze, the wind they created gusting down the corridors.

Under Blayk's kick, dodging Adair's blade, Calloway ducked and thought himself quite the survivor.

Blayk came up from behind and gripped his hands around Calloway's head.

From the front, throwing her blade, Adair aimed for his belly.

Calloway's expression fell pale as he grasped the embedded dagger, his face overcome with shock. Mouth gaping open, he stumbled.

With a final twist, Blayk snapped his neck and Calloway fell to the ground at his feet.

At the gruesome scene, Adair cringed as she watched blood pouring from the open wound, his head twisted at an awkward angle, an occasional reflexive gag the only sign he wasn't dead yet.

Blayk moved to her side, his expression equally horrified.

Blood oozed from Calloway's mouth as the life drained out of him.

The ground shook again, rocks crumbling from the ceiling. "Come on." Blayk grabbed her hand. Together, they sprinted down the maze as it collapsed behind them.

SLAMMING INTO HIS FACE like a series of pistoning bricks, Tromos pounded on Bennett.

Fucking shit, he roared and drove his sword into Tromos' side. Again and again, but it hardly slowed the beast. One of these days, he'd have to pick Ryan's brain about what sort of creatures walked the demon realm. If he survived that long. He hoped to hell there weren't more of this sort.

Feeling like a damn punching bag, he rolled out of reach to adjust his shield.

And quickly learned where vampires got their speed.

For a big guy, Tromos moved lightning fast. Shield raised high, Bennett blocked the next blow.

A grating crunch rang through the air as a crack ran half the length of his shield.

Diving out of the way, again, Bennett ran for the doorway.

Light emitted through a small crack as the team continued their excavation.

Vann's deep voice resonated through the hollow. "We're almost to you, buddy. Hang in there."

"Sure thing." Bennett cringed, leaping out of the way as Tromos aimed to pummel him again.

This time running straight for the beast, Bennett leapt into the air and slammed his shield into Tromos' thick head and jumped out of the way again.

The smallest of the bunch, Lana hauled over the rubble and heaved a boulder from the entrance and growled, "I thought you agreed to wait for us."

Juking another blow, Bennett ducked and spun, but Tromos was faster, his kick nailing Bennett in the ribs. As he gasped to get a breath of air, flying across the room and crashing against the rock wall, he hollered, "This wasn't my plan." Under his breath, he muttered, "Not that anything ever goes according to plan."

He shook away the vibration in his skull and rose to his feet, lifting his sword again.

Legs trembling from exertion, his fractured ribs scraping against his lungs, he ignored the searing pain and stalked toward Tromos.

"I will rise and rule this realm," Tromos rumbled, thundering toward Bennett with his fist balled and ready to deliver another jaw-crunching blow.

"I know. And I wanted a damn prophecy. Be careful what you wish for," he muttered.

Astrid came diving through as the opening widened, her twin swords already swinging as she ran for Tromos.

Behind her, one by one with a furious vengeance, the team came.

Each taking their place, they encircled Tromos, weapons ready, game faces on.

Lana snarked, a wicked grin teasing at her lips, "Really Bennett? He's hardly even wounded. What have you been doing all this time?"

Bennett rolled his eyes before slicing his sword across Tromos' spine. "Ha ha. Shut up and let's finish this."

Tromos spun, aimed right for Bennett. "You will feel my wrath," he roared.

Before Bennett could snipe back with a pithy retort, Tromos fist slammed into his chest and sent him flying across the room. His head snapped against the rock and the world went dark.

Warm hands cradled his cheeks, fingertips gracing along the curve of his jaw. Adair's crooning voice sent waves of relief through his veins. "Hey," she whispered. "It's going to be a miserably long eternity if you die on me now."

Sandbags coated his limbs as he struggled to rise. His eyelashes fluttered. Her watery blue eyes came into view, her bow-shaped lips turned up in the corners. "I'm not dead yet."

"Then get your ass up. We've got a demon to slay."

"Calloway?"

"Dead."

"Nicely done."

She glanced to the fight behind her. "Now the hard part."

Stumbling to his feet, he took in the scene. His team encircled the big-ass monster, each furious, timing their blows, slowly weakening Tromos. Astrid dove under and sliced into his thigh. As she popped up on the other side, Bodie came from the other direction as the wolf and tore a chunk of muscle from his other leg. Ryan's sword, dark as the demon realm, took a gouge out of his arm. From out of nowhere, Blayk rushed in, hammering Tromos in the ribs with a series of kicks.

Joints aching from his injuries, bruises sprouting in areas he didn't even realize he'd been hit, Bennett rose to his feet and lifted his sword, hobbling toward his team.

At his side, Adair drew one of her knives, took careful aim, and launched it across the room. The blade nailed Tromos in his thick neck. Tromos howled and ripped the thing out, sending it flying back.

Bennett caught the next fist with his busted shield. One swiping while another distracted him, exchanging blows, the team brought him to his knees.

Shoving his blade into Tromos' abdomen, Bennett sliced deep and watched as the demon's guts came spilling out. Revolted, his own gut roiling as he remembered the sensation, Bennett stepped back and almost pitied the creature as his wail shook through the cavern like an avalanche up-slope.

Opening his mouth to bellow his final words, cursing his attackers, Tromos tipped his head back furiously.

From behind him, whizzing past his ear, a dagger embedded dead center into Tromos' throat. Thunder stolen from his breathless roar, Tromos' eyes rolled back in his head, a lifeless choke rattling from his throat as he collapsed to the ground.

Turning, Bennett watched as Adair strolled close. "Sorry if you wanted the last hit. I–"

Steel clanging against stone as Bennett dumped his sword and wrapped his shield arm around her, hauling her against him. "Nice shot. You just wanted to prove you don't need me," he teased.

Her bow lips turning up in a wicked smile, she stole a quick peck before sniping back, "I don't. But I really like having you around."

"Like?" Aching in his chest, Bennett knew this was it. Mission accomplished. She could return to her eternity of safety.

Gaze locked onto his, her cheeks flushed pink. "You don't give up, do you?"

"Never," he whispered, nipping a kiss at her lower lip, trying to hide that his legs were about to give out, his arm so sore he couldn't hold on much longer.

Ready, catching him before he fell, she grinned at him. "I love you Bennett. I may die tomorrow or live a thousand years. But I want every second I can have with you. Marry me?"

He unlatched his shield and let it fall, the broken steel vibrating as it hit the ground. Arms free, he wrapped around her and leaned his forehead against hers. Sore from the fight, every bone in his body aching, he grinned. "I have no idea what it will do to you, you might lose your immortality or–"

"Is that a yes?" She grinned, then cradled her palms around the curve of his jaw and pressed her lips to his.

"Yes. That is a yes." He smiled against her mouth and pulled her tighter against him.

Behind him, Lana cleared her throat.

Bennett turned.

"Think he'll stay dead, or is he more catlike, like vampires?"

Arms entwined around him, Adair exhaled thoughtfully. "Better finish him."

Axe drawn high over her head, Lana let it fall and extricated his head from his body.

Vann stepped closer and scowled at the beast. He pulled out a pack of matches and set Tromos truly and irreversibly ablaze.

Hand linked with Adair's, his aches easing with each step, Bennett strolled out of the cavern with his team.

Epilogue

Night was thick on the air, but sunrise teased at the edges of the horizon.

Hands linked with Bennett's, Adair stood in front of her favorite people, and a few she suspected would soon reach that honor, and said the words she'd withheld for too long. The moonlight reflected off the massive walls of windows of the BC home. At the edge of the world on the rocky cliff high above the thundering ocean, Adair answered, "I do."

Quentin, the very hunter that had caught them together all those years ago, the wedge that unwittingly drove them apart, now stood before them and grinned as he watched his godson take his turn. "And Bennett, do you take Adair, to share your gifts with, to cherish and love, for as long as you both shall live?"

Bennett held her gaze. "I do."

Adair heard her brother's whoop as they were pronounced as married, the cheers of the team showering them with joy. Bennett's parents stood arm in arm, Lizzy's hand over her expanding belly, happily looking on as their son settled down.

Leaned in, Bennett teased his lips over hers. Just out of reach, tormenting her with anticipation, he whispered, "Last chance. I don't know if we'll live forever, or if you'll take on the lifespan of a demon hunter like other spouses."

Grazing her thumb along the curve of his jaw, Adair shrugged, "What fun is forever without a little risk?"

As their lips met, the lightning that zinged between sent shocks of thrill radiating through her veins. Their breath mixing, the kiss deepening, the electricity strengthened as if they were the storm itself. Joined, connected in every way, she poured herself into him.

His pulse quickened as he gave her himself, but he shouldered the burden of it. Life, power, thrill filled her.

As the crowd filtered out, the rush of the exchange settling, she leaned into Bennett and waved at her friends. Blayk flashed her a wink and disappeared into the house. Logan gave Bennett one last threatening look, chased with a smile before dashing in behind Blayk, and Adair heard him offering a place to stay, his wife agreeing and insisting. Lizzy and Jonathan grinned at her, waving and disappearing into the house.

Through the windows, Adair saw the massive wedding cake, the plethora of flowers that Lizzy had insisted were necessary. "Shall we?" Adair asked Bennett as she slipped her hand into his.

Rather than turning into the house, he hooked a right and led her to an outdoor stairway that led to a massive deck overlooking the Pacific.

Hands still linked, at the top of the stairs, Bennett strolled backward and grinned, "You know, demon hunter weddings are a little different from human ceremonies."

Flooded with surprise, Adair looked over the deck. Bennett had made a bed on the ground, with plenty of blankets to keep them warm in the spring night.

Meeting his smile, Adair asked, "And what makes demon hunter weddings different?"

"The reception is for the guests. We can join them if you want. But as the connection isn't complete yet..."

Giggling from deep in her belly, she threw her head back and laughed.

Lacing his arms around her waist, Bennett nuzzled against her neck.

Sliding her hands over his shoulders, she shoved the tuxedo jacket out of the way and ripped open the buttons of his shirt. Overcome with need for him, as if only he could fill the yearning that stormed within her, she craved him like nothing before.

Lips trailing across her collarbone, he slid the white satin strap over her shoulder. The short dress slipped to the floor and pooled at her feet.

Groaning with desire, Bennett scooped her into his arms and laid her in the center of the blankets. Sitting back, he stripped off the last of his clothes. Grin tugging at the corner of her lips like a fish on a hook, she sat back to appreciate the view.

Pure ego, he winked as he joined her on the blankets.

As the night drifted away, she tasted every inch of his skin, and rode the crest of fulfillment as he showed her everything that he'd dreamed for her in their years apart.

No alarms alerted her to seek cover. No burning as rays of morning sun filtered over the house and licked over her skin. Soaring together, burning hotter than the sun, they joined as daylight coated the cool morning.

Lying in his arms, her head on his chest, she couldn't have fought the smile if she tried. Hands tracing the contours of her back, Bennett whispered all the words of love she'd refused to hear for far too long.

And would never tire of hearing.

THE END

Carrie Thorne is the author of kick-ass romance novels, specializing in white-hot chemistry, healthy relationships, and a mix of action and dreamily falling in love. Whether it's a sinuous flow down a lazy river or evil bad dudes hot on heels, Carrie's stories will draw you in and ruin your sleep. Happily ever afters are for everyone, and kindness is everything.

She's also an introvert who loves people, travel, fitness, video games, food, and is a true Pacific Northwesterner who lives for rain and outdoors and trees and mountains and ocean, and... she's a total dork. At home, she's lucky to have two creative and confident kids, a witty veteran husband she fell at-first-sight for, and a tiny pup snuggled at her side. In addition to writing romance, Carrie has been a nurse practitioner, a Martian and Earthling geologist, a banker, and she is usually elbow-deep in a DIY project in which she bit off more than she could chew.

Where is she now? Depends on the weather. Cozied up by the fire with a steaming mug of black coffee, or stretched out on the hammock with a frothy IPA in the shade of her forest. Either way, she's working on the next great love story to conquer your TBR list.

www.CarrieThorne.com

www.ingramcontent.com/pod-product-compliance
Lightning Source LLC
Chambersburg PA
CBHW050250110726
47898CB00007B/2355